Feathers, Fins & Fur

Edited & Designed
by
Whitney Scott

Outrider Press, Inc.
Crete, Illinois

All characters, situations and
settings in this collection's short
stories are fictitious.

Trademarks and brand names
have been printed in initial
capital letters

Permissions appear on page 255 and
constitute a continuation of the copyright page

Book Design & Production
by Whitney Scott

Library of Congress
Catalog Number
99-70737

© 1999, Outrider Press, Inc.
ISBN 0962103969

Outrider Press, Inc.
937 Patricia Lane
Crete, Illinois
60417

For my friends who have manes

Table of Contents

Zzzz..

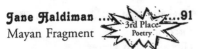

Outrider Press
Award Winner

3rd Place
Poetry

Introduction

Why do animal stories remain enduringly popular? What is the source of pleasure we take from them, whether in the form of fairy tales and myths or in James Herriot's accounts of his days as a Yorkshire vet? Why do the visits of cats and dogs improve the spirits and often, the general health, of nursing home residents and hospital patients? Why do we smile at the sight of baby animals, even those such as tigers and elephants we would not usually consider suitable companions in our homes? Why do we buy our pets special treats, even take them out to dinner and bury their remains in pet cemeteries with headstones?

We've used animal as food, hunting helpers, beasts of burden. means of transportation and more. We've deified them, worn their feathers, skins and antlers in ceremonies dedicated to successful hunts, and have incorporated their claws, teeth and bones into holy objects intended to ensure our survival.

Though we intellectually realize that eating meat, fish and fowl means cattle, sheep, salmon, tuna, chickens and other creatures must perish, we two-leggers, especially the (sub)urbanized variety, are more likely to think of animals as companions, sources of pleasure, comfort and joy than of sustenance. Consequently, many of us routinely speak of "animal friends," often sincerely, sometimes too blithely as we ignore the unwelcome results of humankind's dominance. We have made certain species extinct and endangered many more. We subject animals to cosmetic and medical research that some argue is unnecessary, cruel and ethically questionable.

On a positive note, we see around us some of the world's most well-fed and pampered pets. Take our own cats, dogs, hamsters and pot-bellied pigs: we not only provide the necessities of food, water and shelter for them, but also buy them weather-proof coats, turn on their favorite TV shows, coddle them, cuddle them, delight in them, laugh and fret over them, play with them and love them.

And, because animals are just plain fun, we love to talk about them, often as "members of the family."

Clearly, our relationships with animals run the gamut.

Collected here are writings by 65 authors from across the nation as well as Canada, Switzerland, and Puerto Rico, all on various aspects of the feathered, finned and furred beasts with which we share our planet. Some writers address our fascination with these creatures' innate, seemingly universal, appeal, whether within our homes or in the wild. Are we drawn to them because they may recall a collective wildness lost to us? It that why they so attract, repel and fascinate? Do they evoke stirrings of some less evolved consciousness, of silent stalking, of dark and cold and wet? Are they the stuff that dreams of other lives are made of?

On this note, Kate Boyes, of Smithfield, Utah, whose "Confluence" won First Place in the Prose Division, writes of her life-altering experience at Long Lake in a piece of creative non-fiction that may forever affect the way we view our relationship with "wild" animals in their natural environment. Equally compelling is "Bat Watch," Second Place winner by Santa Barbara's Lucy Aron, an account of a well-organized bat observation filled with psychological insight, information and a sense of awe no amount of human organization can predict or contain.

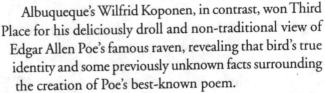

Albuqueque's Wilfrid Koponen, in contrast, won Third Place for his deliciously droll and non-traditional view of Edgar Allen Poe's famous raven, revealing that bird's true identity and some previously unknown facts surrounding the creation of Poe's best-known poem.

In the Poetry Division, Pamela Miller won for the second year in a row, this time for her elegantly-crafted "Fish Story," notable for its metaphoric use of sealife. Runner-up in that division is Cynthia Belmont's "Dinosaur Dreams," musings on the extinct reptiles' vast, eternal sleep. Tied for Third Place were Jane Haldiman's "Mayan Fragment," an image of a monkey god flinging written language into the air and Gregory Stall's "Geese," a spare, elegant celebration of migrating birds and changing seasons.

A number of this anthology's writers explore with great seriousness, others with tongue firmly in jowl, the places we have made for animals in our domestication of them – or theirs of us. Janice Heiss' "Cat Talk," for instance, creates a witty, stream-of-consciousness journal of her love affair with many people's favorite four-leggers. "Pax Canis," a humorous fantasy by Dianne Frerichs, takes readers into a canine training program for puppies, complete with rules, regulations and comic misadventures.

Some contributors have incorporated elements of cross-species shape-shifting into their writings, as does Rochelle Rhodes, whose central character in "Coyote's Chocolate" sees this transformation as simply another way to travel. In the Outrider Press Award winner, "Of Wolves, Ashes and Prairie Gold," by Alice Sellars of Roundup, Montana, the narrator recalls her brief ecstacy as one of the pack howling into the wilderness night.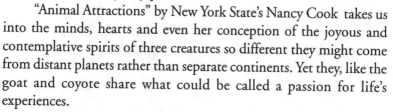

In a decidedly urban context, Puerto Rico's Dominique Slavin uses surreal humor with her daffy scenario of a sight-seeing goat taking on the traffic of Edinburgh, Scotland, and the humans pursuing it. Eight people improbably crammed into a cab follow the trail to the famously upscale Marks and Spencers department store, where shoppers dive for safety as the goat proceeds to break up the place in every way possible.

"Animal Attractions" by New York State's Nancy Cook takes us into the minds, hearts and even her conception of the joyous and contemplative spirits of three creatures so different they might come from distant planets rather than separate continents. Yet they, like the goat and coyote share what could be called a passion for life's experiences.

With this passion, as well as tenderness, exuberance and humor, these writings depict a wide range of emotions as well as a great variety of animals – wild and domestic; stuffed and extinct; naturalistic, symbolic, metaphoric and mythological – each mirroring some part of our human selves. No wonder animal stories endure.

– Whitney Scott
May, 1999

Bat Shower
by Lucy Aron

We sit bat vigil. Out on the grass at Tucker's Grove. About 30 of us, waiting at dusk for them to emerge for their nightly forage. There's a colony of Mexican Free-Tailed (*Tadarida brasiliensis*) under a bridge spanning the creek. Bats like water. They don't like moonlight.

The Los Padres Interpretive Association, a nonprofit volunteer group that works with the Forest Service, has sponsored a public education program on bats. That's why we're here. Other people are drifting out of the park. The day is coming to an end. We assemble on the grass in scattered groups of two, three, some sitting alone – middle-aged, kids, older folk. One man, clearly a *serious* bat watcher, sports a bat tee-shirt and is looking through a pair of binoculars fitted with an infra-red device. The lenses have a spooky glow, making the man appear as though he has red-orange eyeballs on stalks.

Facing south towards the bridge, we gaze at its underside, but in the settling dark can't discern much more than creekside flora – bushes, sycamore and eucalyptus blurring into shadows.

It's mid-June. The babies have only recently been born. Each female bears a single young. The infants roost in masses so thick they can exceed 500 per square foot.

We cock our ears. A lush sound, muted but massive, like hundreds of tweeting, chirping mice or baby birds, wafts up from under the bridge. I imagine a dense wall of bats the color of espresso, pulsating, about to explode off into the night.

The noise of traffic over the bridge, headlights flashing, irritates me. Don't they know something extraordinary is about to happen? I want the cars to go away so I can hear *them*. Even the whispered conversations around me seem blaring.

Seng-Ts'an, poet and Third Zen Patriarch, wrote, "....Nothing is separate, and nothing in the world is excluded." These are city bats. Cars and street lights and barking dogs and people have become aspects of their natural habitat. If they've adapted, so can I.

Colder and colder. I put on my jacket. Darker. It's 7:40 p.m. Thirty minutes pass. I shift my body on the hard ground, trying to get comfortable. Binoculars at the ready. My Nikon 10x50 Stayflow Plus II is powerful but heavy. Its strap bites into my neck. My discomfort, like the fading light, intensifies the anticipation. A place for secrets and subterfuge, the dark has an edgy quiescence, a claustrophobic feel. It belongs less properly to human beings than to creatures with huge, haunting eyes and soundless footsteps.

Will they show? When? Forty-five minutes go by. I look up at the canopy of trees above my head. A breeze shimmies the leaves, now twirling silhouettes against an indigo sky. I turn again towards the bridge. Primarily cave dwellers, bats roost in buildings or under bridges mainly during migration. From which cave, on which mountain, have they come? And where will they go?

Some Native American tribes view the bat as a symbol of rebirth. The Chinese consider it an omen of good luck and happiness. But in the West it's reviled and misunderstood. The myths and legends of a culture maintain the strict boundaries that guarantee the integrity of its cosmology. The imputation of evil originates from the crossing of those boundaries, be they religious, class, sexual, racial, taxonomic. The bat is a mammal, but flies like a bird. It has wings, but fur instead of feathers. Transgression. Evil. Taboo.

We fear what we do not understand. Barry Lopez could as well have been referring to the bat when he described the wolf, another maligned creature, as "not so much an animal that we have always known as one that we have consistently imagined."

Bats do not attack people. They are not blind. Vampire bats (and they constitute just three of over 900 bat species) represent far less potential harm to the human body than Anne Rice does to literature. We rely on bats to pollinate fruit and nut trees, to disperse seeds that foster reforestation, and to control insects. A single bat can consume 600 insects in an hour. They love mosquitoes. If we pay attention, they can inform us about our  own health. The vitality of their populations reflects pesticide and pollution levels in the environment.

Whoosh! Something springs out from under the bridge, flaps toward us, then zips over our heads and away. Was it a bat? Too dark to tell for sure. Flew too fast. Maybe just a –wait, there's another – moth? No, there're two more. Yes, bats.

All conversations stop. It's 8:35 p.m. Another bat whizzes by. Seconds later, a trio. Then a stream of bats. It burgeons into a river. They sweep out from under the bridge, sparrow-size, flying erratically with sharp, angular turns like slightly stoned navigators, yet certain of their course. With a tailwind they can do sixty.

It's like a star shower. They don't shine, but they, too, are gifts of the night. Aggregate, relentlessly onward, evanescent. A bat shower. Hundreds and hundreds and magical hundreds more. They flutter straight towards us, reduced now in our wonder to absolutely silent witnesses.

Now up and over our heads, as though acutely mindful of our presence, but with more consequential business on their minds. Survival. They register us briefly with their exquisite echolocation as they glide off, heedless, finally, of anything but an inexorable purpose. I like the purity of their disregard, envy them their birthright community.

There's something about critical mass that compels. A few bats tweak my attention, hundreds enrapture. The largest urban bat colony in the world, half a million strong, resides under a Congress Avenue bridge in Austin, Texas. The sight must mesmerize nearly into coma.

Cocooned by the dark, there's an intimacy about this spectacle. It's like watching a birth. I almost feel like a voyeur, but can't take my eyes off them. Airborne, the bats ground me, though I feel lighter. They humble me. Because of them, I'm more centered, connected, freer. My petty worries and selfish concerns seem trivial. I've forgotten about the cold and the traffic and the damp grass I'm sitting on. I wish the river in the sky would go on forever. But it stops as suddenly as it began. I look at my watch. The river has flowed for over five minutes. It felt like seconds.

I wonder how many other such events exist in this bountiful bioregion of Santa Barbara, ones of which I have no knowledge? I want to see them all, from the tiniest lichen sprouting in the canyons to the Blue Whales cruising the Channel. In "A Native Hill," Wendell Berry wrote of his rural Kentucky home, "When I have thought of the welfare of the earth, the problems of its health and preservation, the care of its life, I have had this place before me, the part representing the whole more vividly and accurately, making clearer and more pressing demands, than any *idea* of the whole."

I have no doubt that if I learn deeply enough about nature, particularly in my own backyard, I'll learn everything I need to know about life. I love my Macintosh and depend on my microwave and automobile, but technology makes me uneasy. I don't want my reality virtual any more than I want my breakfast or friends or sex virtual. The further I move away from the natural world, the less in tune I become with what counts, with what's life-affirming, and the less in touch I become with my own soul.

Thank you, bats. For reminding me. And for your mystery and grace.

'A Milking
by Denise Bachman

Pre-dawn hours, cold, dark, loudly lowing,
Her bag full and heavy, aching, burning,
Waiting for cool hands to ease its growing,
The early morning chore before churning;
He sits beside her with wooden stool, pail,
Hands reaching, grasping, firmly squeezing now;
Admires her beauty, her soft exhale.
She presses her warm flank against his brow,
Giving herself to him, liquid spun silk,
Eyes wide, breathing deeply, strong hands kneading,
Bucket brimming with steaming, creamy, milk,
Emptying herself, no longer pleading.
Rising from his stool, this chore to be laid,
Ever the farmer, ever the milkmaid.

Raven

by Janet Baker

Yesterday as I waited stuck in traffic
on the on-ramp to Interstate Five,
a raven flew low past my windshield
carrying like a banner in its talons
a two-foot sprig of eucalyptus.

Its glossy black was dull with wear,
the fingered wings outstretched,
as it glided past in a whisper,
smooth and heavy,
brushing the dark hood of my car.

Raven, some say you are a cruel parent
who leaves your fledglings much too soon
while you glide with your flock
called "an Unkindness."
If true, this may be why your croaking call,
so freely given, is so melancholy,
remembering your lonely child.

But your thick beak is so intent today
to build a nest of aromatic leaves
for offspring high among the rocks,
you haul the branch and leave your light touch on me
like thoughts and memories of nurturing darkness
that skim across hard surfaces of urban life.

Pigeon
by Janet Baker

I like to think the pigeon who roosts in the traffic light
at the intersection of Lomas Santa Fe and the Coast Highway
is a conscious work of art offering bird wisdom.

At the end of the millennium she stays nestled facing westward
toward the edge of California and the end of history
her back to the train station
to the chic shops of Cedros Street
to the entire continent.

Posed in pigeon silhouette
in red light flashing only
never green or amber,
she points to some unseen horizon beyond the Pacific
where we will never be
past the ball of sun disappearing into the ocean.

We are forced to stop and gaze
at red light dimmed by bird shadow
here between ocean and railroad
for one long moment
at this conjunction between beginning and the end.
A living light box floats in fluid red
encircled with the flash she has chosen
to say, perhaps, stop, it's over now,
western history or this millennium.

Come On

by Gail Bauman

My motor is running
humming 'cause of the sun
and the fun we will have.
I'm ready to go –
got my gloves, boots, and gun.
Come on, hon, grab yours
and the decoys – oh boy!
I've got the laser for tracking,
you've got the muter for gun blasts,
here's the amplifier
for game sounds
and the pistol laser
with the double sights, and here, cheers,
the lights for night-blinding.
The game feeder needs batteries!
Where are those night vision goggles?
That infrared detector should really
help after we've downed 'em.
We're sure to get more than two,
but what will we do
with all that meat
and foul?

For Women Who Still Sleep With Stuffed Animals

by Cynthia Belmont

You've been told it's time to grow up.
You could swear you did – you're rarely
embarrassed anymore – you don't even
bother to hide them. The lovers
you invite into your bed just pitch them
to the floor, the cat with no eyes
and matted gray tufts of fur sticking out

at unnatural angles, the drooping blue
hippopotamus, the moose
de-antlered decades ago, with his
squashed-in face and increasingly
amused yarn smile. They survived
your grandfather's good-natured threats,
your mother's sarcasm, your college

roommates' dirty pranks. They've seen
you naked, sweaty, writhing around
in sleep, in a dozen arms. They've waited
upside-down for days at a time,
been carried off by dogs, traveled
cross-country on the wrong airplanes.
They've never been washed – they smell

more like you than you do, their layered
odors of skin, perfume, hair keeping
accurate records of years. They don't
love you at all. They know nothing
of interest that you don't already know.
Nobody needs polite company
more than you need theirs now.

Dinosaur Dreams

by Cynthia Belmont

Scaly and unnamed, snorting
in their sleep among low-slung trees,

vast gray bellies like ancient
drums flattening grass, mud-soft

and electrical-storm eyes slitted,
refracting dragonflies: they were

warm-blooded, traveling in packs
or alone like stray cats,

who also own the world sometimes
and dream. Napping, they remembered

light on green rivers, steamy bogs
like hot-tubs, the days

offering their bounty of leaf,
blood, and sun. They did not fear

the slow heave and roll
of earth, hiding its black secrets,

wheeling into a colder morning.
They did not wake sweating,

suddenly lucky, on the other side
of nightmares, or grow old overnight.

Samson! Where's Delilah?

by Steven F. Bigden

After being awakened by the whine of the alarm clock, my flippant feline, Lucifer, shrieked with sounds of starvation. He pounced on me every time I moved my body, letting me know it was time to get up; his meal had been missed.

"Okay, Lucifer," I groaned, knowing there wasn't a morsel of food in the house. Lucifer, thrilled I was getting out of bed, ran to the kitchen. He lay sprawled by the empty cat food tin with a look of complete despair, screaming again, letting me know he was weak from hunger and wanted to be fed immediately.

"Lucifer, you won't starve to death while I go to the store, so stop walking around with that sullen look." I knew I had to hurry, because my famished feline was starting to eye Gabriel, our little goldfish.

I decided to go to The Fish Bowl, a pet store that had just opened for business at the corner of Belmont and Seminary. I'd been there the weekend of the grand opening and wondered if Noah himself had populated the store. There seemed to be two of every animal: beautiful exotic birds, dogs of every size, cats of every shade, fish from every ocean on the globe. I saw insects to feed other animals with and insects you kept around the house.

The owners were Italian immigrants, husband and wife, who spoke excellent English. Vito and Donnabella Parisi were warm and friendly people who kept the shop clean and inviting, with colorful animal posters alternating with tall stacks of 50-pound dog food sacks.

Feathers, Fins & Fur _____

When I arrived at The Fish Bowl, I studied the many aisles of products before finally reaching the cat food aisle. I picked up a box of Iams (Lucifer's favorite), but noticed it wasn't in the usual packaging. As I was reading the ingredients list to make sure Lucifer would eat it, I felt something brush against my face, and heard a low hissing sound, almost a drumming. I turned my head to see an enormous green and brown snake that was probably bigger than Godzilla. It had pried off the top of its aquarium and was now staring at me face to face and licking me.

My bodily functions stopped one by one. My muscles tensed. My heart raced. My whole body shut down in panic. The room started spinning, with the snake still coiled there, licking my face. I was finally able to turn my head and glance over to Vito and Donna, who were smiling and standing at the counter. I gave them a look of terror, praying that one of them to come and rescue me.

"Oh, don't you worry about a thing," insisted Vito. "Samson is a very friendly snake and won't hurt you. Besides, he's a python and not poisonous."

Not at all reassured. I looked at the snake, looked at the Parisis, the snake, the Parisis. . . suddenly the room started spinning so fast I couldn't keep my balance. I stumbled around, only to have Samson follow me. I wasn't sure if he was trying to catch my fall, or make a midday snack out of me.

I fell into a display of dog food that was stacked almost to the heavens. It started a large game of dominos, knocking over other displays one at a time. Ping, Crash, Shatter is all I heard from what seemed like miles away.

I was in for it. The snake was going to bite me, and eat me. There would be no more Lucifer, no more anything, for me. Blackness seeped into my vision, blocking everything out.

Then I was drowning in a bright, white light. Everything was gone, except for the light. Overwhelmed with a sense of serenity, the voices I heard seemed far away.

"Samson, get back in your cage. What did I tell you about causing trouble?"

"I didn't mean any harm, Vito. It getsss boring in thisss cage, ssso I thought I would liven thingsss up around here. In fact, I haven't had thisss much fun sssince I talked Eve into biting into that apple," Samson boasted. "How about I wrap mysssself around him ssso he getsss a clossse up when he wakesss up?"

"No, no and no. Now get in your cage. After you left Eden, you promised me you'd be good. And what do you do? You sneak in baby Hercules' crib and almost ended up getting killed yourself. Then what happens? You…"

"I was only trying to check on the baby to sssee why he wasss…" Samson protested.

Furious, Vito interrupted the snake, "Yeah, right! Then why did that Irish-Catholic, Patrick, drive you out of Ireland? Deeds I am too embarrassed to mention to this day, that's what! If I only knew that you would behave this way, I never would have let you move to Chicago. Will you never learn?"

"Pleassse forgive me, Vito. I try to be good, but it is ssso difficult. I am only looking for a friend. You know how I feel about the sssnake I'm paired with. Delilah just makesss me crazy. She iss ssso hideousss it gives the rest of us snakes a bad name. I can't be myself or have any fun when she is around. I would have been much happier paired with a big macho lion or sssomething."

The voices were growing louder and I could see shadows in the white light. Did I die? Am I in heaven, I wondered.

"Maybe I should try and apologize to SSSSebassstian for my sssilly waysss. I did not mean to ssscare him ssso much."

"I don't know, Samson. I think that you have done enough already."

"Sssebsssstian. SSSebasstian, I would like to have a word with you. I only need a sssecond."

Suddenly I could see Vito and Samson standing in front of the light, but now Samson had a bright, pink bandanna around his neck.

"Am I dead or is this a dream, or what?"

"Does it matter?" responded the man.

"Yes, it matters! Did Samson bite me and eat me?"

"I mosst cccertainly did not," said Samson, in a tone that indicated that he was insulted.

"Well, I didn't mean to suggest…" I started to talk, but Samson interrupted.

"I know what you are trying to sssuggest. I am a big, ugly sssnake, so you asssssumed that I would attack you and devour you like sssome sssort of wild animal. I would never do a thing of the sssort. I wasss trying to make your acquaintanccce. When you came in the first time, I noticed how sssexy you were, with your icccy blue eyesss, and sssstraw-colored hair. I thought that we could be …friendsss." He waved his tail seductively.

29

"Friends? You wanted to be my friend?"

"Well, friends, whatever you humans call it these days. You do not know how awful it isss to be a gay sssnake in the twentieth cccentury, let alone being matched with that dreadful ssserpent, Delilah. I think there should be a rule, or law, or sssomething, that preventsss usss from ending up in sssituations like thisss. *'One of each ssex and ssspeciesss'* — that'sss a laugh. Mosssesss didn't know what he wasss talking about when he wrote Genesssisss. If *he* was ssstuck with Delilah I am posssitive he would have

thought differently. *'Man shall not lie with man,'* sssaid Leviticusss. You know he only sssaid that because he wasss just a crotchety old man who didn't like pork, and wasss insssecure about hisss own sssexuality."

"Gay snake? You knew Genesis and Leviticus?" I asked apprehensively.

"Yesss, dear, on both accountsss. I am a gay sssnake, indeed. In fact the Greco era proved to be my mosssst favorite time. There were many ssstimulating thingsss happening then." The snake stopped talking and winked at me. "Besides, Delilah only has one thing on her mind, and it is the one thing I have no interessst in giving her."

Vito shrugged his shoulders.

"So how old are you then? You must be pretty old if you've seen all of that. I just can't believe..."

"As I was saying, there is nobody to hold a decccent converssssation with. Humansss and other sssnakes run away from me, because I'm ssscary looking and, of course, gay. And you thought you had it rough, hmm? At any rate, I am ssso sssorry if I ssstartled you. I really didn't mean to."

Samson's eyes swelled and he started to cry. "I am ssso tired of being forcccced to live with Delilah. I only want to meet my true sssoul mate, sssomebody I could talk to, share my life with. You know the routine."

"Oh, uh. All of this is news to me. I had no idea there could be gay snakes or that you even had emotions..."

"You sssilly boy. Oh courssse there can be gay sssnakesss. There are gay animalsss in every ssspeciesss. It'sss only those right-wing radicals that believe otherwisssse and try to forcccce their beliefsss on the ressst of the world. If you can be gay, why can't I?"

"I guess, well I never really thought about it before... Hey, how did you know I'm gay?"

"Darling, I've been around sssince the dawn of time. A sssnake my age knowsss thessse thingsss. I can ssspot one a mile away. Who do you think taught Mosesss to shake his ssstaff like that? I'm the one who whissspered in SSSigmund Freud's ear one night and sssuggesssted that whole sssnake sssymbol thing," Samson boasted.

I tried to digest all the information he was giving me. "Apology accepted," I said, finally. "I'm sorry, too. I didn't mean to hurt your feelings. I guess I shouldn't have panicked the way I did. Friends, then," I said.

"Friendsss for life! I wasss beginning to think nobody would ever asssk." Samson started swaying up and down with excitement.

"No, I mean *just* friends. I'm afraid I'm going to have to leave you with Delilah. I've already found my soul mate."

"Figuresss." He looked down. "Ssssee what I mean, Vito? All the good onesss are either taken or ssstraight. Oh, when will I be able to get rid of that pain in the tail, Delilah?" Samson groaned.

"I'd better get going. I promise not to scream next time I see you around. Good luck with Delilah."

The snake rolled his eyes and snickered.

"Vito, I'm also sorry for knocking all of those displays down. I just got dizzy and..."

"No problem. I am just glad you're okay and nobody was hurt. I thought Samson was going to hurt himself when we tried to catch you! Hey, don't forget your food for your Lucifer. He gets pretty ferocious when he does not get his way, that little devil!"

Samson and Vito winked at each other.

"Tell him that we said hi," said Vito.

I turned around looking for a way out, then turned back to wave good-bye one last time. The white light was consuming Vito and Samson. The light slowly flowed away to reveal the top of the ambulance I was being loaded in.

Did I dream that, or am I just going crazy? I wasn't sure; it seemed so real.

Then I saw Samson slithering by the ambulance with Vito chasing after him shouting, "Samson! What did you do with Delilah?"

Maybe I'm not crazy after all.

The Feathers of Man

by Donna Black

Have you ever seen a living Quetzal? Neither have I. Perhaps the only place they will survive is in national zoos. They are being lost to the world at an alarming rate. When Quetzalcoatl the ruler of the Aztecs or Mayans, I forget which, was alive, his people would trap the Quetzals and take their wonderful, shimmering green tail feathers to use in their headdresses. The bird was then set free to grow more tail feathers. The Quetzal was a revered part of their rituals and his feathers were considered to be worth more than gold. To receive the Quetzal feather from the ruler was the highest of honors. To see a Quetzal in flight meant extremely good fortune for your day.

How do I know this? My Grandfather told me. That's why today I have a photograph of a flying Quetzal on my mirror so every morning I start my day with good fortune. On the other side of the mirror I have one of my Grandfather's hunting licenses. The license gives him permission to hunt "Game Birds, Migratory Game Birds, Game Animals and Fur-bearing Animals." Sound a bit contradictory? That's Gramps! He loved hunting "with the guys." The hunting license I have shows him to be 71 years old at the time it was issued. I happen to know they were hunting ducks. I personally cannot think of sitting in a duck blind with a bunch of wet men in the cold, before the sun is awake, drinking hot coffee (sometimes with a little something added for warmth), for hours. The wooden ducks float outside the blind in the cold water, which you have sloshed around in setting up these "decoys." They are just barely seen in the dawning sky when the music of the ducks is heard calling. You now respond with your little duck sound horn, which always reminded me of a kazoo, and blow them out of the sky as they respond to your call. Then you gather them up and take them home to stuff or eat.

Feathers, Fins & Fur

If you eat them, no matter how well you clean them you always miss at least one piece of buckshot. Dentistry flourishes. And unless your wife or mother is an exceptionally good duck cooker, they usually taste like the decoy.

If you stuff them, they stand around wherever you've put them until the wife or mother or yourself finally says "When are you going to get rid of that moth eaten old eyesore?" and out they go into the trash. I think I'd rather stand in a mist-shrouded forest and watch for a Quetzal.

Gramps also loved to go pheasant hunting. He convinced me that this was a good thing, because not only were they good eating, but also because you could make hats out of them. In those days we all wore hats. Have you ever made a hat out of pheasant feathers? Well, neither have I. I made half a hat. It cost me more than buying three or four hats would have and I never finished it. First of all it takes lots of pheasants to make a really pretty hat. Gramps brought me lots of pheasant wings and pheasant heads and parts and stuff. I took a class in hat making. I bought a form and all the necessary hat making tools for working with feathers still attached to pheasant parts and stuff. My sister Susie managed to make a really beautiful hat, but mine never quite got off the ground...so to speak. Also, just as an aside...pheasant tastes like chicken only smaller. My choice is still mist and Quetzal.

Gramps' second choice of sport was fishing. I love to eat fish. Yummy!

He took Susie and me stream fishing once. He stood in the middle of the stream with these waders (really high boots with rubber overalls attached to the top) and cast his line while Sue and I stood on the shore with sticks and string with fish hooks attached. We used some sort of clay-like goop on the fishhook and never caught anything because we spent too much time playing around. Gramps was really good at fly-casting. We liked watching him do it. He didn't catch anything that day either. But it was fun, and he didn't get upset with us for horsing around and scaring the fish.

When he retired, Gramps got a summer job up in Wisconsin at one of those fishing places. As the bartender he had the whole day to do whatever he wanted. Sue and I went up with him; well, actually Sue went up often, and I went up once. Boat fishing is boring...boring...boring.

You get up before the sun is awake, yes, just like duck hunting, and you get into the boat and go out to where "the fish are biting." Then you sit in the boat with your line in the water and every once in awhile you lift your line out of the water to see if the worm has managed to escape. And you sit it the boat…and you sit in the boat…and you sit in the boat. No rocking, no loud talking, no dipping your fingers in the water, no putting your feet over the side. The only movement you're allowed to partake in is slapping the mosquitoes. A Thermos holds coffee, and in our case milk, but you still have to be careful not to rock the boat and let the fish know you're there.

When it got warm enough and a trickle of sweat ran down my nose, I carefully went over the side. We were wearing shorts and I slipped off my tennis shoes so it was okay from that standpoint, but Gramps and the other fishermen in the area were a touch unhappy. Hence, my one visit to the fishing camp.

It turns out Susie loved fishing. Egad!

We have some 16mm film from Gramps that I recently had put on tape. Eighty percent of it was Gramps and Susie fishing and swimming at the fishing camp. I guess if I wanted to be in film I should not have jumped out of the boat.

He and Sue brought home huge coolers filled with ice and fish and we would have a cookout. That was the best part of fishing as far as I was concerned. The worst part was cleaning the fish but that was an unbreakable rule. You wanted to eat it….you helped clean it. Fair, but yucky!

I have made Gramps sound like a sportsman and nothing else. He was many things. He consistently surprised me as a person. When I was about seven and Sue was six, Gramps came over to our house with a pickup truck loaded with pipes and chains and wood and paint. By the end of the day he had built a swing set for us with two swings, a trapeze bar, and a swinging seesaw. It was magnificent. It was also large enough so that when we were twelve and thirteen we were still using it.

He also built a playhouse for us. It was big enough to stand up in and had windows with glass that opened and a door with a lock and key. He made a bunk bed set, a kitchen table and chairs to go in the house. The roof was shingled and had a chimney and it looked exactly like a real house, in miniature, up to and including shutters on the windows that worked. And he made a two-story dollhouse. It was wired for electricity and was carpeted and tiled and had kitchen cabinets and a sink and stairs leading to the second floor. Doors that opened and closed into the separate rooms. I grew up knowing that my grandfather could do anything

Gramps was my paternal grandfather. Mom's dad had passed away in an automobile accident before I was born. When Mom and Dad got their divorce, he took over and made sure we were well taken care of. I don't know for certain, but I think he helped Mom out financially many times. When she remarried, he was still our Gramps, and our stepdad welcomed him as one of the family. I never knew how unusual that was until I grew much older.

Gramps was a widower; Grandma died when I was still really young. He worked for the railroad as a switchman. Every morning he would get up and make his own breakfast, before the sun was awake, of course. The breakfast was always the same: two eggs sunny side up, two pork chops and fried potatoes. It never varied, but lunch, now that sounded exciting. He ate his lunch with his working partner on the caboose of the train they would be on for that day. They would be moving along and cooking their food on the caboose. Cool! Now there are hardly anymore cabooses. Too bad. No more Granddads cooking lunch on a caboose.

I would like to tell you one more thing about my wonderful magical grandfather. How I got his hunting license. I work in a dental office. One of our patients actually recognized me from when I was a child. After we talked a few times, he said he collected duck stamps (the stamp they put on the back of the licenses) and while he wouldn't give me the stamp he would send me Gramps' license if I wanted it. I said I would love to have it. It never came and I assumed he had forgotten.

About three months later, I read his obituary in the paper. Two weeks later I received the license and one small turquoise duck feather in an envelope. The man's daughter had sent it to me. The short note thanked me for the flowers I had sent and said her father had asked her to mail the license to me after he became ill. Seeing my name on the flowers had reminded her.

That license saying my Gramps was 5' 7 1/2" tall, weighed 163 pounds, had gray hair and brown eyes and was 71 years old and is signed by his own hand is worth more to me than gold or Quetzal feathers.

That's why a duck hunting license and a photo of a Quetzal are both on my mirror to see as I begin each day.

Confluence
by Kate Boyes

I hold my time on Long Lake like an amulet. It is a charm worn smooth by frequent recall, hibernating in memories until my need for strength wakes it again. Then, I remember...

A disk of ice, formed in my cup during the September night, sounds a faint chime as I drink to the morning sun. I stir the fire and watch the crust of frost on my boots thaw slowly in the thin warmth of last night's last bright coals. But I am too impatient to let the boots, still wet from yesterday's hike, warm through. Nothing can cool my enthusiasm today, for I am off to explore some high falls near the lake's headwaters.

A light morning breeze stirs the lake and the patches of water plants along its edge. The rasping of sedge to sedge and the lapping of water against shore whisper "shh, shh, shh." Perhaps other creatures are lulled by this; I seem to be the only one awake. But with days changing so fast, I cannot bear to sleep too long. Autumn began and has almost ended in the short time I've camped here, the whole season passing in one week. Green trees fired to peak color in four days and were denuded by wind in another two. Now the bare branches seem exhausted, resting on the seventh. Nature, working feverishly at this latitude and altitude, has managed to squeeze a season in edgeways.

I see something strange up along the spit, just at the base of a tall cedar. From this distance, it looks like gray stones strewn in a rough circle around a core of white litter. I guess that these are the fire pit and trash of hunters here for the opening day of bear season.

But when I cautiously approach the site, I find an open cache of empty, bone-white turtle eggs. Lumps of hardened clay surround the cache, still lying where they were scattered in some creature's haste to dig up the eggs. Each edge of the lifeless shells draws in on itself, like a scroll, as if

37

resigned to predation, and the shells are almost translucent now after weeks of exposure to sun and wind and rain.

Past the spit, the edging of clay gives way to an intermittent path, part substance and part sloshing, which straggles northward and upward, along the stream. Picking my way through willow thickets is even slower than wading through water, so the frequent moves from land to stream lend variety and not vexation to the walk. Besides, I am also here to fish, and I accept that fishers' feet are always wet, our boots forever molding to and on us.

The warm afternoon sun welcomes me when I untangle myself from the last stand of willows and climb the final rise before the falls. Here the stream widens and slows, as if relaxing from its recent rush over granite cliffs. I can see those cliffs up ahead, but in this quiet spot, the falls' roar is faint, subdued by distance.

Exploration can wait. I lean my fishing rod against a pine, wade into the water, and scramble up a boulder to relax, like the stream. I sit quietly for a while and then doze, sit and doze while high clouds drift overhead and change the expressions on mountain faces. Water foams white over the falls, creating currents that pirouette on stage marks only the stream can see. Tangles of trees elbow each other all the way down to the shore. The sun's warmth soaks into my bones. Even occasional flashes of brown trout against the streambed's bright agate can't tempt me to leave my position as watcher of the day.

Then, on the far shore, a shadow one shade darker than the rest emerges from the trees and grows distinct. Bear. She bear, I think. Sun's fire reflects on fur, glossing the bear with a cinnamon glow. My lingering drowsiness veils the implications of the bear's presence, so her shuffling amble from the forest to the stream and the playful way she rolls rocks over to search for insects seem amusing.

The bear stands when she reaches the water's edge, sniffs, and then moves, half upright, into the stream. As her lower body submerges, her front legs extend on the top skin of water, never seeming to break the tension. I am awed by her transformation from lumbering clown to graceful swimmer, her bulk no handicap in the buoyant water.

She crosses the water without swaying; only the long fur fringing off each forearm on the downstream side indicates the current's strength. All of her strokes are facile, effective, sure. The bear is unperturbed by a force that could drag me under and bobble my body along like a chunk of pumice. She heads in my direction.

She is heading toward me, and now I am awake. My eyesight is not enough to understand the bear: my whole body takes her in; my fingers trace her movement through the water; inside my boots, my feet follow every bear stroke. Thought, flesh, and feeling focus together; my life watches the bear.

As the bear swims toward me, memories and physical sensations flash simultaneously through my mind, the past inseparable from the present. Campfire stories. The bear's delicate head nodding above the water. Park flyer warnings. Corrugate waves splashing on the shore behind me. The newspaper account of a woman mauled, her two arms severed and scattered among the flame leaves of fallen autumn foliage.

At first I am afraid. But I struggle to push away thoughts of panic reactions; swim, run, climb – no use, I know. The bear would win any race I start. And so I let go of control in the presence of this creature, gratefully, like a cloistered novitiate, my loss losing significance in the resulting freedom and peace of mind. My past becomes faint as the remnants of a wind-worried cirrus cloud. To be me, here, now; there is nothing else. Fear is gone. She could open me like a cache of turtle eggs and litter me about, or she could pass by. That is fact, that is all. While I wait for her decision, I touch my truest friends – mountains, water, and trees – once more with my eyes.

The bear pauses four feet in front of me and slightly to the right. She lifts her head and seems to puzzle over this odd being on the rock. Her eyesight is not enough to understand me; she rises on her back legs and swings her head slowly from side to side. Her head moves smoothly in a rhythm some stray fragment of instinct allows me to recall a rhythm so familiar it seems I have felt it before. The motion and the gleam of her eyes fascinate me, but I remember, finally, to look away, my head slightly down. I am no threat, and it is important to both of us that I signal my submission.

The bear drops to four legs and moves forward, still to the right, until she is beside me. I watch her with everything but my eyes, the bone, muscle, and hair on my right side following all her moves. We are close enough to reflect each other's warmth, creating a heat that heightens the scent of cedar smoke in my hair and pine pitch in her damp fur. She stays beside me while the streams of water sheeting from her fur lose their force, become trickles, and then slow further until no sound comes from her direction but the last drops' sporadic dappling of the stream's surface.

She expels a deep breath. The sudden sound surprises me and I gasp. Air which exchanged oxygen in her lungs moments before is borne my way, a pulse of life on the breeze. Her breath is drawn with mine.

I wait for the next sound, but only silence comes from her direction. The lack of sound touches me, absorbs me, carries me out with it across the water, expands, and, in expanding, makes me light. Each cell fills with silent space until I am translucent, my face the visage of this place, my body, lake and sky. I disappear – what harm can there be? Clearly, now is the time to turn to bear.

No bear stands beside me. I look down at the water, so recently ruffled by fur, as if expecting to find her essence swirling there in a small eddy. Only the sky and I mirror back. Still, I look down at the water, watching my face shape-shift in the current, watching two stones, bright and variegated as onyx, glitter back at me like eyes.

By the time I wade to shore, several fading impressions in the clay are the only evidence of the bear's passing. I follow her sign until I find a place, just at the edge of the trees, where she stopped, turned to face my direction, and then continued into the forest. I crouch down and place a palm flat in one of her tracks. We pause in the same place; our paths touch here; we both move on.

And then I realize with surprise that I am singing. It's possible the song began as I shambled over stones on my way back to shore; a small hum may have leaked out while my concentration was on footing. But now the song grows in volume and complexity, and it carries me back down the stream to my camp in the near dark of late afternoon. Whole passages flow out of a well of gladness newly tapped. This day has toned my life.

I hold my time on Long Lake like an amulet. It is a charm washed with the amethyst of an autumn sunset on calm water and softly fogged by the opalescence of cedar smoke rising through still night air. In distress, it quiets me until my life is the silence of owl's flight. Again, it resonates with the heartbeat of a bear and with my own pulse, the bear's gift. And always it takes the shape of a waxing gibbous moon, and glows with bits of light captured from that moon which hung above my camp, reflecting the better half of fullness.

Legacy of the Chat Noir
by Harker Brautighan

Behemoth is a terror. I should have known better, naming him after Mikhail Bulgakov's gun-toting human-sized black cat. In *The Master and Margarita*, Behemoth is the devil's companion. So, I'm afraid, is my Behemoth.

Nonetheless, I have been curiously bonded with him all these years. Perhaps that makes me some sort of witch.

When Behemoth was a kitten, I woke early one morning with his fangs sunk into my right eyelid. Throwing up an arm in defense of my sight, I cast the demon off of my pillow, and ended his privilege of sleeping curled around my neck. I think that moment marked the transition for Behemoth from kitten – stuff of children's dreams – to monster suitable for grown-ups' nightmares.

The first year of Behemoth's life, we never spent a night apart. His first Christmas, we went to my parents' house, and I carried him in a sling against my belly up and down the ladder, trimming the tree. We were always together.

Later, when I first left him in another's care one sweltering August day, he lunged at her throat – and just missed. She came back in jeans, cowboy boots, a heavy leather coat, and leather work gloves.

There was once a man in my life who was over six feet tall, and who weighed 230 pounds. He had a brown belt in karate, and, as a law enforcement professional, he carried a gun. Before he came to my house to pick me up, he would telephone to ask, "Where is the cat?"

"Which one?"

He would say, "You know which one. I'm coming over now. You'll make sure he's shut in the kitchen before I get there, won't you?"

You see, I'm not the only one who has seen Behemoth's black and powerful soul.

41

On his first New Year's Eve, we went to visit Sara and Geri. The first thing Behemoth did was open all of their tightly closed closet doors. He had mastered the concept of doorknobs at an early age. He would neither be locked in nor our, particularly if his intentions were bloodthirsty. Sara and Geri's doors proved no challenge for Behemoth, despite being heavy enough to challenge either one of those humans, who would presumably have greater strength than a mere cat. Underestimating Behemoth is a grave mistake.

Later that evening, Geri came scuttling out of the bathroom screaming, with her pants around her ankles. Apparently, Behemoth had stalked her into the bathroom, then jumped out from behind the toilet just while she was most vulnerable. Behemoth was not invited back.

On his second New Year's Eve, Behemoth became ill. I had to take him to the emergency animal clinic since my veterinarian was home for the holiday. By the time the exam was over and shots administered, the doctor at the emergency animal clinic had become the third veterinarian to recommend that Behemoth be put to sleep for my own safety.

How could I explain to them that this wretched demon was my best friend, my beloved companion, my soul mate? Did that not make my soul black, too? By now, I knew Behemoth was not your ordinary feral cat. I knew he was a deeply mystic being with a spirit centuries old. His power was far greater than mine. And though I could defend myself from his venomous bites and his hell-raising growls with a nudge of the foot or a sharp rap with a finger across the nose, I knew there was an unmarked boundary beyond which I could not cross.

In his physical manifestation, Behemoth is, after all, just a cat. Not even a notably large cat. Weighing in at eleven pounds, he somehow seems larger and more ferocious than an ordinary house cat. Everyone knows cat bites can be dangerous because cats can spread disease. No one would go out of their way to be bitten by a cat. But most people would brush your typical growling cat aside with one side of their foot or a broom. A simple clap and a "no, kitty" will do it for most cats. But Behemoth is no typical growling cat.

His screams are like something freshly risen from the dead. They are as loud and gruesome as the voice of someone fighting for her life – and losing. His cries betray the pain and indignity of murder; grow out of centuries of enslavement of souls like his; are testimony to the brutality of his use as a forced companion, a novelty, a plaything. He does not need words to demand, "What gives you the right to deny me my freedom, to breed out all that is good and unique and primal in me, to threaten me with that ridiculous contraption of stick and straw? I will bite that stick in half. I will shred your throat. I will be my own self. I am not a thing. I am not tame. I am me, beautiful, majestic, awful and powerful."

❖ ❖ ❖

I am alone and I am hurting. My right paw was hurt so badly when they took away my claws...I lick it and lick it, but nothing brings me any relief. My jailer takes me to men and women who look at my paw, squeeze it, and fuss at it. They always say, "There's nothing physically wrong with him. I don't think pain medication will help." She looks sadly at me, and does nothing. I love her so much, but she is my captor. As if I am not trapped enough, sometimes she puts little blue pills in my food. I never see them until it is too late. Even in tuna, they taste so bitter. After the pills, I feel dazed and naked. I'm sure I am completely vulnerable and all my enemies will attack me. I am too stoned to fight; I would be ripped to shreds in combat. I feel so lethargic, like I am trying to swim across a raging river, but I just keep slipping farther and farther downstream. She did this to me; surely she will protect me. I jump onto her lap and curl myself around her neck, like I did when I was a kitten. (She always used to let me sleep with my body thrown across her throat, my face nestled in her hair. One day, I tried to wake her up, tried to make her eyes open, and she cast me away. Why? How can I ever trust her again?)

She tries to put me down, tries to get up. "No, you can't leave me this way. I'm dizzy and confused and tired, and someone might hurt me." She picks me up again and holds me till I sleep. When I wake and she's not there, I cry until she picks me up and holds me again till the little blue pill torments me a little less. When will she free me?

At night, she sleeps next to him now. It was always just the two of us. The others always went away, but not him. He sleeps with his head close to hers, where I used to sleep. I have to crawl up above her head now, and nudge at her till she makes room for me. It is so cold and lonely without her; how can she expect me to sleep alone? She thinks my mate, a timid calico she calls Zephyr, is sufficient company. But my whole life is her – my mother, my friend, my soul mate, my jailer. He shifts closer to her on the pillow. She's mine! I hit him hard with my paw, but no beads of blood raise up on his forehead. "For your own protection," the man in the lab coat said. The man with the knife. "If you don't put him to sleep, you should at least do this. And give him the medication. Feral cats can be dangerous."

He doesn't move off of our pillow, so I hit him again. I growl at him; he doesn't move. I hiss, growl louder, raise the pitch, hiss, hit, bite. "Goddamnit," he says, whacking me with the back of his hand. I bite the hand. I lose my footing as he pushes me off the bed with a pillow, onto the cold wood floor. I hiss and curse at him. "You bastard," I growl, "She's mine; she's always been mine; she'll always be mine. I won't let you have her. She claimed me for hers, and I claim her for mine. She and I are bonded to each other. She enslaved me; she declawed me; she drugged me; and she has a duty to care for me. If she has to choose, she will choose me."

❖   ❖   ❖

Behemoth knows me better than anyone. There is a deep understanding between us. We know our roles and our responsibilities. I don't cross his boundaries, and he doesn't cross mine. I fear the day that my soul mate and my life partner can no longer tolerate each other, but I pray there are better and stronger drugs for that. You see, the second vet that wanted to put Behemoth to sleep gave me a choice. Death, right then and there, quick, easy, and painless. Or a spiritual death, dragged out over time. A slow dulling of the senses, cultivation of dependence, breaking of the spirit. Being more familiar with the latter option, I chose it. I chose another form of slavery for my companion. "What gives you the right?" I hear in his whimpers as the little blue pills steal off with pieces of his mind (his soul).

Heavy Daybreak

by Harker Brautighan

He creeps in like night,
As I sleep on my back.
His breath wakes me;
My eyes open.
He will want to cuddle –
I am trying to sleep.
He will press his nose into my ear;
I will pretend not to awaken.
He will be insistent
And he knows I love him.
He slips closer to my bed;
my teeth are clenched tightly
He thinks he is stealthy,
but every footfall rocks the graying dawn like thunder.
Little gusts rattle through him as air bursts
from his lungs to his nose.
My fingers close around an invisible ball in my hand.
He makes soft wet sounds with his tongue.
He is very near.
My fist unfurls in a last desperate reach for sleep ...
Sleep, in turn my own elusive companion;
Sleep, the reluctant player in my nighttime drama.
Sleep, who so erotically recedes from my outstretched hands,
who so mockingly defies seduction.
Sleep, that tantalizing lover,
bends toward me in a fleeting kiss.
My eyes close and my jaw goes slack.
As my open mouth catches the dog-eared corner of a dream,
that cunning watcher of my brief affair makes his move.
His weight falls on me as he jumps
above my bed and drops himself on my chest.
My teeth snap shut onto a yelp of surprise.
Fingers fumble stupidly with sheets as I try to push him off of me.
But as he settles his weight more firmly on my stomach,
my fingers fan out, trail over his ears, caress his shoulders.
He begins to knead my chest with his padded paws,
and his sandpaper tongue sends a shiver down my neck
as my ears fill with his sputtering purr.

A Fetching Picture
By Lisa Brosnan

A new mailman came to my door the other day with a pale blue envelope and a question. "I have a letter here," he said. "It's addressed to someone named Shuggie. It has your address on it. I wasn't sure…"

"It's for me," I grumbled as I snatched the envelope from him. "I mean, it's for him." I nodded to my German shepherd who was at this point obtrusively nosing the mailman's bag to see if it contained anything of interest.

The mailman grinned in his effort to humor me. "Of course," he said.

An urge to explain came over me. "My dog gets quite a lot of mail: no bills or junk, but good mail. Brightly colored cards and packages come for him on his birthday and on all the major holidays. Sometimes he gets long letters from my relatives and people he's known from other states. He also receives invitations to parties and more attention than I do at the beach. And yes, it is a little annoying."

This particular letter was from my friend Gretchen in Los Angeles. She had stumbled across an item on the Internet pertaining to dogs and Prozac and thought she'd pass it along. In her letter she stated, "when I saw the article, I immediately thought of Shuggie and his little obsession/compulsion disorder." She was trying to be helpful.

There was a time I suppose when Shuggie's passion for the game of fetch did concern me – just a little. He would pick up a stick from the yard, toss it at my feet, take a few steps back, and then whine at me until I threw it for him. If sticks were scarce, he would pick up whatever was convenient: a stone, a leaf, a cigarette butt. I tried to discourage him by ignoring his offering. This never worked. With his muscles tensed in preparation and an intense look of expectancy in his eyes, he would wait and he would whine. His was no ordinary whine. It was a whine made of fingernails against chalkboards, dentist drills and car alarms. It was a whine that could not be ignored for long. There was nothing to be done about it except to throw the stick. Of course, he would bring it right back again.

It didn't bother me so much as it bothered Gretchen. She said it wasn't normal for a dog to fetch so much. Having never met one before, I didn't know what a "normal" dog was. I tended to believe that when you love someone you put up with their little idiosyncrasies. As long as he wasn't hurting anyone it was no big deal to me. After all, there were worse things he could be doing. To assuage Gretchen's concern, I went so far as to call a pet psychologist on a radio talk show. Backed by his degree in animal behavior, his books and his syndicated show on NPR, the doggie shrink told me, "There's just some things that some dogs like to do." Shuggie wrote back to Gretchen. He keeps up with all of his correspondence. Not gainfully employed, he doesn't have much else to do during the day. This is the letter Shuggie sent to Gretchen exactly as he had written it.

Dear Gretchen,

Hello! How are you? I am fine. Thank you for your letter and the article on those poor, psychotic pooches and Prozac.

I found the article very interesting, in particular the part about the Bull Terrier who had an obsession for sticks and wood. It is comforting to know that a dog like that could be cured by modern medicine. The article mentioned that the Bull Terrier was featured on the television show, "TV Nation." I missed that program because my owner doesn't allow me to watch television. Goddamn noisy box she calls it. I wonder why a dog with such a problem would want to advertise it on national TV. I would be embarrassed. Perhaps he just wanted to tell his side of the story.

It concerns me: your reason for sending this particular article at this particular time. It is always nice to hear from you, but I can't help feeling that you are trying to tell me something. Am I reading too much into this, or do you think I have...a problem?

Sure, maybe I fetch a little more than other dogs do. Is that so bad? I have memories from my puppyhood of people throwing things for me to fetch. I'd bound after them like a hapless fool. I didn't know what I was doing. Everyone said it was cute. What? Now that I'm older, it's not so cute anymore?

I remember the time back in Los Angeles, when I ran off the side of a cliff after a poorly aimed tennis ball. It took my owner almost an hour to get me out of there. Hey! Now that I think about it — I could have died back there. Maybe I do have a problem.

You know, sometimes after I chew a stick to little bits and swallow the pieces, I don't feel very good the next day. My owner has to walk me every ten minutes because I'd have a tummy ache. She always told me that it was my own damn fault for chewing up the sticks. But I never listened.

It embarrasses me now to admit that, on more than one occasion, I've stolen toys from other dogs who gather in the park just so that I would never run out.

When my owner walks me past the tennis courts, I can't enjoy the nice weather or the beautiful scenery because I am always on the look out for stray tennis balls. The worst part is: I have a whole bag full of tennis balls at home.

I'm pathetic. I feel like I've hit rock bottom. I should be doing something more constructive and meaningful with my life like leading a blind person, or assisting a police officer, or herding sheep.

I realize now that the road to recovery starts with recognition of the problem. Your letter has opened my eyes. Maybe there is hope for me. Maybe it's not too late. This is after all, the first day of the rest of my life. I wonder if there is a twelve step program for dogs like me. If there are a lot of dogs like me, we could form a support pack. It would be nice to know that I am not alone with my problem. If that doesn't work, I'll see if my owner will take me to the doctor to get some Prozac. I want to get better. I want to be a whole dog again!

I've heard that "chipping" Prozac can make me more creative. I could write a book like Millie did: I WAS A TEENAGE FETCH MANIAC, or DOGS WHO FETCH TOO MUCH AND THE OWNERS THAT LOVE THEM, or how about I'M OKAY — YOU'RE JUST HUMAN?

Looking back, I can't help but wonder how my life would have been different if only my owner hadn't thrown those sticks to me when I was too young to know any better. It seems to me that her need to throw the stick is as great as my need to retrieve it. Do you think she may be co-dependent?

Already, I'm starting to feel better. Fetching would be okay if I could learn to do it in moderation. I am looking forward to a life free from this seductive monkey on my back; this fetching addiction.

Thanks again for sending such an informative and inspiring article. In return, I am sending you a biscuit and one of my favorite ratty old shreds of a tennis ball to show you that I am sincere in my desire to kick the habit. I will keep you informed of my progress. Hope to see you soon.

Love, Shuggie

P.S. Please remember that there are no bad dogs, only bad owners.

Bolsa Chica

by Anne Clifford

The smell of salt water and campfires blows
over the four-lane highway and across the wetlands,
lifting the hair-like feathers
at the base of a blue heron's neck.
The heron poises like a pointer,
its eyes set in rings of yellow, of red.
It waits until the sun strikes the scales of a fish.
Further out, fish break the surface
like handfuls of thrown stones.
A cluster of white pelicans rustles on the water
and the tips of their wings flash black.

In the breeze, the reeds bend
away from the sea,
away from the highway.
Ducks with feathers like brown velvet
filter through soft green algae with their beaks.
The males have turquoise beaks –
but only in summer, only right now.
A snowy egret shakes a black leg, a yellow foot, a black leg
poking step-by-step through the silt.

Far above the water
a tern cries. It dives,
surfaces, and takes flight again,
a silver fish in its orange-red beak.

As the sun sinks
the air cools
the colors warm
the tide recedes.
And the night herons come down from the trees
to the water's edge.
And they sit there on the rocks,
like old men waiting for another day to end.

Force of Habit

by Cathryn Cofell

He pulls the pillow down tight
around his ears like a nun's wimple
but still he hears her hum
through the oily two a.m. night.

At first he thought
it was that same bat
returned again night after night
through some mysterious hole
in his dreams, returned
in a flurry of tennis rackets,
paper bags, screams.

Now he knows it is just her
at war with her own bats,
her own sonar throat
humming a tune with no last line,
finding no bare walls in the dark.

He puts one hand across her neck.
Strokes her like a cat.
Wills her to stop, fears she will.
He kisses her softly
above the jaw,
tastes talcum and candle wax,
a hint of wings.

The Exclusion Process
by Cathryn Cofell

Three summers in the house,
three bats.
The last one dies slowly,
slides through a knot under the basement steps
surrenders like a faulty smoke alarm,
disappears.

Tomorrow the exterminator will come,
but bats are not the killing kind.
He will cast his nets,
anoint the attic with mothballs,
heal the small cracks in our framework.

Next summer, we will split
our house in two searching
for signs that it is finished.
Recoil, revenge, regret,
it is the thing you fear the most
that holds you at night.

Someday I Will Become a Woman

by Cathryn Cofell

and forget
I am really a giraffe.
It's easy to see how,
long sultry legs compressed
into squat pink snowpants,
body thick and clumsy
and eager to be less,
eager to be out

in Wisconsin's bitter season.
Someday I will lose the grace
of running naked
through the dusty grass,
drinking without two hands
and a cup,
ruminating over a dinner
not picked or pickled
from grandma's garden
and not because
I have three more bites to go

before leaving the mesa.
Someday I will hear that empty space
before the lion pounces
and not know
he is not a boy in a parka
fighting a snowball war,
that he runs for my
twitching spotted rump.
That it is hot and real,
closer to the end
than ever was
in a fenced backyard of Band-Aids
and trips to the Milwaukee zoo

not know that I run
on all four legs
for my life.

Animal Attractions
by Nancy Cook

1. Otter Infatuation

You know what it's like, it's like spilling down a rainbow. You jump without thinking, and you slip along your back on water smooth as moss. All around are colors, blue and green and silver. You think your eyes are wide open the whole time, but they blink... *Pop*! ... and every blink brings a tiny shudder. You stretch, and stretch again, body in a grin, lifting your head to meet the sky, inviting the sun to reach down and touch... It's a short slide, a bullet ride; you never look down and you never look back. Falling is a flash of color.

Down you go, like a whistle. Head first and eyes slit. Knowing what to expect and never ready for it. The body-breaking bottom is hidden from your sun-struck eyes. You have to trust. Or block the need to. Then you hit. *Womp*! You plunge with pleasure, and *ooo ooohh* you squeal. This is what living is. This is sweet joy, this is pure love, to feel so free.

You dive in deep. No colors any more and hardly any sound but what's within. No one can see you now, not really, you've gone too far. For a moment it's still and you tense. You doubt yourself, you want to turn back. But *hussshh*...do you hear something? Muffled clapping maybe? The flapping of furry wings? Applause, like *hubba hubba*. The music of *Yessss*... Then *blpplp...blp blp blp...plp blp*... and something like laughter escapes from inside. Bubbles rise, slowly at first, then faster. They burst through the surface. *Ha*! A thousand giggles.

When you come up for air, you're brand new. You shine, and don't you know it. You toss your head

57

and the water flies, *whhssht*, a spinning crown 'round your uplifted head. And there you are, that happy body, that sleek, sassy grin. Were you scared? Will you go back for more?

2. Snake Lust

She was going home, and it was late.

There would be a moon tonight, as full and alive as the sun. She slowed her slithering pace until she could see its outlines grow into a shimmering eggshell, a glistening platinum globe of light, light she wouldn't need as she traced the familiar ground below, the ground that was the road home. She knew what was waiting for her, knew without thinking it; and without realizing it, she imagined seeing him there, everywhere, in the gulleys of the moon, in the flickering branches of the cottonwoods, in the shadows like rivers curving and curling over the dry earth. Now she had no desire to think, now she had no need to see; it was late, and she was going home, skimming the dusty humps, not looking, not thinking, only sensing the darkness.

The darkness, suddenly it was there, a vapored blanket, descending like mist from the open space above, and settling on the ground. To the west, low on the horizon, a thin ribbon of orange blazed, separating the rich brown earth from the blue-black sky. She stopped, scanned the stillness. She smelled the air, a weightless wind, adrift from the river, dispatching tiny shivers. She let the coolness enter her skin. She loved the silence and the stars.

Closer to home she came now, home, that was just a little hole in the ground, that and nothing more; and she slipped on, passing through the grassy range, avoiding the cattle guard, keeping her eye on the apple tree to the left. The tree would soon bear fruit again; its branches shook off silver petals in the breeze and they fell like snow. Already tonight dew had spilled onto the grass. Like a thousand tiny mirrors, the splattered drops caught the moon's light and glazed the earth with stars; the grass had become the sky. It drew her in. Come play, it said. Come play.

She would leave the dusty road, but only for a moment; she knew what was waiting at home.

She slid into the slick grass, felt it cooling her hot skin. It tickled. She pressed harder, thrust her sleek, tapered body between the prickly blades, making circles in the dew. Now she could feel the dust on her back and she longed to roll over, wished to let the grass rub off the tension, scratch the dryness of the day away. Minutes passed, moments of unawareness...

Then, as suddenly as it had taken on the heaven's disguise, the earth lost its celestial texture, became the grass again. She gathered her thoughts, regained composure, remembered. She knew what was waiting. She eased back to the road, followed it to the end.

She came to rest just inside the entryway and caught her breath. He was home. Inside the hole it was dark, darker than the open sky; but she could sense the nearness of him, could feel the ground move with his soft slipper of a glide. Inside the hole it was moonless, starless. She felt her way towards him, her skin, still wet with dew, blending into the dampness of the floor and the walls. She was very late.

They came together, she and he: limbless, skin to skin, wrapped in moistness. Bodies coiled, sharing their heat. She lay her head against him, rested. He barely moved, let his shape yield slowly to her wordless will, each stirring guided by a heartbeat. She stretched her bowed throat deep into the dark above. In languid motion they swayed, alone, together, a breathless, shudderless rhythm. She loved the silence and the stars.

3. Elephant Love

On the best mornings, the sun awakens me. I open my eyes gradually, as if I were afraid, as if the mere flicker of my eyelids might disturb the sun and prompt its hasty departure.

I like to hold on to my dreams. They are a comfort to me in my old age. I remember them, and I know they are my fate. Once, I dreamed I was a lion, and all around were trees with broad, silky leaves of purple and crimson. I lay in the sun while she brushed the hair of my yellow, shaggy mane with her coarse tongue. One stroke at a time, slowly, ever so slowly, one stroke following upon another, until my mane was gold and glossy, and every leaf had turned to brittle rust.

Now the sun teases me, or so I imagine; it lights upon the leafy canopy above my head and dances there until the leaves are all aflutter, then it slips through the morning air, warming it, and comes to kiss my cheek, nestle in my ear, touch my naked buttocks.

Sometimes I think that she is like the sun, all warmth and innocent power. When she stirs, and her heat touches me, I am reassured, and I am awed.

But she is the tree, too. And it is the tree I see rising every morning, straightening limbs thick and solid as trunks, lifting an awkward, cumbersome weight to its full height, lacking grace and ease of motion. There is hesitation in her movements, a shyness that seems quaint for one so large. Often when she catches me looking at her, she will turn her head away, glancing an ear against her shoulder.

Once, she followed my gaze to her legs. Self-consciously, she touched the sagging skin. I know something about gravity, she said, her smile not hiding, or meaning to hide, her embarrassment.

In the summer, I have seen her eyes rest upon the roses, and I have watched her pluck lilies from the green lake, and I know that she has envied. She does not know how her beauty can stop my heart. But I know. And anyone who would cherish the lily or the rose above all others has never seen the cactus bloom.

I want to touch her. I always want to touch her. Her skin, with its razor-fine lines, its husky feel, its soft, after-storm grayness, tempts my tongue. I want to rub my forehead against her side, and feel the hairs, dry like the savannah grass, bristling my nose. I want to see her kneel, and watch the flesh stretch and grow taut across her knees. I want her on her back; I want to see the dust lift with a sudden thundering shift of her body, and I want to hear her belly moan.

Now I sleep again, and again I dream. And in my dream I hold a piece of ice-clear quartz, shiny as a mirror, and a bit of her thin gray hair, and no illusions.

What Dumb Animals?

by Lee Cunningham

They stood off to my far right just as I opened the door for Lacey, our longhaired, white-gloved black cat who loves to go outside between naps. Three squirrels sat stark still on the sidewalk that crosses in front of our house, focused on the newly arrived cat who had not even noticed them. An aura of fear and desperation hung over their almost frozen stances as the somewhat arthritic older squirrel subtly placed herself behind the two stronger and faster youngsters. Their journey to their maple tree home had been interrupted by danger. Now what to do? They chattered among themselves in short, staccato phrases with brief pauses between.

The oldest squirrel moved slowly between and behind the two younger ones, neither of which ever took his or her eyes off the cat. The sparse hair on the old squirrel's tail and her molting coat spoke of her age, as did her jerky movements. Her days of frolicking, running, somersaulting, wrestling, and playing flying leap games in the trees must seem like foggy dreams in her old, forward-bent head. Grey squirrels can live more than twenty years.

Lacey suddenly turned full face toward them and froze in mid-step, one paw poised in the air. She sized up the situation, and then continued on her way as though she had decided they would be no threat to her. She was right. Some more squirrel conversation, crisp and humorless, came across the lawn. They had planned their strategy. The objective: to get the older squirrel, possibly related to them, safely back into their tree. It stood a driveway's width beyond the door where Lacey had begun her foray — about 50 treacherous feet for them to travel.

Their plan of action began when one of the younger protectors flashed his tail and took off at a dead run across Lacey's path. He chattered and made little playful charges in the direction of the cat. She loved to play and took the bait. She moved toward him, doing her crouching "I'm sneaking up on you" forward motion, head tight to the ground and all four "elbows" rising above her backbone; she slid herself forward on her tummy in the tall grass.

Back on the sidewalk, the guard squirrel and the old one moved slowly so as not to attract Lacy's attention, always with the younger squirrel between the cat and the elderly one. As soon as the cat's range of vision did not include them, they sped up, using the target tree as a screen between them and the distracted cat. Lacy kept her eyes glued to the crazy squirrel that was running up the other tree, around the back and down the front to flash his tail and grin at her almost on her eye level. It was too much for Lacy. She made a bounding run at him. Up the tree he went.

This maneuver gave the other two just enough time to get to their tree and climb up to safety. Even then, the younger squirrel maintained his position between his charge and the cat. As they moved up the tree, he stayed below near the ground as she carefully and slowly climbed up. The biggest danger had passed.

When she was safe, the decoy squirrel made a zigzagging, whoopee-shouting dash across the grass between the trees and scurried up the maple tree with them. Lacey sat down and looked disgusted. She knew she had been foiled, but then realized she had been given the respect of being seen as a danger to them! So with tail confidently up, she continued her normal morning patrol.

I watched this whole thing and still couldn't believe it. I had witnessed a strategy planning session, an executed deception, coordinated maneuvers, and victory. The squirrels had openly given their elderly relative value in their society, and, along with that, Lacey was having a beautiful day.

Marmalade

by Joanne Dalbo

Stretched out so long, a crescent on the grass.
Creamsicle stripes against cool leaves of green.
Your eyes large orbs of lazy golden glass.
No movement, save to lick a white paw clean.

But then in jungles deep with marigolds,
Ears up, alert, paws poised, you pause, then pounce.
The softened crescent tautens, becomes bowed
No moment wasted, every movement counts.

The small prize hanging limp in your tight jaw,
You place at my feet, proudly waiting praise.
I wanted to scream at the mouse I saw,
And prayed that this would be a short lived phase.

What message do you have for me, what facts?
Work purposefully briefly, then relax.

String Figures

by Jeanne Desy

With the divorce I took the cat
from house to apartment. The cat
did not like change,
and cowered behind a chair,
and when it was lifted, streaked
under the bed and huddled
unblinking until I captured and boxed her
dust and all.

      I'd bought her when I was lonely. But now,
when I studied, she sat on the page.
She nibbled my thesis; she jammed
the keys, calling me Burmese names.
She climbed to my shoulder, heavy,
and purred louder than Kant or Hume,
louder than thought. The cat
was impossible.

      I was no longer lonely. The cat
startled my phobic lover from hidden places,
and bulked, insistent, against his legs.
When we passed string between us, figures growing
under our hands, the cat
hooked the cradle and pulled.
I knew what she wanted –
the simple dance,
the marvelous twitching and lift
and her own leap, catch.
Her teeth tangled our figures time and again.
One could do nothing with her around.
She wailed whenever we talked.

      I wish I had kept her when we married,
but she was a hindrance just then.
I was sure she would always survive,
I thought if I had to replace her,
I could, I thought
I would never be lonely again.

On Looking at Precambrian Fossils

by Jeanne Desy

Translucent
      simple creatures,
economical grazers,
      colorless prints
            in sandstone.
Cloudina,
      Pteridinium,
Kimberella,
      innocents,
            softer lives.

      Repeated cries
      of poets, *To be silent,*
      without names, without words!

Oh, to be Rangea,
      browse plankton,
Phyllozoon, rise
      from the seafloor,
            undulate through
      speechless waters
or be anchored there.

Breakfast

by Jo Lee Dibert-Fitko

This morning
black birds
crowd each other
out
for the few pieces
of stale and
crusty bread.
Semblance like
spreading piles
of dark thick tar
across the fresh
green summer
grass.
Their hungry
pitch strained
screeches
smother
the air
then succumb to
a muted drone.
Searching beaks
clean the
ground laid table
with one
picked up swoop,
departing as
promptly as they
arrived.
I'm left staring
with an empty
plastic bag dangling.
My guests' gratuity
paving the sky
for a hundred runways'
crisscross view.

The Dog From Three Blocks Over
by Jo Lee Dibert-Fitko

He or she startled me.
I jumped with the wet licks
behind my knees.
Milky Lab.
Toasted edges around
perked up ears and tail.
    "Don't follow me."
You became my walking partner.
Catch-up companion.
Following me home.
No collar. No I.D.
Slopping up water from
a dirty green bowl retrieved
from my kitchen sink.
    "I don't have time to play."
Emptying contents for a
makeshift Frisbee.
A round of fetch with
broken up sticks.
Last year's tennis ball
asking to be chased.
    "Go home now."
As if I expected agreement
or compliance with stranger's commands.
You curl up on the outdoor mat.
Afternoon's welcome nap.
An autumn sun makes your coat
gently warm.
    "You can't stay here."
Belly rising with slow easy breathing.
Lids closed over fudge brown eyes.
Tail thumping in metronomed pace.
My lunch on a plate by your side.

The Perils of Pasta, St. Bernadette and Casanova

by Alexandria Elliot

I know where Easter eggs come from…" Connie announced, hand on hip, tiny nose uptilted. At five she reminded me so much of Mom, especially when she brushed her long brown curls from her shoulder, all arrogance and drama. "…Bunnies!"

"No way – what about these?"

Connie narrowed her eyes just like Dad, and rebuffed our 12 year-old sister. "I mean the ones the Easter Bunny brings." Defiantly, she dunked a finished red egg into the green egg dye. Green splashed all over me, the white Formica tabletop and newspapers, and Anna's high chair tray.

The baby's tiny fingers were reaching to smear the dye when I grabbed her hand in midair. "Connie, stop making a mess. Kim, quit arguing with her. Hand me a towel before Anna fingerpaints. This stuff really stains, and I'll have to clean it with bleach before Mom and Dad get home."

Casanova jumped onto the table, narrowly missing a cardboard tray of dried, colored eggs. Though two years older than Anna, Casanova seemed an eternal kitten, always eager to dip into the fish tank or turn over whatever glass of milk, beer or straight scotch was nearest. He usually stayed close to us girls, and remained wary of any man, except for Dad.

Dad had discovered him as an emaciated kitten devouring dried-out spaghetti in our garbage can. He carried the dirty little thing into the house, saying. "Mutter, mutter, look what I found," in his most coquettish voice.

"Leo, you're as bad as the kids. I can't even pee in peace." Mom regarded the baby kitten on the floor, then Dad, busy cutting pasta into a saucer, leftovers from Pasta-Egg Soup.

"Mutter, he's so hungry," Dad said, as if he were the one who was starving.

69

"He won't eat pasta."

"I caught him eating s'ghetti in the garbage. He must be Italian," Dad said, smiling as he poured the yellowish soup stock with bits of egg over the pasta. Sure enough, Casanova licked the saucer clean.

He became Dad's dinner companion, growing huge until their bellies matched. This gray Persian knew whose hand fed him, and would stand on his hind legs behind Dad's chair and beg for a morsel by poking him with one claw. Dad would oblige several times, then tell someone to fix Casanova a dish. Along with the rest of us, Casanova ate pasta three or four times a week since we were Italian, and poor. I tired of it, but not Dad and Casanova. They loved their pasta. Dad's favorite was cheese-filled ravioli; Casanova's was Mom's homemade spaghetti and meatballs.

Connie's shrieking startled me back to the catastrophe confronting me. "I am *not* making a mess. Don't boss me around, Regina, you're not my mother" – Connie's favorite line when she didn't want to listen to me, although I was 10 years older. "Bombs away." She aimed an orange egg toward the blue food coloring, hitting the bare edge of the tabletop instead. Cas shied away, knocking over a cup of red egg dye that bled over the newspapers and dripped on the white floor. Anna's quick little hands reached across the edge of her tray and splashed happily in the stream of color.

"Dammit, this was a bad idea," I said, trying to catch the drips with whatever sheets of newspaper remained dry. "I should have spread papers all over," and, on seeing Anna, "and on your *hair*." Kim removed the dried, colored eggs to the safety of the counter.

Connie poured the blue into the pink container, then emptied the murky purple mixture back and forth between the two cups, spilling lavishly.

"Stop," I shouted as Dad walked into the kitchen carrying a cage with straw poking out of the sides. Anna started to whine at the sight of Mom and Connie was caught with her fingers in the green dye trying to fish out the old red egg, now brown.

I looked to my father for support. "I'm trying to color eggs and Connie won't listen to me. Look at the mess she made." Casanova jumped from the table, leaving a wet trail of tinted tracks on the linoleum. One side of his white whiskers was green and red.

"Dad…" Kim's dark blue eyes grew wider in fear as she made the sign of the cross and backed up against the wall. The tabletop was soaked with rainbow-colored puddles and streams. By now Anna had smeared the egg dyes all over her high chair tray, hair and mouth, giving her a greenish, sickly look. Her right cheek was slashed red.

Mom's face paled beneath her fiery hair rolled up in pink sponge curlers. "Redd-gina," she slurred.

"Don't worry. I'll clean up." How much had she been drinking?

Dad's face purpled. "How're you gonna get those stains up? You don't deserve what I brung yous for Easter."

"You didn't bring anything," Mom sneered. "Rocco the Shark made us take it. He said they'd have stew, and you fell for it."

"But Mutter, it had no mutter. It's a poor, mutterless little thing," he protested.

"Jush open the cage," Mom said, steadying herself with a large gesture that almost clipped me on the chin.

Connie was off the chair and peering into the cage in an instant. "What's in there?"

Dad lowered the cage to one of the few dry areas. Connie, Kim and Casanova drew closer.

"Keep that cat away," Mom warned, her finger shaking sternly in my direction.

Kim reached into the cage and opened the box. Inside huddled a small, trembling white rabbit. Kim, who had a dramatic and not necessarily healthy streak of religiosity, breathed, "Ooh. God's answered my prayers. I'll name her Bernadette, after the saint. We'll have her blessed." I rolled my eyes and wondered if she might kneel.

Casanova crouched, ready to pounce. Terrified, Bernadette squirmed out of Kim's arms, leaped out of the kitchen, through the dining room and into the living room. Cas was right behind. The rabbit zigzagged, crazed with fear.

Mom screamed, "I told you to wassch that bunny."

Dad yelled, as if the cat would listen, "Casanova! Come here."

"Cas is gonna eat St. Bernadettel" Connie's screeching penetrated our eardrums. Kim made a beeline for the rabbit, chasing her as she bounded from one corner to another.

I put Anna on the floor and followed. "Connie, help me get the damn cat." Anna started to whine.

Kim was down on her stomach, reaching for Bernadette under the couch. Connie tackled the cat just as I intercepted him from the front. "Got him," my sister announced, squeezing the poor chunky thing under his paws, forcing his fur to fold into accordion-like waves. All scrunched up, he looked as if his front legs jutted forward from his head. The rest of his body swung heavily like a pendulum as she carried him off to her room. Mom stooped down to pick up Anna and soothe her, but almost toppled over.

Dad stared at me. "You'd better help your mother. She don't look so good."

"Sshhh. St. Bernadette's scared," Kim said. "She's shaking." I took Anna from Mom, who stumbled to the couch mumbling something about making an Easter cake.

"You sleep. I'll feed the kids and make the cake." Go ahead; pass out, I thought. Leave me with everything again.

Dad's eyes were bloodshot from drinking with Rocco the Shark. "I'm gonna take a nap."

"Okay." He'll be out for the night.

Kim sat by the couch with Bernadette, speaking softly as the furry body calmed.

I carried the baby into the kitchen and surveyed the damage. It was bad. The cage sat on the linoleum, surrounded by pools bleeding color one into the other, a larger version of the high chair tray. Soggy papers littered the tabletop. When I reached a free hand to toss them into the garbage, I saw reversed black newsprint staining the white Formica.

❖ ❖ ❖

Damn my mother, Easter, *and* this cake, I swore silently, fighting to remove it from its molded pan. Damn its long ears, threatening to break off. Three hours on my feet, scrubbing up, mopping the floor, feeding the kids, making the cake and washing dishes while it baked, and now the cat wants food.

Cas stuck his paw into the bunny's cage, sending Bernadette digging under the straw for protection. We're out of cat food. Wouldn't you know it. Hey, there's always leftover pasta and sauce. "Here. Eat, and leave her alone."

Finally, I pulled the rabbit cake from its pan and stood it upright. It would look great after it was frosted and sprinkled with shredded coconut, surrounded with Easter grass and jellybeans. But with the first dab of frosting, the head broke off. When I lifted it, the left ear fell into pieces. My anxiety grew as the music from "King of Kings" swelled from the living room. Don't panic – toothpicks and frosting could do wonders, I thought. I heard Jesus intone, "Forgive them Father, they know not what they do." Casanova's slurping distracted me, and the bunny's tail crumbled at my touch. As I toothpicked the head to the body and glued them together with frosting, its nose fell off, and when the right ear followed, I broke down and cried, realizing I knew not what I was doing, either. The noseless, earless, tailless creature stared lopsidedly at me from a precarious angle.

I had an amputee rabbit for a cake and no hope in sight. I sobbed my way into the living room, exhausted and ashamed, careful to step around my sisters asleep on the floor.

"Mom," I managed, interrupting her snores. "Wake up. Something terrible's happened." She momentarily opened her eyes.

"The rabbit. I tried to stop it, but when Casanova –" I gasped. "Its tail came off, and then its ears – both of them. And the whole head, too." A fresh wave of tears overtook me.

Mom's eyelids flew open. "Christ, no," she screamed, waking the kids. "I tried to save it, but it's all in pieces."

The sound of Casanova's claws raking the metal cage drained the color from my mother's face. "Cas," she croaked hoarsely. He walked in, red staining his face and whiskers.

The girls stared at him, shocked. Connie's long howl shook the windows as she dashed to the kitchen. Kim screamed, fleeing the room and reappearing seconds later, frantically crossing herself and grasping her jar of Holy Water. "My bunny, my little St. Bernadette," she cried against the background of Anna's drowsy whimpering. "I have to baptize – what's left of her." The cat licked his paws. "Murderer," she accused from the doorway. "I can't go in there."

Dumbfounded, I watched Mom sit up, gripping the seat for support. "Casanova – how?" she said.

I looked at him washing away the last of the tomato sauce and at last understood the commotion. "No, the bunny – "

"Is right here," Connie said, walking in with Bernadette, alive and in one piece.

"A miracle," Kim proclaimed, flinging Holy Water. The rabbit flinched under the assault.

"The frosting wouldn't fix the cake – " Laughter overcame me.

Mom's face turned from tragedy to comedy, comprehension shining in her eyes. "You're hysterical," she giggled. Weakly, I lowered myself to the couch beside her, and Kim continued showering Connie, Cas, Baby Anna, the rabbit and everything else in sight with holy blessings.

Pax Canis

by Dianne L. Frerichs

Hello, Pup, welcome to the pack! As a puppy and the pack's newest member, you need to learn a few things. Life here can be fun, but first, you have to catch on about the two-leggers who think they are the bosses.

Over there's Number One, the pack leader. This is the one you obey above all the others. Your relationship with this two-legger has a lot to do with you. If you enjoy a good tug-of-war and an enthusiastic Frisbee catch, this one will be your best buddy. Number One doesn't like the cuddly fluffy four-leggers as much as the tough ones. It's a hunter thing, I've been told.

Next in the pack is the Number Two. This is the human you must get on the good side of because this one is the guardian of the food. Even if short two-leggers set down your dish, human Two is ultimately responsible. This human likes cuddlers and kissers. Knowing this, you can use it to your advantage. But be careful, Two hates accidents in the house and canine trash inspection spread all over the floor.

The final type of pack member is the short two-leggers, small humans. They're more like us than anyone would care to admit; so watch the rest of us for proper technique. If you're clever, the short two-leggers can be blamed for something you did. But they can be a great source of fun, games, and snacks. So follow them around and enjoy yourself.

Remember, you are a puppy, so exuberance is always fitting. Jump up and down, roll around, chase your tail, and wag your entire body. All of these are acceptable behaviors in public; in private, act your species, not your age. The one behavior that must be carefully controlled is barking. Now the main two-leggers have accepted certain barking situations: danger, stranger, and woodland creatures invading your yard. All other barking should be the joyful "I'm with my people and I'm having fun" barks.

75

Yard is something a dog can truly appreciate. If offers freedom of choice. You can stalk other creatures, chase others away from your fence (a job approved of by humans) or you can just soak up the sun's rays. All this, and the smells of nature too. A fun place to visit and roll around in, but I wouldn't want to live there.

This brings us to living indoors. This kind of doghouse has a variety of spaces but they break down to: play areas, dining areas, den areas and emergency areas. Play areas are all around. Number One may throw your toy and you can drop the toy by other two-leggers and get more of them involved or just grab the toy and run, playing keep-away. Letting the entire people pack chase you can be great fun for all. But don't spoil them, take a lesson from the cat: aloof attitude and cool disdain can keep the human pack humble.

One concept we can't forget is mealtime. But the dining areas of the house are closely guarded since the humans here don't like to share their food. So don't skip the chow in the bowl. If small humans are present, luck is on our side. Small humans are sloppy; they lose food. Cute works here. Look adorable and hungry, but not aggressive, and do *not* frighten the small ones. Let them drop things down to you. They think it's a game and we let them, while at the same time, we snarf their food.

Den areas are just about the most important. Where will you sleep? As the rookie, you need to know your place and that is at the bottom of the pack both literally and figuratively. Pack piling in bed is a joy, but I am number one dog and selecting my sleeping arrangements come first and I choose people snuggling.

Sleeping positions in the pack bed are "H", puppy curl and Velcro, my personal favorite. You are probably used to puppy curl. This can be done at any spot in the bed usually without disturbance. "H" can cause trouble if a human can't move because they will move you. The same can happen with Velcro position. Trapping your human on the edge of the bed will, I promise, bring results you don't want. That covered foam basket in the corner is the result of an edge-clutching human's vengeance. It might be better than the floor, but it can't beat soft, warm people snuggling.

The final space in the house to worry about is the emergency area. I mention this only because you are so young and things happen when puppies get excited. Cold hard floor surfaces are the only acceptable accident surfaces. On the newspaper is fine unless it is on the carpet or if the humans have not opened it. They get to play with it first, then we can use it. Rugs covering cold, hard surfaces should be avoided since these will cause more work for humans and that doesn't make them happy. And never leave a pile in a corner. If you must have that kind of accident, be subtly obvious. Leave it near the door, but not in the human path or directly in front of the door. Always remember, as a puppy, you can use cute to bail yourself out of a lot. You need to remember what works for each different human. Sad Pitiful Face may work for one, but "What? Who, me?" may work for another. Don't look to the rest of us to help you out here – every pet for himself on toilet errors.

Since you are new to this pack and young, the two-leggers will think you are undisciplined. You can use this, but don't stretch it too far. As a pup in training, you will be able to knock the garbage over and carry it around the house, but only for about the first three weeks. After that, even cute can't save you. I remember when Valdi and his brother, Sigfried, got caught by a telltale meat price sticker stuck to a back paw that no amount of paw shaking could remove. Through waves of human laughter, they were both punished, even though these humans thought longhaired dachshunds were so very, very cute.

If the two-leggers take you to training classes, beware. Trust me, they will expect better behavior and slips will not be tolerated. The training usually covers your basic pack survival skills: sit, come, and stay. The real tricky stuff is the heel walking. My advice is, if Number One has your leash, do everything perfectly. As soon as this human stops, drop to your best sit position, watch the human's every move, and don't move until told to. Now, if any other two-leggers have your leash, stop but don't sit down. This little bit of personal independence does wonders for your own canine psyche. You must remember to choose your battles and your victories carefully. You don't want to break the spirit of the humans.

That is the most important point to remember. Don't break their spirit. Humans can be strong-willed, but also gentle and loving. For always, the word pet is a noun and a verb and unconditional love goes both ways.

Tiger
by Cynthia Gallaher

Bands of color dance
from the center
of the picnic table umbrella,
or race from a flag end to end.

These are the tame stripes,
the domestic variety,
not like yours
dabbed on and jagged
from bristles of an angry paintbrush.

Your scary suit
is so thick a mat,
I wonder if you have
a real heart beating
between ribs,
along your furry underside,
glowing in a higher candle power
    of white,
finger deep in fur and
    hand deep in tiger flesh.

Orange and white and black
in the USA
mean Halloween,
pumpkins,
ghosts,
cats,
but in India,
it can only mean you,
tiger,
fire, mad stripes and terror,
making a jungle purge
of extra rats and
things that go bump in the night,
between your flaming teeth.

Whale Song
by Cynthia Gallaher

My ears ride
the backs of whale songs,
dreams climb
through whale arteries
vast enough to hold
my giant-sized yearnings,
to listen to lowdown
lub-dubs
that might have read
a healthier pulse
of the deep sea.

I see 2000 faces
of people from the coastal town,
waving from shore,
their weighty and windy words
could pull oar and fill sail
for generations,
but like Jonah, I want to throw off
the same tonnage in thoughts,
heavy in whale days
that may not be as numbered.

Nations could either hold hard to harpoons,
continue to cut to the quick
and the capture,
or hold tightly to pens like these,
waving whale melody like
breath rising fast to surface,
roving without keen edges,
as do eyes, camera lenses
or memory.

Finding Home
by Margaret Glass

Personally, I never could quite understand which came first in that great philosophical question about the chicken or the egg. Nor did I find humor in the joke about the chicken crossing the road. However, I am convinced it was to find home. Searching no doubt, like myself for the perfect place, then poof, having it evaporate like water on a hot sidewalk. I realized this a couple years ago when I decided to move to Chicago, selecting an apartment in a very family oriented, ethnic neighborhood. My building manager offered to find me a husband when we first met and invited all his single European male friends to help me the day I moved. Matchmaking was apparently the part of my lease written in Russian.

My first two nights in my new apartment were marked by strange bird sounds late at night. I dismissed them as just pigeons. A few more days passed before I saw my building manager, Lufka, raking leaves and I decided to ask about the sounds.

"Lufka, I hear birds outside my kitchen."

"Birds, good outside, no?"

"They bother me."

"Okay, I fix." He smiled his big tooth speckled grin and bid me goodnight, leaving me with a false confidence that he would attend to the problem.

The next evening, a wide grin graced Lufka's face as greeted me at my front door. He held up the trophy of his catch, five dead pigeons. Their feet bound together by heavy baling twine, he offered them to me like a wilted gray flower bouquet. The effect was more like a feather duster with eyes.

"I bring you the birds."

"I don't …Thank you." I stumbled for words to express my thoughts. He had gotten rid of the problem; however, a new one now faced me. What does one do with dead pigeons, I wondered silently?

81

"You have no husband. I know good man you can meet. He can catch birds just as good as me."

"Well, I don't really need the birds. Would you like them?"

"My wife, she good cook. I'll give them to her. You need husband, I call Edgar... you a little too skinny, but..."

"But...." I was too late. He had taken the birds and headed up the stairs toward his own apartment to give the birds to his wife and no doubt call Edgar without delay.

I opened my back door to allow the fresh spring air to seep into my newly painted apartment while I prepared my fried chicken for dinner. Relaxing to the sounds filtering in from laughing children playing in the side yard and the soft music on my radio, I thought perhaps I had found my home. As I sat down in my dinning room I heard, "Tap, tap, tap, tap." Then a loud, rustling turmoil, almost like a scratching sound came from outside my screen door. Edgar? Already? I got up and looked outside to find nobody there.

Perhaps there are more pigeons, I thought. Poor Lufka thought he got them all.

A fluttering commotion caught my eye just outside my dinning room window like something flying around as I returned to my chair. Probably a piece of paper caught by the wind, I thought to myself as I picked up a drumstick of my now cold fried chicken. However, the noise at the back door returned, this time definitely sounding like someone was knocking.

Damn pigeons, I thought as I rushed toward my back screen door. "I'll teach you!" I yelled.

"Bang!" I slammed opened the screen door expecting to surprise the gang of pigeons. Instead, a small, white hen raced inside my warm, inviting apartment. She flapped a few times, giving her enough lift to land on my dinning room table, making a spectacular centerpiece performance. Stunned by a bird's appearance, "Oh, Shit!" was the only thing that came to mind. The hen adjusted her small frame boldly on top of the green and red apples in a basket, cocking her head side to side, staring at her new surroundings. I glared at the small white intruder, amazed at the peaceful look it seemed to have as it sat unaware she was disrupting my dinner or that I was eating some distant relative of hers, or perhaps even a close friend. A few minutes passed before it occurred to me to call Lufka about the bird. Surely, he would remove the hen and return it to her owner, whoever that was. I gave him a brief summary of the events but he did not seem to follow at all what I was talking about.

"Chicken?" He apparently did not recognize the word chicken, I thought.

"Lufka, a hen."

"Hen?"

I attempted to mimic a chicken. "Cluck, cluck, cluck."

"Pigeon?"

"Lufka, no pigeon, chicken."

"No catch chicken, only pigeons. Over here, chicken come from store."

"Lufka, you don't understand. I have a chicken in my apartment."

"Sorry, not pets allowed, Miss G. I go eat now. Thank you."

As he hung up another brilliant idea came to mind. Call the police. Surely they have a division who handles this kind of thing in big cities. Smugly, I dialed 911.

"Chicago emergency line. How may I assist you?"

"I have a chicken in my apartment."

"Miss, it is a serious offense to call this number for false emergencies."

"It is not a joke. I really have a hen in my apartment."

"Is this chicken threatening your life?" Her voice had a definite edge to it.

"Well, no. I want someone to come and get it."

"How did it get into your apartment, miss?"

"I opened my back door and it ran in."

"Ran in."

"Yes."

She paused. "Was it being chased?"

"I don't know. I didn't see anyone else."

"And where is this bird now?"

"Sitting on my fruit basket in the center of my dinning room table." She paused again, longer this time. "Miss, have you consumed any drugs, alcohol, or inhaled any fumes in the last hour?"

"No. Do I sound like I have?"

"Well, miss, it is not for me to say. What do you want us to do?"

"Send someone by to pick up this bird."

"I am sorry, miss, the Chicago Police are not allowed to transport farm animals in their squad cars for health reasons."

"Health reasons? Whose health?"

"Miss, that is not for me to say."

"Is there anyone else who can help me get rid of this bird?"

Feathers, Fins & Fur

"We are not equipped to handle such emergencies. I can dispatch officers to your residency to give you the current zoning ordinances about having fowl within the city boundaries without a special permit."

"What good will that do? I want to get rid of the bird, not start a farm."

"Well, miss, then you will understand the $500 ticket that they will issue to you for having a chicken in your apartment without the proper permit."

"But I just told you, it ran into my apartment."

"How can I know you are telling me the truth? You have a chicken in your apartment, is that correct?"

"Yes, but..."

"Miss, my suggestion is to catch that bird and throw it outside before the officers get there. So let me verify your address..." I panicked and slammed the phone down.

Now I had to capture this bird and get rid of it before Chicago's Finest came to ticket me. How was I to catch a chicken?

"I could put it in a bag...no, a box!" I thought out loud as I looked around my apartment. I dropped a small paper box over the hen, trapping her like a gift. A soft clucking came from under the box. With the hen enclosed and a lid on tightly, I began my quest to find the owner of the little white bird. So I began to knock on back doors. The first door opened.

"Are you missing a chicken?" I smiled and lifted the lid to show the hen. The door slammed. I took it as a no. The next two apartments had no response. I thought a large family lived above me and headed up the front stairs. I could hear a television game show, voices of children yelling, and smell something like a cross between sweet potato pie and stale beer. It reminded me that I now lived in Chicago. I knocked on the door.

A loud, strong, crackled voice called out, "That you, Babe?"

"No, I live downstairs."

"Too loud?"

"No..."

"Then go away."

"I came to ask if you lost something."

"Say what?"

"Did you lose a ....pet?"

"Just a minute." I heard the rustling of children being pushed away from the door.

"Be out there in a minute." The door opened to reveal a sweet, kind face of an elderly black woman. "Now youngins get in there, this has nothing to do with yous." She turned to me and said, "Well, honey, what ya find?"

84

"A bird."

"Let's take a look." Her snow-white hair gave her a wise appearance. She pulled off the lid with one hand and swooped up the hen with the other faster than I expected. Quickly she brought the hen into a bear hug to her large, sagging body and said, "Henry, honey, you've come home."

"I think you're mistaken. It's a chicken."

Her face creased into a broad smile. "Henry, you old cock. Knew you'd come back. Wait 'til I show Mattie. She thinks ya dead and buried. I knew you'd be back, baby."

"I think you are little confused."

"Mattie!" She began to scream over the television, over the crying children, and sounds of running feet.

"Momma, where you'd get that thing?"

"Ain't it sweet? Sweet little birdie. Lookie kids, Granny got Henry. Like to see us dance?" She swung around into make believe dance steps from some other decade.

"Momma, now put that down. No telling where it's been. Kids, get back before I whoop you all."

"Can't I keep the sweet little birdie?"

"No."

"Who's Henry," I asked.

"My beloved husband." She beamed fondly at the memory. "Dead 15 years."

"Um…I can tell this isn't your bird. I'll just take it and go now." I struggled to get it back from the woman's tight hug.

"Is it yours?" snapped the younger woman.

"I found it."

"No pets allowed here, lady. Momma, you get your ass back in here."

"Sure was nice of ya to bring your bird up to visit." The door slammed in my face.

I glanced out one of the stairway windows and noticed a white Chicago squad car parking in front of my building. I raced down the remaining stairs, popping into my own apartment to cut through to my back door and outside to evade the police. As I shut the door, I heard my doorbell ring. Grasping the box tightly, I ran toward my car parked in a back lot, imagining the police arresting both the hen and me for breaking city laws about farm animals. Finding home was not going to be as simple as crossing the road I thought, as I quickly opened my car, tossing the box with the hen into the back seat and sped off.

Swimming at the Reservoir

by Leonard Goodwin

Three of us
      bounce along the dirt road
      in the stationwagon
Jonathan assures me
      it's a great place to swim
      as I swerve around a rut
Max tries to hold his balance
But his claws have no place to hold
      and he slides

We park at the end of the road
      walk through bushes to a broad sandy beach
      Max trotting on ahead
A clear blue lake
      motionless in the morning sun

We leave our clothes on the vacant shore
Jonathan walks to the water with Max
      encourages him to enter

Max advances slowly
      until the water laps his neck
We continue, while Max hesitates
      his shepherd courage waning
We call
      but he slowly turns toward shore
      sits near our clothes
      recedes to a spot
  on the landscape

From that small spot
      begins a howl
Not a bark, but a howl
It grows in volume across the water
A long, lonely, mournful
      forlorn call
Compressing into sound
      all the sadness and sorrow
      of separation
I turn back toward shore

Off the Bay of Fundy Trail

by Leonard Goodwin

Max runs up the wooded path before us
Returning now and then to check
     as befits a shepherd
But gone too long, my daughter calls
Max bounds out of the woods
     panting from his arduous, self-appointed tasks
Rachel pets him, saying, "Good dog"
     and he disappears in the underbrush

Suddenly, loud barking below to the left
     reaches a crescendo, then silence
We move quickly to the woods
     down the slope where the last sound was heard
Max is in a clearing
     crouching on the ground, twisting his head
     vainly pawing at his mouth
     Rachel runs to him, but stops
     as she sees blood dripping from his jaw

With great effort
      we pin him on his back
      force a dead branch between his teeth
      hearing the crunch of wood
I reach into my pocket for the pliers
Extract six quills from the roof of his mouth
      four from his nose

Twenty feet away
      in aristocratic disdain
A giant porcupine
      hoists himself higher in a tree
Freed, Max scrambles to his feet
      shakes himself, runs to the tree
  barks fiercely at the disappearing form

I return the pliers
      to my pocket with a sigh
Knowing the difficulty
      of living beings
      to learn certain things

Mayan Fragment

by Jane Haldiman

Thick-lined howler monkey god,
scratcher of stones, you squat
egg-eyed and smiling,
crouching like a jaguar over
a kill, flinging lines, codices and ink
over dull white clay.
Rain falls from a fishscale cloud.
You – everything about you is a mess.
Slobbery, ecstatic deity
of writing, a hairy gray muse,
your life sketches a raucous scenario
over the clean clay sky.
Howl your imitation jaguar's
voice to the green sun.
The blood you scatter from a
maimed stone tablet fills the air,
hardens into black lines all around.

Cat Talk

Dedicated to my cats, Sleeping Beauty and Tinkerbell

by Janice J. Heiss

> *In ancient Egypt, the cats of the rich were embalmed*
> *and buried in mummy cases often ornately decorated with gold.*
> *Why did the Egyptians worship cats?*
> *Because cats allow themselves to be worshipped.*

Daily Life

If I keep talking and talking to my cat, one day, out of the clear blue, I'll bet she'll talk back in perfect English. What, oh what, will her first words be? "Are you my real mother?"

Are cats too body conscious? Too vain? Story goes that Queen Cleopatra learned how to do her eye make-up from some Egyptian tabby.

My cat walks down the long, narrow hallway of my apartment with intent. Carefully avoiding the thick, wool runner, preferring the cool hardwood strips, she could be any corporate lawyer getting to work right on time.

I knew a woman who could tell time by measuring her cat's purrs.

My cat puts her paw into the sunspot on the rug as though she were dipping into a pond.

The sunspot is a material object to my cat. She wouldn't bat an eye if I picked one up and moved it to within sniffing distance.

Once, I saw Tinkerbell trying to reach a sunspot on the wall; another time, she tried to find one under the bed.

Would it put an end to world hunger if we put cats to work kneading bread?

Observing a strict daily routine, my cat follows the sun through my apartment. She prepares to take off for her final sunspot of the day, the setting sun burning through the living-room windows, as one would get ready to go to the beach.

Cats bat balls around as if they were part of a World Cup soccer team.

Cats can be so finicky. Some turn up their nose at any food that spills out of their bowls.

Feathers, Fins & Fur _____

My cat climbs the plastic-basket-shaped monumental rectangle of laundry on the bed. Up, up she goes. One misstep and she could land at the bottom of the heap on the pink bra where she started.

Funny Feline

Do you worry that catnip interferes with your cat's short-term memory?

Is a cat in the dog's house double jeopardy?

Here's an ad for a rental placed by a cat landlord: 3-bedroom, 1500 square feet, numerous sun spots, custom-made, built-in litter boxes. All yours for 300 lbs. of kibble/month…NO PEOPLE! NO DOGS! Birds ok.

I picture a group of tough, macho guys hanging out at a bar until the wee hours, too embarrassed to admit they are afraid to go home because they ran out of cat food.

No matter what she's in the middle of – she could be competing in the International Cat's Wimbledon finals, or the world could be hanging in the balance – when you need to lick yourself, you need to lick.

I have a premonition that one day my cat – just as the Wizard of Oz appeared from behind the curtain – will unzip her coat, discarding it like an old garment, to reveal a long-lost relative.

What do you call someone who copycats cats?

Us

A lawyer in San Francisco marries people to their cats. When I marry Tinkerbell, our wedding party will shower us with cat litter, not rice.

I'm afraid my cat just wants me for my body.

I worry that my cat finds me boring since she frequently greets me with a yawn.

Sometimes, when I enter a room where my cat is lounging, she grants me a crumb of acknowledgment just as my grandmother who, before her death, scarcely grunted and nodded when I entered her room.

I'm startled, now and then, to see the face of my deceased grandmother, especially her dark, drinking-well eyes, when I look at

Tinkerbell. We lock into each other's questioning gaze, and I feel Grandma's palpable presence. Is it common to see the beloved in the beloved?

Tinkerbell's fur is as soft as air. Petting her is like stroking a warm, summer breeze.

After my cat licks herself, I love to bury my head in her fur for a deep whiff of fresh, moist laundry mixed with light, spring rain.

Suddenly, I understood my destiny in moving to California. To get together with my cats!

My cat has a nose shaped like a valentine. Will she always be mine?

At times, when I'm petting my cat, caressing her fuzzy tummy, sensing the warm body bag beneath, loving her all over, she abruptly leaps off my lap. Does she feel what I feel after an intense orgasm: panicked, afraid she has fallen too far out of herself, she rushes to collect the pieces?

I've never wanted children, but, if I could have a litter...

What's It All About, Kitty?...

Do cats ever fret over what to do with their free time?

My cat might not know what I'm doing but she always knows *when* I'm doing it.

Cats don't have plans.

Science cannot explain the mystery of cats. Cats only purr in another being's presence or when injured.

A cat's love must be earned. Petting a cat, waiting for her to purr is like those tense moments waiting to hear how a new lover feels.

Purring... Love-current? Exquisite static?

Is purring audible endorphin delivery?

Her purr is as silky as deep sleep.

When I was little, I thought all cats, being feline and the epitome of "sheness," were female. Even now, it is difficult to dispel this belief.

For the true meaning of bourgeois, behold the way cats check out a new apartment! If cats were people, all their homes would look like something out of *Better Homes and Gardens*.

Cats are Republicans, conservative; they don't like change. (Cat owners beware: Don't try to rearrange your furniture.) They are motivated by self-interest. Unlike dogs, they will rarely do anything for you.

Cats like additions and hate subtractions.

Cats think we're their mothers; dogs think we're the leaders of their packs.

Catshots (Cat Snapshots)

My cat, curled in repose, is all swirl.

My sleeping cat's tail wraps her up like a gift ribbon.

Cats' paws, with their cupped claws are, like baseball mitts, equipped for the catch.

My cat's ears monitor her sphere like radar.

My cat is a slinky when she walks down the hall.

When cats turn their heads to lick their shoulders, their shoulders seem to move toward their tongues, like the cart pushing the horse.

What groomers cats are! They, not people, should be the subject of Renoir's "The Bathers."

My next-door neighbor bought an orange tabby the color of her hardwood floors to match her apartment decor.

My cat smells first and decides later; only her nose knows.

The caterwauling cats make other-worldly sounds like a toy doll being raped.

My cat always looks like she's dressed in long johns.

My cat's anus looks like the vortex of a kaleidoscope.

Talk about a perfect fit. My cat's coat was just made for her. Nevertheless, my spoiled cat bought a brand-new winter coat this year.

Though in her fur coat, Tinkerbell is technically nude.

Cat Years

Sleeping Beauty, as she aged, got plumper and plumper, spreading out like a pancake over the entire surface of the pan.

When my 17-year-old cat, Sleeping Beauty, was dying of kidney disease, I asked my vet, Dr. Hansley, if I could donate a kidney. He said that no one had ever asked that. I was surprised.

Though Sleeping Beauty died, she's still here – the faint click of claws on the linoleum, the hoarse meows, the vibration of her landing on tables, chairs, beds. Her soft swish in mid-air. Scratching of fleas, couch, chair, and carpet. The sandpaper tongue. The crunch of kibble. Gagging on hairballs in the middle of night. The quiet lick of water. Blessed breathing, breathing beside me.

Maybe Sleeping Beauty disappeared inside a closet and I just haven't been able to find her.

Ten years after she dies, I dream I open the bottom dresser drawer, and there she is! Cats never die. They just hide.

Take It

by Shari Hemesath

she's looking for paradise
atop her white horse
Ride it cowgirl
Ride
the prairies and
plains and
mesas and
steppes

ride into paradise
on your mare
cities paved in gold
milk and honey
cream and sugar
latte
give that girl a latte

in paradise everything's free
even the lattes flow from waterfalls
like champagne at a wedding
looking for paradise
in tulle, chiffon and sateen
fluttering and rippling
over her gelding's back

she's riding into paradise
a fairy princess
she fancies a
black, pin-striped
bow-tied
aqua velva-scented
tomboy
YUMMMMEEE

paradise
this is where it's at
peaches and cream
lavender buds
starry, starry night

paradise
from her trusted charger's back
ride on into the city
Take It by fire
Take It by force
Take It
just TAKE IT
and stand tall
stand proud
in her curving, saddle-filling hips
full of hope

Gators In the Sewers

by Tina L. Jens

When Phoebe saw the baby alligator swimming in her soup, she realized she was quite mad.

It was homemade vegetable. The soup, that is. Made from the last pickings of a late garden. Which is to say, a few scrawny potatoes, a rogue carrot and lots of onions.

The alligator – yes, it was still there – had climbed upon an onion log and was sunning itself in the glare of the bare, 90 watt bulb that hung over the kitchen table.

Phoebe wondered where its mother was. She had jumped to the conclusion that it was a baby, based solely on its size. But considering its current location, there were infinite possibilities. Phoebe chose not to consider them just now.

The alligator yawned widely, exposing a mouth full of tiny, pointed teeth – about the size of sewing needles, but not nearly so long. Suddenly, the little thing snapped its jaws, ripping a fleshy hunk out of an unsuspecting creature floating past. The surprisingly loud snap scared Phoebe, and she jumped back in her chair with an "Oh!"

The vicious attack on the innocent canned mushroom was a good reminder that while tiny, the alligator was still a wild, dangerous creature.

Phoebe mellowed as she watched the gator wag its tail and chew happily. A herpetologist might have told her that alligators don't wag their tails, exactly. But Phoebe didn't know any of those sort of people.

Phoebe pondered what to do. She lived alone. There was no one to call into the room while she pointed excitedly at her dinnertime discovery. She wasn't a dramatic person, but it would have been nice to have another witness to the strange event.

Even if she had someone to summon, they wouldn't see it. Phoebe instinctively knew this was one of the fundamental laws of nature. She

101

was no student of metaphysics, but she'd seen the Abbott and Costello routine. If Abbott couldn't see the bullfrog in Costello's soup, nobody was going to see the alligator in Phoebe's bowl.

You can't think clearly on an empty stomach. Phoebe had heard that once. It made sense to her. And it *was* her soup. The alligator would just have to share.

She dipped her spoon into the bowl gently, hoping she wouldn't scare the creature, but he slithered off the onion and dived to the bottom of the bowl. Oh well, she'd find him as the soup level went down.

She checked the contents of her spoon carefully – nothing moved. It did contain the mushroom the little gator had been eating. Phoebe felt guilty for stealing his dinner. But he could find another piece.

She went on like that for a time, checking each spoonful before slurping the broth. It occurred to her that there might be more than one gator in the bowl. She spooned frantically through the soup, looking for creatures. Finding none, she continued to eat.

She began to wonder if she'd imagined the alligator. But no, she spotted him in the dregs of the bowl, hiding under a cabbage leaf. She set the tip of her spoon down in front of him. He stepped gingerly onto it. The tip of his tail hung off. He looked uncomfortable – but Phoebe didn't have a bigger spoon.

She lifted him until they were nose to nose. They studied each other intently. The view made her cross-eyed, so she lowered the spoon and set it on the table. The little alligator crawled up the incline and rested his front legs on the tip of the spoon.

Phoebe knew she couldn't keep him. The landlord didn't allow pets, and she already had one contraband kitten that lived in her bottom dresser drawer. But that didn't stop her from fantasizing about raising the little reptile. It'd be cool to have a full-grown alligator slouching through her house. She'd have to put a sign up in her window, "Beware the watchgator."

If she set it loose outside, it would freeze to death. Or get run over by a car. The nearest swamp was states away.

The cat would enjoy playing with it, but that seemed cruel. It was just a baby. And the cat might get hurt, too. Phoebe shuddered as she pictured the creature sinking those needle-sharp teeth into the kitten's soft, pink nose.

Finally, she resorted to the standard method of urban gator disposal – although she did not, technically, live in the city. She flushed him down the toilet. She waved good-bye as he swam away.

Fish Fantasy
by Fran Kaplan

Part 1 – Do Fish Sleep?

I was up at four in the morning. So were they. My three fish were swimming in the mini-aquarium for Aqua Babies, my fourteen-dollar bargain from Thrifty's. They looked wide awake, frisky to me. No matter what time I observed them, they frolicked in bottled water, cobalt blue gravel, in and around a dark green spiney plant. Didn't they ever sleep?

I named the largest, a Dwarf Top Minnow one-and-a-half inches long, Aunt Minnie because she reminded me of my real Aunt Minnie, whose height never exceeded four feet ten inches and who also showed aggressive tendencies at mealtime; first to dive into the largest portion for herself. I knew the sex of the smaller Dwarf Top because the male minnow is only one-and-a-quarter inches long. I rather enjoyed that differential and called him Uncle Harry.

The third, a guppy with a lyre-shaped tail and sharply defined black stripes, flipped and cruised in its tank's left front portion. His devil-may-care attitude recalled to mind my bachelor brother Murphy, who enjoyed his own company doing what he wanted when he wanted.

I had purchased them one week before my first sleepless night. They didn't seem to sleep. I began sleeping less and checking up on them more, every evening at a different time.

They never looked tired. Do pets mimic their owner's habits? Had my insomnia influenced them? Don't be foolish, they're only fish.

One midnight I tip-toed into their room with a small triple-A-batteried flashlight shielded by my hand, hoping to catch them napping.

Up. All three, fluttering, swimming, diving. Aunt Minnie and Uncle Harry, especially perky.

Another time, I left a bright light on all night, thinking eyestrain would make them tired enough to sleep. I had set my alarm clock to ring every two hours so I could check them. They weren't as active as usual, drifting in down-time toward the lower part of the tank. Definitely awake.

Fish have no eyelids; they're unnecessary because the eye is constantly bathed in water. Certain fish live in the dim light and are nocturnal, open

103

at night, closed during the day. What is closed during the day? Without eyelids does it mean their brains close down to browse?

Their brains are divided into three parts: forebrain, midbrain, and hindbrain. All that in an inch? With that much brain, they'd always be thinking. Wouldn't that make them sleepy?

I feed them every other day. Is it enough? Why do they always look hungry? This morning I poked a toothpick through the air hole on top of their mini-tank to wet it. Then I stuck the moist part into the tiny plastic bag of food and re-inserted it into the air hole. Whatever food stuck to the toothpick became their food until the next mealtime. Aunt Minnie and Murphy went right for it. Where was Uncle Harry? I turned the glass cube slowly, as if it were a lazy Susan with ravishing foods. I looked for my third fish. I found a tail between the gravel and a green frond.

Common knowledge is that the best food for fish is other fish. Did they eat him? Did he die of neglect because I should have fed him oftener? I always feel guilty when a pet gets sick or dies, like my gerbil, Milton. I didn't even like him, but I knew it was my fault.

I never suspected illness. Sick fish are listless and swim abnormally. They became emaciated, with sunken eyes and pale gills. My real Uncle Harry was emaciated with sunken eyes and pale cheeks, but my fish looked healthy. A symptom of disease is rubbing against hard objects and having difficulty breathing, sort of like Uncle Harry when Aunt Minnie rubbed against him and my mother told them, "Do that in private, please."

If I knew that a fish had no chance of survival I would dispose of the unfortunate animal with as little pain as possible. I didn't have time to consider draconian methods. Uncle Harry's head was off without my input. Aunt Minnie never liked Uncle Harry. I view her with suspicion.

Just to be on the safe side, I removed the plant and set it aside, then carefully poured the water into a bowl, using a cup to catch the water with the fish so they wouldn't be chummed down the drain. I rinsed the rocks with bottled water, wiped down the sides of the tank to remove any algae and felt relieved to protect Aunt Minnie and Murphy from catching a disease. I yawned and took a nap.

Part 2 – A Fish-Eye View

Here comes that flashlight again. Doesn't she ever sleep? Every time I have a water problem to solve, she bothers us. When I settle into a meditative state, she stares. Yesterday she fed us twice. Is she trying to kill us? Why does she buy gourmet, ground, dried fish flakes that smell like fertilizer? We yearn for an old-fashioned grated fish cake.

Communal living is unbearable. We have no choice of companionship in this closed society. The only way we can get out is by the Aquarist's decree. She doesn't change the water often enough, and when she does, it takes so long that it's hard to breathe. We have an active lifestyle which makes us unsuited for aquarium living in this undersized container.

I have no sex life in this bowl; I'm stuck with a minnow and a swordtail. What's a libidinous guppy to do?

If our insomniac feeder were stuck in traffic, or late for a meeting, she'd know how stressful it is for us to be chased with a net, captured, and lifted out of water. Our gills could collapse from lack of oxygen. Can't she hurry when she changes our water? Confinement in this space without adequate solitary areas brings out aggression and anger. I need a cave or a crevice. My brain's tired of sharing. I feel imprisoned without benefit of parole.

There was her gerbil on the treadmill . . . it used to be on the next shelf in a cage . . . constant track, track, twirl, turn. The noise drove us crazy. The gerbil didn't like her; we didn't like the gerbil. He nipped her fingertip last week when she pushed food toward him. The next day she wore gloves, but he didn't move to the food or toward anything again. Suicide is the only way to show our discontent. Don't eat, don't suffer; make the feeder feel guilty of culpable neglect.

'Course, with Uncle Harry we helped him out. We couldn't stand any more of his complaining about the food, or his rubbing against Aunt Minnie.

Betty, the cockatoo, sang like a chanteuse and talked all night, but she didn't like to be told, "Sing 'Farmer In The Dell,' Betty; Say good morning; pretty bird; good-bye now." Our owner sang off-key and bribed Betty with extra birdseed. One afternoon, Betty sang the words to "Bye-Bye, Birdie." Then, in a loud, strong voice she chirped, "Good morning pretty bird, good-bye now." She dived from her high perch, landed on her back, her white crested head, still; her legs sticking straight up in the air.

Our owner seems frustrated too; she puts her face up close to watch us. We dart and cavort and then hide behind the rock while she talks to us as though we're babies and mimics our yawning mouths. Peering into our bowl is an invasion of privacy; fish living in glass houses can't throw back anything but stares.

She looks tired, with sunken eyes and pale cheeks. She needs a good night's sleep.

The Shape of Things – 1

by Tanya Kern

Stags everywhere the first fall after her father died.
On the feast of all souls, this one. Jewels to heavy crown,
his many points, lifted pride and swagger. Lips'
tender velvet twist.

Trees watch the doe. Her sex utters a wounded heat,
draws three stags. The doe hides against an earthen haunch
behind the woman's house. Stags drive away her fawn.
The woman's girls decide to play inside.
Afternoon, its downward suncourse pays in green
as gold as any heat.

The woman listens to the tongue, the blood. Deer. A woods
talking to itself. She wondered once what animal
she might have sex with. Not a dog, the smell all wrong.
Maybe a lion, intensity unhinged, might swagger
like the angry boy with northern eyes. How he held
a pool cue, sucked his teeth when she walked by;
how a stag might ride a woman. This thought pronounced
by woods scraped after noon by many antlers.

The stag drives off the younger males, turns to the doe.
She comes to him now. Grace hesitant until she licks him.
He enters her blood violent, hipshot as any man.
The woman's pulses hurt and falter without language
to call the stag to her.

The Shape of Things – 2

by Tanya Kern

She turns home, feeds her children, sorts and cleans.
Practices the shape of it in voice and echo, tongue to need
and yearning when the moon is thin. Willing to penetration.
Willing to antlered pride. The third year moves her blood
from human courseways. Here the entrance beyond hours,
here the distant recognition. The window in the west.
The wound she calls between her legs slashed warm. Intense grace
slowed by loss, her lumbar curve.

She follows a languid mixture, night bird, scratching dark;
glances back. The man. The children calling. Mama!
Come quick. A deer! She saunters on. Those can lose her
for an hour. Disappears to unlit space: what the forest makes
where deer breath touches frosted air. The stag speaks.
Her way back to her house is lost unless the moon leans blind
against her heart. Darker light tracks longing not quite gentle.

Her daughters watch for her most mornings, slide long fingers
deep in hoof prints, her last sign. Her daughters
in their lost age. When girls begin to bleed they still can choose.
Become woman. Become deer. Through these years she comes.

Quoth the Raven, "Mortimer"

by Wilfrid R. Koponen, Ph.D.

A candle guttered in the open window. It was dank and near midnight. I figured I'd freeze if I stayed outside, so I flew in. There was a handy perch above the door: a bust of Pallas Athena. What's that? Who told you ravens have no culture? I alighted and looked around.

A man in disheveled clothes scribbled at his desk. He looked the worse for wear, as if he hadn't had a good night's sleep in days. I'm no ignoramus. I recognized the famous writer at once. He was all the rage. Everyone was talking about his poems and stories. Daguerreotypes of him were in all the newspapers and literary magazines. Who was a stranger to that mop of dark hair that looked as if its owner had been tugging at it as if trying to uproot it? Who hadn't observed images of those brooding, bloodshot eyes? The circles under them looked like a caricature. Did I spy a decanter of brandy, or was it Laudanum?

No, it was not the elaborate fountain pen in his delicate hand, the crumpled papers overflowing from the wastebasket, nor the mess of ink on the blotting paper that made me perceive that I faced none other than Edgar Allan Poe himself. He paid no attention to me.

At first I hesitated to say anything. I mean, would you have wanted to be the neighbor who called on Coleridge when he was writing "Kubla Khan," pushing the Muse far out of reach, with the result that Coleridge had to use the word "fragments" in the subtitle? At long last, my tactful silence ignored, I spoke. "Mr. Poe, pleased to make your acquaintance." No response. I waited, then offered, "Thanks for your hospitality." Still nothing. I added, "So nice of you to leave the window open."

Poe looked disconsolate and distracted. He's not the only celebrity who's self-absorbed, I mused. I thought to myself that he was the host, after all, and was being rude. If he wasn't in a talkative mood, fine. But he could at least ask me my name. I waited and waited. I dozed off. Suddenly, he shouted, "The Raven! That's it! I knew a parrot would establish the wrong tone – too bright and gay." The perfervid scribbling resumed.

Finally, I gave up waiting for him to ask my name. I said my name aloud: Mortimer. No reply. Then again. Same thing. "Mortimer," I kept repeating. "The name's Mortimer." Not that he asked. He kept referring to me as The Raven, which bugged me. What if I just called him Man?

"What?" Poe asked, looking up at me, like a tugboat emerging from a bank of fog. He was all stuffed up. He had a terrible cold. This must have affected his hearing. "Why does that damn raven keep saying 'Nevermore'?" He shook his head as he turned back to his desk.

"Mortimer! Mortimer!" I insisted, having really lost my temper. I thought this guy was really out of it! Why doesn't he lay off the Laudanum, already? Geniuses and creative types can be pretty stupid when it comes to imbibing mind-altering substances. I kept these thoughts to myself.

Then I thought Poe had heard me, but he was saying "Lenore," not "Mortimer."

Who the hell's Lenore, I wondered.

Poe became voluble, asking me question after question. Not one was, "What is your name, Mr. Raven?" I exacted my revenge by pretending that he kept asking me that very question over and over.

Poe's response was to say aloud, "Quoth the Raven, 'Nevermore.' "

I'd had enough and flew back out the window. I never bothered to find out what resulted from his midnight musings. For all I cared, they might all have been used by the parlor maid the next morning to kindle the fire.

"Mortimer, Mortimer." You'd think he would have gotten it eventually.

Her Choice for the Evening

by Jill Angel Langlois

Instead of going home to Gizmo, her thirteen-year-old Siamese cat, she turns the 1969 Ford Fairmont into the parking lot of the local library, hoping to meet the book-smart man of her dreams. She puts the car in park, turns on the light and reaches into her make-up case to freshen lips and cheeks, running fingers through her short graying hair. Casually slinging her purse onto her shoulder and grabbing her sweater, she steps out and locks the door. She inconspicuously scans the horizon, wondering if anyone is noticing her. In rhythmic step, she quickly reaches the entrance to peer into the window and flick the hair from her eyes one last time. This is it, she is ready; he will be here.

She will talk briefly to the clerk behind the desk, making her presence known. Eyes will move from scrutinizing art books to gaze upon her, smiling and carefree. She will cross the lounging area, skirt rippling as she walks past the fireplace toward Poetry. There, she will finger all of her favorites; Browning, Chaucer, Dickinson, Frost; moving toward Tennyson, then, finally, Whitman, further down to the right. She will choose this one then, pulling the book from its home on the third shelf. Carefully turning the pages, her eyes will drink in the words and images, fusing them with her dreams. She will melt into a sea of fantasy.

She will feel him watching her and slowly turn to catch the wave of his smile and the sparkle in his sea-green eyes. They will speak, all the words coming at once and she will blush, tongue-tied. He will laugh at the awkward moment, then will begin again, speaking of Eliot and Poe. He will describe the Rocky Mountains and the cold of Alaska. He will tell her Rembrandt was his first name and that he was Dutch, then reach for her hand, inviting her to tea.

She will decline, naturally, explaining Gizmo will be waiting for her. She wouldn't want to seem too eager. But he will insist, carrying her books

111

to the counter, and she on his other arm. Her stomach will flutter in excitement as they continue discussing "The Love Song of J. AlfredPrufrock." Her feet will not touch the ground as they leave the library and come to Cafe 23, his favorite tearoom on the corner of Chesapeake and Montgomery. He will open the door for her and motion for a table for two by the window. He will order two cups of Darjeeling, cream, sugar, scones and currant buns with jam, whipped cream and butter, when the waitress asks, "Can I help you?"

"...Can I help you? Ma'am, can I help you?" The clerk calls to her from behind the desk. She meets the young woman's eyes, slightly confused, hitching her purse back onto her shoulder; an impatient line forming behind her. Silent, she pushes her choice for the evening onto the desk. The clerk checks her card, gives her a curious look, then slides back *The Old Man and The Sea*. She nestles the book inside her purse, bows her head and shuffles to the exit.

Outside, a chill is in the air, rustling the autumn leaves. Dusk will be upon her soon and Gizmo is waiting. A cold gust penetrates her, stinging her moist eyes. She wraps her sweater around her shoulders and hastens toward the car.

She maneuvers into her parking space, catching a glimpse of Gizmo positioned in the window. She nears the apartment, hearing the cat anxiously meow at her arrival. She fumbles with the key, then stops, turning to absorb one last look, one panoramic view of the outside, before re-entering her world. The door to her efficiency apartment opens and Gizmo welcomes her, weaving through her feet as she makes her way to fix his canned dinner. After setting his dish on the newspaper, she prepares

 chicken soup for herself, then reaches for the gas stove to heat the kettle, enjoying the familiar appreciation of the purring cat.

Teacup in hand, cat on lap, she settles back into her easy chair. She turns the pages of "The Old Man And The Sea," melting into the familiar scenes. Tonight she will keep company with Santiago; he is familiar and comforting. He is also alone and tired of braving the raging tempest. She understands him. As she daubs the tear-stained fur with the corner of her afghan, Gizmo positions for better comfort. Turning a few more pages, she wonders if Santiago likes tea.

Holding Animals
by Lyn Lifshin

The warm fur, like
a quilt or bunting.
Memento on the
velvet squares, a
warm potato or stones
travelers would
wrap in wool for
sleigh rides the
first night it
snowed or put in
dark beds in icy
mansions. A child
in tears burying
her neck in some
smelly dog's neck.
The waves of breath
like waves smooth-
ing ragged edges.
My aunt, after her
19 year old child
is buried clutched
the ragged black
and white cat to
her as if what she
held held her

Geese at Midnight

by Lyn Lifshin

as if a feather
quilt exploded
a white you can't
see in the dark
but breathe, a
wind of white
rose petals,
wave of fog
in the shape of
flying things.
Like radio
voices on
the pillow,
 lulling, keeping
what's ragged
and tears at
bay, the geese
pull sky and stars
in through glass,
are like arms
coming back
as sound

Geese in Coming Rain

by Lyn Lifshin

only a few blood
leaves on the maple.
Grass nibbled closer

to the house. The
geese move in waves
toward pewter, a

clot on the edge.
Sky colorless on
the skin of water.

Grey reeds. Circles,
pale ripples, ash
colored. Only the

mallard's jade
and the last leaves
bright as crushed

berries

Cat in an Empty Nest
by Ellaraine Lockie

He comes when my last daughter leaves for college. A two-pound package from the Himalayas with Paul Newman's eyes, politically incorrect fur coat, the voice of an oboe. Undeniably needy. As I am. He laps up baby talk, caresses, kisses, all my mother smother. A symbiotic pair. Only I can feed, groom, medicate him. I glow with pride, exclusivity, indispensability. In return he nuzzles, purrs, lap dances into my void. I carry him bottom-side-up in my arms. Cradle comfort.

At night he's four live pounds sleeping on my belly while I have pregnant dreams. He follows from room to room expecting entertainment, nourishment, safety. He gets it all. Discipline too, for climbing the Christmas tree, licking the butter, internally examining the piano, shredding my latest blueprint.

At six pounds we take excursions to a nursing home where strangers say he's beautiful. As he hides in their pillowcases. To the vet for shots, neutering, camaraderie with other mothers. We talk toilet training, toys, cat videos. We brag. One prodigy covers a cat calendar. Another is descended from Morris. Mine covers emptiness and is descended from me.

Eight pounds takes me away. A two-week return to a mad cat. Our first fight. He gives me silent treatment, middle-of-the-night oboe squawks, then misguided affection. He doesn't give mother love. Knows another kind, instincts uprooted from the Himalayas. He mounts my arm. I substitute a stuffed animal, happy there's no great-aunt visitor. He performs his sterile welcome-home ceremony on the kitchen table. I tell him it's okay, that it won't cause blindness. I catnip him to sleep.

At ten pounds he takes his own trips. Leaves me for mice, squirrels, birds. Sometimes prowls all night. I fret. He comes home for breakfasts. My daughter comes home for the summer. She's glad I have a cat.

117

The Odd Couple
by Bobbi Mallace

Shorter, rounder and plumper than the rest of her littermates, she was appropriately named Miss Piggy. Teddy, her brother, was a bit taller and thinner. Miss Piggy was a bit slower to react to things. Teddy was very bright and quick. These two were our "odd" couple who went everywhere together, side by side.

Through the years Miss Piggy and Teddy spent much time playing, wrestling, arguing, and eating (Miss Piggy's favorite sport) together. They socialized with the other dogs in the house as well as the family, but they always seemed to do it together.

As they approached middle age I noticed that Miss Piggy would lag behind Teddy at times. Teddy would check behind him to see if she was there. In time she no longer ran at Teddy's side but stayed close behind him while Teddy periodically checked to see if she was following. We wondered why Miss Piggy would do this. After exams by our local vet and an animal eye specialist, we received the news that Miss Piggy was losing her ability to distinguish objects, but could still see strong contrasts of light and dark. "Of course," I thought, "Teddy is black, so she is able to follow him."

For the next few years Miss Piggy would follow everywhere behind Teddy as though they were glued "head to rump." In spite of Miss Piggy's impairment they were quite the happy couple.

One day Teddy just stopped eating and appeared listless, but the vet could not find anything specific wrong. The problem continued in spite of our trying different medications and diets. After extensive testing we were told he had cirrhosis of the liver and had only a short time to live. I had noticed that every time we had to take Teddy to the hospital, Miss Piggy would howl and cry for several hours before she would settle down.

Realizing this, we decided to bring Teddy home with medication and a proper diet that he now would eat, so he could spend the time he had left with Miss Piggy.

Six weeks passed, and Teddy seemed comfortable, and comforted by Miss Piggy. They didn't run anymore but cuddled up together. Then one day Teddy stopped eating and began "digging" at the floor. He "dug" all day only to stop when we called his name, but then continued on his mission. We tried to comfort him but he would have none of it. We would learn later that in the wild, a dog will dig a nest in which to die. Miss Piggy grew still and left Teddy alone. She knew what was going to happen.

At two o'clock in the morning I got up to check on Teddy. He lay quietly, worn out from digging. I detected a faint heartbeat and called the vet who told us to meet him to the hospital with our dog. As I picked Teddy up I realized he was no longer in any pain or even discomfort – he was gone. Miss Piggy remained quiet and wanted to be left alone. This time when we took Teddy to the hospital, she didn't cry or howl. This time she understood what had taken place, because it had happened at home, where they both had lived.

❖   ❖   ❖

Miss Piggy grieved for many months. In time, though, she began to try to find her way around without Teddy. Slowly she learned to follow one of the humans who lived in the house. She never adopted another dog to follow although there were several from which to choose. She now appears to be relatively content and we help her as much as we can both physically and emotionally. We spend time cuddling and talking to her, but we know she will be happiest when she goes to be with her beloved Teddy.

Good Dog

by Terry Martin

*"Did you know
that a good dog in your house
can make you more thoughtful
even more moral?"*

Stephen Dunn:" Some Things I Wanted to Say to You"

Good dog in my house,
what's it like to be you?

Leaning into life, full-out,
wagging your welcome to the rest of us,
easing into deep stretches of dog lassitude.

You seem to live in present tense,
attentive to only the here and now,
but I wonder.

What worlds live in your sighs?
Are you, too, obedient to echoes?

Perhaps in your dreams
you conjure fields of rising birds,
cats that disappear, leaving
only soft twitches behind.

Without words, you ask
clearly for what you want
and almost always get it.

Routine receiver of affection
from usual and unexpected sources,
of touch that wholly satisfies.

Even strangers smile and soften,
remembering their better selves
in your presence.

Daily, you remind me
of the limits of language,
occasionally barking your curious news,
blessed with uncomplicated beauty
and the grace of forgetfulness.

The Visitor

by Karen Laudenslager McDermott

The roof resounds with that thumping again. It's him. He looks down at me, tries to fix my eye.

He came to us on a hot June evening, when I was thirteen. I had been daydreaming in the hammock; the dog was flopped in the shade. From the corner of my eye I saw her get up. She was a retriever, not a pointer, but there she was, tail straight out, one foot raised in the air. She darted into the hedge, mucked around, then backed out pleased with her mouthful of feathers.

She carried her catch toward me, but veered away, unwilling to give it up. I grabbed her tail and made her drop it. She caught it again and I screamed for my mom. "The dog's got a bird!" When the dog finally did let go, she barked frantically. What a ruckus! Even the trees seemed to be screeching.

The little fellow, well he was pretty big, a crow, I guessed, must have fallen from his nest. He scampered back and forth, trying to find a way out. The dog kept him cornered until my mother came with a pair of gardening gloves and a shoebox. Mom was nervous, so it took her a few tries to hold the bird firmly enough to stop his fluttering. She picked him up, put him in the box and, all out of breath, slapped down a piece of cardboard. Carefully we poked holes in the lid. Mom and I looked at each other. Now what?

My mother called the Ornithological Society while I went for a shovel, to dig worms.

Since the bird was not injured, the man on the phone asked if we could care for our little foundling since the Ornithological Society was overworked and understaffed. He gave my mom instructions. She hung up the phone quietly, looking kind of shocked. I said I'd help. She told me to forget about worms.

The bird needed space and light. It was about ten inches long, too big for a shoebox, fully feathered in coal black, its dark eye ringed with gray. It was an eye that seemed to know things. Like fear.

We bought cod-liver oil from the pharmacy, and fresh hamburger to mix with egg yolk. My heart pounded when I had to hold the bird while Mom pressed open his mouth and forced the hamburger mixture down his throat with wooden tweezers. We had to do the same with water, from an eyedropper. He was scared. He'd see us coming, three times a day, and try to hide in the corner of his shoebox-house.

My project was making him a cage. I didn't like to call it that, so I said it would be his pen. It would have a three-foot high wooden frame with a lid like a hamper. It would be covered with chicken wire and have a perch. Until it was ready, we kept the bird in his box in the dining room with the window open, closed off from the dog, because she still thought he was hers.

From the third day, that eye began to look smart instead of always afraid. He'd still back up when we came with our gloves and tweezers, but he started to open his mouth by himself.

On the day we planned to transfer the bird to his new home – the one I'd cut and hammered and screwed together – we woke just as the sun came up, to a terrible noise in the dining room. When I opened the door, the bird was throwing himself around his box. I looked straight at him but he wasn't saying anything, although the eye said, 'oh-oh'. The squawking was coming from the fireplace. There was no bird that I could see, but instructions of a very definite sort were coming down the chimney. Our little bird recovered confidence and added his voice. By the time he ate his hamburger breakfast, whoever it was at the top of the chimney had gone.

He liked his pen, found the perch and settled in. We covered the bottom with straw and put leaves down hoping he'd find insects. But he never once tried to feed himself.

After a week and a half, the dog had accepted our new visitor and I thought the bird would like to be outside. We easily moved him in and out. That's how he came to pass his days on our terrace and nights back in the dining room. We passed our dawns listening to him shout to the bird in the chimney.

One afternoon, we left the bird out on the terrace and took the dog swimming. Hours later we tumbled from the car to find 'blood' on the tiles around the pen. Little pits gave it away. Someone had been feeding him! A few minutes of hiding behind the door and we saw it happen. An enormous black crow brought cherry after cherry and fed her lost baby. He sat on his perch, straining through the wire to reach his mother's mouth. I thought his eye looked real happy.

We stopped the forced feeding and moved the pen against the terrace wall. Mama-crow took on the whole job.

But this little fellow had to learn to fly. He seemed to be over his fear of us. That eye would fix itself on me as I talked to him when I moved him around. I told him about flying. He cocked his head and listened, but he didn't blink, not once.

One evening my mother put on her gloves, took the bird from his pen and climbed onto the terrace wall. Using both her hands, she gently wafted him into the air. And he wafted straight down to the ground. He didn't know he had it in him to do more. Mom ran down to scoop him up just as the squawking started. Up near the top of the tree closest to the house, the big crow was watching.

We decided to try again. He wafted into the air and came down gently, but he hit the ground running. First in circles, then toward the mama-crow's tree. They screamed at each other, and she flew into the next tree. He ran on the ground, then tried to climb toward her. He wanted to get to her so badly. That took me by surprise – I thought we'd been doing a terrific job. In the middle of all that fussing, I felt

hurt, but my mother understood. She put him into a tree on a branch as high up as she could reach. He fell right down. We were all frantic. The bird voices were mixed up with the dog's wild bark from the house. We could only watch helplessly as that big mama-bird tried to lead her baby toward the gate, away from his captors, us. Finally we put a stop to it – after all, she couldn't protect him if she did get him out. She would have to be content with an early morning chat and feeding her baby through the chicken wire.

And so it continued. Each night when the evening star showed, my mother put on her gloves and threw our baby crow off the terrace wall while the mamma watched and squawked.

He tried spreading his wings. One day, he flapped them, and just like that he was gone. We were not prepared, even though our tasks had been whittled down to nothing more than moving him in and out; even though we knew it wouldn't last forever. I never said good-bye. And I didn't see what the wonderful eye looked like. Maybe he was sorry, too. Maybe he thought there was something just as magical about us...

Well, I'm sure it's him up there. He taps on the roof tiles and looks for me over the drainpipe. He comes to tell me that he remembers.

Euthanasia

by Karen Laudenslager McDermott

You know the routine,
The waiting place,
the examination room –
up on the table and down
then out the door.
But this time I struggled
to tell you, and walked you
to another room
another table
another world

I have to do something
with your bowl
your bed
this terrible burden
of silence.
I hear you breathe
and reach down to stroke your nose
I see you everywhere,
imagine we could have had
one day more

Over and over, it plays in my mind
I hold your face, your eyes
look back at my sorrow,
so calm, so easily
you lower your head
to those once fleet feet
I whisper I'm sorry
so, so sorry
but you are already gone.

Gigantic Frogs Will Come from Fire

by Pamela Miller

> *"'The Last Frog' examines the unexplained phenomenon*
> *of mass deaths of frogs all over the planet.*
> *While reports of grotesquely deformed frogs*
> *in Minnesota lakes grab headlines,*
> *researchers are baffled by the sudden disappearances*
> *of scores of frog species,*
> *even some that live in pristine areas."*
>
> – Ad for a 1996 National Geographic TV special

On the day the new millennium unfurled its flags
gigantic frogs arose from fire,
straddled the globe like squiggly pagodas,
baby-faced and furious,
to rescue Earth from the world.

Spurred by the healing hug of their legs,
the earth grew back its
hacked-off forests,
the blackened rivers skimmed off their toxins
like small boys spitting out squash. Nudged
by their towering wise-eyed heads,
the ozone layer reknit itself,
exquisite and proud as a wedding dress,
an invincible star-spangled bandage.

128

The deformed frogs from the factory towns
rose from their Lazarus lakes to be cured,
their hideous pinwheels of extra legs
cauterized by deft tongues of flame.

On the day before the Frog King rested,
all the world's cities turned to
placid ponds. Billions of tadpoles
surged up from their depths,
cavorted and jigged like "Jabberwocky."
Humankind faded away
like a rash. Except for
one virgin in her boat of blonde hair,
who once hid a frog
from dissection class doom,
chosen as the one pure breeding bride
for the brave new Buddha-shaped prince of fire,
the gentle green Vulcan of peace.

Fish Story
by Pamela Miller

At night I release all the fish
from my hair. Shore-leaved from me,
they grow big as zeppelins,
swim down the airwaves
of a dozen all-night oldies stations,
head out over the city
leaving trails of smoke and pearls.
They sail off to places
my sisters would never approve of,
wrap their gills around long white men
like squirming strands of spaghetti,
send a message to the man in the octopus tuxedo
to report to my bedroom pronto.
The moment his tentacles
glide down my gown,
the whole room fills with seawater. Later
I trim his beard
on the carpet which has turned to a coastline,
shiver to one last scherzo
of suckers down my spine. When he goes
he leaves his love knob
for me to scrimshaw in the morning
as fish after fish after homecoming fish
pokes her joyous face through the walls.

Bravo
A Novel Excerpt by Eliza Monroe

It wouldn't be long before Pepper would have to put Bravo down. To make him stop working too soon would be cruel to the horse. Yet Pepper had to watch for the point at which he could no longer perform – became scared of water, plastic bags and the blind spot between his eyes – could no longer be trusted in crowds. This was a responsibility that Pepper didn't look forward to, and although she knew it was inevitable, she hoped it would happen later rather than sooner.

As she mounted him, the morning air at Aquatic Park felt clear and cool. To the west she could see the ocean out to its farthest flat end, and to the east every little island in the San Francisco Bay and the San Pablo beyond it. She swooped down and got coffee at Majeski's and noticed the tide was low at the bottom of the stairs, widening the beach. Through her legs she could feel Bravo's heartbeat. He eyed that smooth hard sand, snorting, his shoulders jerking forward past his center of gravity, overreacting to every possible indication that Pepper wanted him to perform.

Pepper usually needed to ask Bravo to go down steps. She'd urge him down just by wanting him to until it became his idea. But today he had a mind of his own so she let him have his head. Pepper leaned back for balance as Bravo, goat-like, negotiated the concrete steps that were too deep for humans to take two at a time.

Once on the slick, hard-packed sand, Pepper took a deep breath of seaweed air. They were alone on the beach except for a single seagull, which extracted food out of the sand the old-fashioned way instead of waiting for a handout from a tourist. Mutant, thought Pepper, slipping her feet from the stirrups the way she'd done in training. Without reins, she held her arms in front then out to the sides, moving them in circles like a bust exercise. Next she leaned her whole torso over the horse, up

131

and down like sit-ups. When she leaned over the saddle and touched her toes, Bravo chewed and dropped his head. He wanted to go to work, but was accustomed to Pepper's routine – bowing to one's partner before a dance.

Pepper anchored her feet back into the stirrups. Bravo responded by bowing himself, and Pepper petted him on the neck. She pretended that Bravo's feet and legs were her own. Her body livened up and he began a smooth four-beat gait forming a narrow figure eight the length of the beach, Pepper's hands floating in the reins until he'd warmed up and reached a canter. She prepared her body for the stop ahead of time and when she asked him, it came down smooth. Then she spun him around in full circles until the sand gave way and they dug a triangular pit. She backed him out and he sidestepped, knees high, on harder ground.

A large driftwood trunk had floated in the night before and lodged itself in the sand next to a soggy tennis shoe. The log made a perfect jump; jumping had always been his best event. It was that airborne moment they both loved when their centers of gravity preceded them and met up with them again on the other side. Pepper spun Bravo around again and brought him to the far end of the runway. But when she asked him to go, he stopped short of the jump and collapsed in the sand.

"No." Pepper rolled off the horse and looked into his eyes. She knew he couldn't see her. He was still alive, still breathing, but overly lathered. "Come on, sweetie, come on. Keep breathing." She removed the bridle and tugged at the saddle, but the full weight of the horse lay on the straps, so she reached for her pocket knife. She sliced the straps and threw the saddle and bridle downhill, which rolled twice toward the ocean and stopped. Then she knelt in the wet sand and hung onto his neck with her chest and one arm, afraid he'd go into spasm. She rang the Coroner on the radio with her other hand but since the horse was down the steps on the beach, he said he'd call in a chopper.

Bravo was the last of the retired racehorses Pepper's father had donated to the Horse Mounted Patrol. He'd been born when Pepper was three, in the stables in back of their house, before her mother had died, before her father had begun drinking. It had been a happy time when she was little. Her mother had horses all around her. Pepper had been too young to remember, but as Bravo lay old and dying, her arms around his thick, still warm neck, the dampness of the sand seeping through her police uniform, she thought she remembered a foal being born, but it resembled feeling more than memory.

❖ ❖ ❖

A pregnant bay mare had paced all day in the sunny Marin pasture. When her mother lifted Pepper up to pet the mare's soft fur between the withers, to feed her wildflowers, to calm her, a few flies departed but the mare pawed at the ground and threw her head toward her hindquarters.

"She's going to foal tonight." At night when it felt safe, away from predators, in the safety of the herd, in the safety of the stall, wood slats surrounding her, not burning.

Pepper'd had to take a nap that afternoon so she could stay up late for the birth. After dinner the mare lay down, warm hay against her belly, her uterus contracting in waves to push out the foal. Pepper's mother pointed to the mare but Pepper looked at the red fingernails of her mother's callused hand instead; she had hands that could wring the last drop of water out of a washcloth.

"No, look at the horse's tail," she said, stroking Pepper's shoulder.

Pepper watched the place under the mare's tail open into a big red circle. Clear fluid spilled from the opening - a smell like broth on the stove - the blood vessels tree branches straining across the mare's abdomen. Then a white sack slipped out, long and narrow at first. Pepper gripped her mother's hand. The sack widened, the foal's head and shoulders came, then the rest of the foal slipped out quickly and fought to break the sack.

"Come on, sweetie, come on, breathe."

The mare broke the umbilical cord as she turned to lick her foal's nose. Breathing on its own, it thrashed out of the last of the sack that was strangling its hind legs, and as it kicked it seemed to pump life into itself.

"It's a boy."

Spring had neglected to bring in the fog, and the air felt balmy. Pepper's mother grabbed a blanket and turned off the light. She cuddled up with Pepper in the corner and they went to sleep to the smell of damp, warm hay and the sound of curious horses in neighboring stalls swishing their tails and snorting. In the morning the mare and foal were both standing, the foal's fur no longer slick but brown and fluffy, and he'd found the mare's udder.

"Bravo," her mother said.

❖ ❖ ❖

The sound of the chopper brought the pirate street performer James – parrots clinging to his shoulders – to the top of the steps. The wind from the blades stirred up such a wind that James had to back off, but he could see Pepper and a man from the Coast Guard strap Bravo to a harness. He felt creepy as if someone were behind him, watching him watch, but he shrugged it off. Pepper climbed into the chopper and gave James a nod – too sad an occasion for thumbs up. James saluted and Bravo was carried away, a dark shape hanging, his head limp over the light blue ocean – nothing left on the beach, except deep gray-green trenches Bravo had carved in the sand, and one lone gull mounted on Bravo's English saddle, chewing the reins. When the wind ceased, James went down to the beach to scoop up the leather. He walked up the sandy steps and placed Bravo's tack in the International for safekeeping.

The calm that usually hovered over the Wharf in the mornings stayed all day. The spot on the sidewalk where James stood never livened up, as if the whole Wharf were mourning the passing of Bravo. By three it wasn't worth hanging around. Besides, Preskar, the owner of the shopping center, apparently did not share James' sense of grief, and had phoned up the Health Department, complaining of parrot shit on the sidewalk. A couple of Health Department agents showed up and looked around, but they said they really couldn't distinguish parrot shit from pigeon shit, and that they were going to see that Preskar got a bill for their time.

On any other day, this would have cheered James up. After they left, he headed across the street past Sierra, the crab girl, into Capurro's. When he walked in he found Pepper sitting alone in a dark corner, out of uniform, nursing a beer, her hair in a braid hanging over one shoulder. A weak voice upstairs attempted to sing the songs that belonged to someone else. James slammed his pewter mug with the dragon handle on Regina's bar, and she filled it up with a little Coke and a lot of rum. He grabbed his mug with one hand and with the other perched the parrots on the back of a chair near Pepper's table.

"How be ye doing?" he said, and sat down across from her for the first time.

She looked up at him, her skin grayish under her eyes. "Had to put him down," she said.

He looked at her braided hair. About ten times a day, whenever he saw a good braid, he'd declare that it was a rope and hang his blue-and-gold macaw from it, but the current mood would clearly not permit such behavior. "Aye," he said, "when an animal dies, it leaves a hole."

"I never thought of it that way," Pepper said, and new tears smeared her cheeks.

Oh boy, am I glad I didn't try that rope trick, thought James. "There, there, don't ye be crying now," James said, and produced a red and white scarf. "Here, blow yer nose in this. That's what I do."

Pepper laughed, but only long enough to let a smile form and disappear. Then she took the scarf.

"Blow yer nose. There ye go. If I cried for every bird that died on me, the drought in the entire state of Californee would be over."

They sipped their drinks.

"What are you going to do without Bravo?" James said, dropping the pirate jargon. He knew that the difference in his two voices, his two personae, was as baritone is to tenor. He saved his non-pirate voice for times when he didn't mind being vulnerable, or to honor someone with his real self, though it seemed debatable which of his two selves was the most genuine.

"I'm on leave for the rest of the week," she said. She looked at the wall. "I might have to transfer. I don't think I could do this beat without him."

"Know what you mean. I may have had a lot of birds die on me, but if I lost Dominique or Reggae, I'd close up shop. Thinking of quitting anyway. Things haven't been the same since the Cable Cars shut down. Besides, Preskar's on my tail."

"To the end of an era," Pepper said. She dried her eyes and they raised their mugs. "There's been talk of phasing out the horses here anyway."

"Yeah, who needs you." They caught each other's gaze. James couldn't decide which self to be. He'd never asked anyone out before. He was too shy, so he just pretended to be a pirate until some wench asked him. But he didn't feel like being a pirate today and this woman was clearly in no condition to ask anyone for anything. "Come on," he said finally, "why don't you come to my place and I'll show you where I bury my birds."

"Okay," she said. They got up to leave. James set his parrots back on his shoulders and as he passed the bar, Regina the barkeep looked at him blankly as if to say, "What do you think you're doing? She's not your type."

I know, thought James, she's not my type and I don't know what I'm doing.

A Bird's Eye View
by Rita Naughton

Some may call me a lean, mean, bitin' machine, but my name is Daytona. My roommates include Harley, a big, fat, spoiled Golden Retriever, Babe, a psycho nut German Shepherd, or as I like to call her, the Furred Beast from Nazi Hell, and Ruby, our mom, an over-the-hill, out-of-shape lady, or Big Mama as I refer to her behind her back.

All of us spend the day playing games and figuring out new ways to play tricks on each other. The first game of the day is Ruby coming into the kitchen, saying good morning, and trying to take off the sheet that covers my cage for the night. As she pulls the sheet towards her I grab a section, yanking and tugging, and finally I let her win so she doesn't get too stressed, and more important, so she can feed me once she's calmed down with a cup of coffee.

With my morning seeds I get fresh water, great for my daily bath. Washing up in my water cup makes a big mess, and I get to splash as much as three feet in all directions, and sometimes even on Ruby if she's not fast enough to get away. She has to get me fresh water all over again, because she'd be dumb to think I'd tolerate dirty water.

Morning cereal, if I'm lucky, is steaming, hot oatmeal or Cream of Wheat, but if Ruby's rushed, I have to settle for dry Cheerios or Wheaties. There are my seeds, of course, but not before I fling a bunch of them out of the seed cup and all over the cage, the floor, the kitchen stove, the microwave oven, and if she's within range, Ruby, too. This helps me practice my aim. I give myself one point for each millet seed I hit her with, three for each kernel of corn, and five points for each sunflower seed, which makes the best *ping* sound when it hits her glasses. Like hitting the jackpot. Honestly, it makes my day when I get four or five hits like that. When I reach 30 points, I preen and preen as Ruby takes her headache pills.

137

𝕱eathers, 𝕱ins & 𝕱ur _____

Sunday's the day we all get a big, hot, cholesterol-heavy, bust-your-arteries, to-die-for breakfast of bacon, eggs, buttered toast, and sometimes, pancakes with maple syrup. When I see Ruby take my special blue bowl out of the cabinet, I know it's big-time Saturated-Fat City, and I bob up and down, doing a little dance while she cuts my food up and puts the bowl on top of my cage. Once she's unlocked my door, I let myself out, making a dash for that breakfast. For dessert I like my peanuts and almonds, and occasionally walnuts, but only walnuts if Ruby cracks the shell for me 'cause otherwise they are so big I might hurt my African Grey Parrot beak. That seems funny when you think that if I bite you I could apply 900 pounds of pressure with that same beak.

My buddies Harley and Babe don't usually get breakfast. They just get fresh water while Ruby's rushing around, trying to find her car keys and briefcase. I think that if she got up at 3 a.m. she'd still be running late. While Ruby is dashing all over the house, the dogs go outside and when they come in they play with their toys, leaving them in strategic places so they can trip her, adding to her morning exercise and activities. Before leaving the house in the morning, she picks up the toys and puts them back in the "toy box," an old hospital bedpan. But by the time she gets home, everything's been dumped all over the kitchen floor.

Still, the bedpan's a nice touch of décor in here, right next to Ruby's designer wrought-iron microwave stand. I view things with an artist's eye, you see, maybe a little unusual for a parrot, but I used to model at the School of the Art Institute. My dream is to be a top interior decorator, and I'm starting with our kitchen.

When I lose a feather, which happens a lot when Babe attacks the cage, I pick it up and shove it through the metal bars to accent the floor. Otherwise it's so plain, but Big Mama's decorating taste is not her strong point. When my cage door's open, I sit on top of it so my droppings land on the linoleum, usually in interesting patterns I've given a lot of thought to, though Ruby tries to re-arrange them by scraping them up with her putty knife. Another thing I do to beautify the area is take my whole wheat toast, dunk it in my water dish, and throw it against the wall. I don't mind covering that ugly flowered wallpaper she paid $78 a roll for. It's the least I can do for Ruby.

Some of our games give her a real pain in a lot of places, she says.

Harley's special game is hanging out in the living room when Ruby needs to get him locked into the kitchen so she can leave for the morning. Harley's on the sofa and doesn't want to give up its comfort, but also Babe is in the kitchen growling to let him know he is not welcome, so even if Harley wanted to go into the kitchen with us, Psycho Nut does her best to keep him out. That is Babe's part of the game. I add to the general commotion by screeching and tearing up the paper on the bottom of my cage and flinging it wherever I can. It makes a nice effect, I think. Ruby doesn't agree with my sense of aesthetics, but she's too busy tricking or bribing Harley into the kitchen to complain.

When she comes home from her appointments, I've had my morning sleep, and it is usually lunchtime. We share whatever she has, especially my favorite, gooey grilled cheese sandwiches. I take lots and lots of that. It sets me up for naptime on my swing. Ruby takes her nap on the love seat, with Harley on the couch, and Babe on the floor next to the love seat by Big Mama. Ruby says she needs her naptime because of the stress we give her, but even that is not too relaxing because she jumps up when Babe and Harley begin barking at the kids coming home from school. When they start barking, I start talking very loud, the louder the better. I want out of my cage and I want out now. Ruby tries to calm us down, but we are so loud she can't even be heard.

So she opens my cage door and I am at liberty. I like to sit on top of my cage and enjoy freedom. I don't bother anyone, but I can't say the same about Babe. She keeps coming over to my cage, jumping against it and sometimes makes me lose my balance. If I am fast enough I can fly into another room and find safety, but I often end up on the floor in the corner of the kitchen, right out in the open. Now I have the two furred beasts, the one from Hell and the fat, spoiled baby, in front of me barking and lunging at me. They're crazy to think I wouldn't tear their eyes out. Of course, they'd tear my whole head off. I am squawking my fool head off and after what seems like an eternity, Ruby comes to my rescue. She picks me up, and I don't even bite her because she is rescuing me from my tormentors. Becoming an item on their menu is not my idea of a fun time.

If Ruby runs afternoon errands, Harley and Babe give her a big welcome by racing through the house like maniacs, barking, jumping on the furniture, and knocking into my cage. Once they crashed right into Ruby, knocking her down as she came in the back door. She sprained her wrist over that one.

Eating supper's fun for sure, and comes with its own set of games. Ruby used to hand feed Harley because Babe (or Psycho, Nut Case and Brat, as Ruby sometimes calls her) intimidates Harley so he won't eat. Then she can have his dinner, too. I don't understand why Ruby worries so much about Harley because rumor has it Harley can stand to lose a few pounds. But Ruby is so worried about him, that if she's not hand feeding him, she stands guard so he can eat in peace.

We all love it when Ruby gives us special treats like pizza, steak and potatoes, tacos, chicken, and even White Castle hamburgers. When she gives me spaghetti, I eat some from my bowl on top of the cage, but am very careful to save enough for my "environments." That's what I call the sculptural creations I make by draping the spaghetti over the top bars of my cage.

Our evening consists of Ruby returning her clients' phone calls or watching TV – or should I say trying to. It's hard for her to do either over my screeching and talking and my four-legged buddies barking, dashing around and jumping on the furniture, especially if that means jumping on Ruby who's sitting on the love seat. At times she gets annoyed with all that racket because she can't hear the TV, and it is always at a good part when we make the most noise.

At bedtime, Ruby says "nite nite" to me, covers my cage, turns out the lights and goes to bed with Harley and Babe. Well actually only with Babe to start with because Babe (or Bully as she is sometimes called) won't let Harley into the bedroom. I may be covered (with that tacky sheet, but I plan to change that eventually), but I still hear it all. Harley cries this yelpy bark, and Babe growls, and then sometimes I hear the two of them scuffle while Ruby yells at them about how she can't take any more of it, and threatens they won't see their next birthday. The crying, barking, fighting and screaming goes on for as long as a half-hour, and then it suddenly quiets down, and I hear Ruby say, "Good, Harley, you've figured out how to get into the bedroom for the night." Now we have some hard won peace and quiet that will last through the night until the sun begins to shine. And so begins another day of fun and games in the lives of Ruby, Harley, Babe, and of course me, Daytona. Remember the name. You'll hear from me – probably on Oprah, as Chicago's first feathered designer.

I Want to be a Dogsled Driver

by Ellen Nordberg

I want to be a dogsled driver. Hurling down mountain trails at 17 mph, chasing the sound of howling dogs and sled runners scraping ice. Running behind the 550 pound sled, then leaping to brace myself perpendicular between snowbanks and sled rails, as I effortlessly guide the sled around a tight curve. I could do this job.

During a January ski vacation, my boyfriend Jon and I have taken a day off from the slopes of Aspen Mountain for our first-ever dogsled ride. Jon has agreed to give up the bumps for today, if only to silence my curiosity about the sled drivers.

Our driver for the afternoon, Jeff Martin, a compact guy built of solid muscle, pushes back his jester hat and examines our garb through his Oakley wraparound shades.

We have dutifully donned the required jumbo mukluk boots, which made our trek down the hilly slope to the sled area like trying to stroll through one of those moon-walk bubbles at the county fair. I peer out at Jeff through the snorkel face-hole of my enormous yellow parka, certain he is appraising me as a potential driver comrade.

Twelve Alaskan Huskies stand or sit in six rows of two across in front of our sled, all in brightly-colored harnesses attached to a central wire. Two of the dogs in the last row shift their focus from the rear end of another dog in order to check us out: a fluffy black dog with one blue eye and one brown, and another with a single eye and a fur patch where its mate should have been. Their names are Claire and Cyclops, Jeff tells us.

He puts Jon in the sled, and shoves him so he's sitting braced against the wall of the sled, legs apart. I'm next, knees up, facing the dogs, wedged back into Jon's crotch by a push of Jeff's huge thigh, then enfolded in blankets. Already my butt begins to feel numb, but I have an awesome perspective on the dogs in front of us and the trail on either side. Loud grunts come from behind me.

141

"I've got about the same view as Cyclops up there," Jon's muffled voice says. "Half of some dog's butt."

I move my head to one side, and we can feel Jeff moving around behind us, positioning himself on the sled rails. Let's go! I think, squirming restlessly under the blankets. Suddenly his voice calls out, "Penny! Elle!" and the two female dogs in front yank into gear, leading forty-eight paws joyfully through the snow in unison.

The 200 or so remaining dogs, each with their little house or platform, strain howling at their chains, disappointed to be left behind. Surprisingly, their noise sounds less like the barking of suburban dogs, and more like teenage girls screaming at a Leonardo DiCaprio sighting.

We come out of the woods as the dogs race along the catwalk of a Snowmass ski slope with "Caution Dogsled Crossing" painted on yellow signs. I glance over the edge, down the steep face of a black diamond run, realizing for the first time how much trouble we'd be in if Elle or Penny stopped paying attention.

"Ever get into accidents with skiers?" I ask.

"Yeah, occasionally they don't hear the dogs, don't hear the driver yelling at them," Jeff says, as I look up, picturing an expert skier flying over the crest above and landing in the midst of twelve moving dogs.

"A few bad accidents," Jeff continues. "But the dogs always come out OK."

We continue tumbling down the trail, like in a rollercoaster drop, careening across little bridges spanning creeks and ditches, the dogs gleefully churning up snow in their wake, and intermittently biting off chunks from the banks to quench their thirst. Jeff leaps off to man-handle the sled around a corner.

"How'd you get to be a dog sled driver?" I ask eagerly as he jumps back on behind us.

"I came to Aspen, racked up a big bar tab, and had to find a job to pay it off." Cool.

"No, actually I got tired of being a programmer in Corporate America," Jeff says. "And I'd met one of the drivers here, and it seemed like a good time. Penny, Penny, GEE," he calls out, as the dogs veer right and across a mountain-rimmed meadow.

I ask about the qualifications, certain that my stint as a water aerobics instructor would make me a shoe-in. Behind me, Jon flaps his arms and wiggles his feet in an effort to generate circulation.

"Well, you generally have to be big, and pretty strong," Jeff replies. "A lot of the guys are over six feet."

I could grow.

"I was a power-lifter and a wrestler," he continues. "So that worked in my favor. Hup Elle, Hup!" he yells to the dogs over our heads. "And you've got to be able to lift the dog food barrel - 350 pounds of lard and kitchen scraps from the restaurant on the hill."

I'm not so sure about the lifting. Then Susan Butcher, four-time winner of the Alaskan Iditarod dogsled race, and snacker of butter sticks rolled in pure cane sugar, comes to mind.

"How many women drivers are there?" I say.

"Uh, actually, none," Jeff says. "Not yet anyway."

"What do you do in training camp?" I ask, undaunted, envisioning 11 manly men and me running the trails in heavy boots, bench-pressing sleighs.

"Chop wood for the restaurant, dig out the sled trails, train the dogs, and run them to get 'em back in shape after the summer," he says as I nod. Yes, I could do these things. The dogs would love me!

"Oh, and shovel poop," he adds.

Poop?

"You start out each morning at 7:30 with a shovel and a bucket. You fill the bucket, and then fill the wheelbarrow," Jeff says guiding the sled away from a snowdrift.

I wrinkle my nose.

"Where does it all end up?" Jon's muffled voice inquires from behind me. I'm intrigued by the topic with which he has chosen to break his silence. "Some kind of mulch or manure pile?"

"Ah, yeah," Jeff says. "Something like that. We just call it the Shit Pit."

Then Jeff tells us it's time for dogs and humans alike to take a rest, as the dogs love to run so much, they'd run until they drop without a forced break. The dogs stand panting, and Jeff pries me off of Jon, where I promptly collapse in a heap at Jeff's feet in the snow, pins and needles pricking at my useless thighs. My Wonder Woman Dogsled Driver image seems to be developing a few chinks.

While we stretch our legs, Jeff feeds the dogs pieces of bacon, and we ask him about the off-season. Does he have a different job? He tells us he takes the summer off and travels around the country, and I wonder about the other drivers, are they Baywatch lifeguards or street lugers in the summer?

"Well, there's one guy who's a conservationist," he says. "And there's this other guy who's an exotic dancer." So much for the manly men.

Jon studies a pair of impatient dogs as they climb back and forth over each other in line. "Is the breeding controlled?" he asks.

"Yeah," Jeff answers with a smile, dropping bacon pieces and patting dogs, "By the dogs. Sometimes a dog gets loose in the yard, or their chains are too long. And sometimes, they just get really creative while hooked up to the sled." He leans to untangle Cyclops' leg in his harness. "Sometimes you look at them, and think, 'how the hell did they do that? I've gotta try that one.'"

Jon snickers and I focus on mastering my moon boot walk. Jeff trundles us back into the sled and we prepare for our return ride to the kennels. As the dogs fly across the trails, Jon gets Jeff to describe the various hazards of his job: broken thumbs from heavy sled motions, concussions from being flung off backwards, slipping on the ice while carrying the food barrel.

As we arrive back at the base, I swivel my snorkel jacketed face around the area, searching for the Shit Pit, having second thoughts about my new career. As Jeff pulls the sled up short, a chorus of barking ensues, all the buddies of Elle, Penny, Claire, Cyclops and gang welcoming them home. As I stagger out of the sled, another brawny driver approaches us with an armload of fur.

"Would you like to hold one of the puppies?" Jeff says.

I push back my hood, extend my arms. Ice blue eyes stare up at me out of a gray and white face. Fur as soft as cashmere rubs my chin, and a tiny tongue traces a trail along my cheek. I look over at Jon, green eyes grinning at me over his own furry handful. I want to be a dogsled driver.

Tim

by Nancy Nye

Where would these people take me? We were crowded into their car, the bigger, quieter ones in front, the smaller, squirming, excited ones in back. The girl held me, and without intending to, I lost my lunch in her lap.

It hadn't been a very good lunch, the usual dried nuggets with a bowl of fresh water, but I always ate what was available in case someone forgot to feed me altogether the next time.

When the people stopped the car to clean up the mess I'd made, the girl put me on the ground at the side of the road. I could smell a dozen things I'd never smelled before. Something made my mouth juicy and my stomach want to climb right out of me, but in a good way. Other smells made me want to run like I might be able to catch up to them. And other things smelled sweet and growing, nothing I'd eat but maybe I'd sniff just for the fun of it.

I was tempted to make a dash for the bushes I could see across a field. The little girl probably couldn't catch me, and the bigger people were busy wiping out the car. I wanted to run as fast as I could. I didn't even know how fast that might be since I'd been in the Pound for so long I'd almost forgotten about running altogether. I could feel it in my legs; they twitched a little to encourage me.

"Run for it," the front legs seemed to say, and I scratched at the ground a bit.

The back legs weren't as eager. They seemed to remember how good a run would feel, but they were reluctant to leave the little girl, and so was I. She reached down to pat my head, or my back, or my rump. Her hands were small, and the touch of her fingers was light, like leaves drifting out of the sky. Her words were soft too, and magic since they kept me from the freedom of running across the field.

145

"Good boy," she said, and I felt guilty for even considering escape.

"When we get home, I'll show you my room," she whispered, as if it were a secret garden she would reveal. (Perhaps it was. I've slept there every night for six of her years and forty-two of mine and never had a nightmare I remembered.)

"We're going to call you Tim," she said as she talked to keep me still beside the road. "Tim," she said again, and it meant nothing to me, good or bad, though it sounded true coming out of her lips.

The people climbed back into the car, and the man lifted me and put me on the little girl's lap.

"He has worms," the man said, and it sounded bad.

The little girl didn't seem to care. She kept her hand on my head while I slept the rest of the way.

In their yard, the boy showed me a ball bigger than my head. "Tim, here Tim, Tim, Tim, Tim," he called and tossed the ball a few feet where it dribbled to a stop.

The grass on the lawn tasted good and settled my rocking stomach. It smelled good too – wet and cool and fresh. The boy called my name again like a rhyme, "Tim, Tim, here Tim, come on Tim, Tim-Boy, Tim, Tim," as if I were in another world, and he wanted me to come back to life. I knew he wanted me to lift my head, turn and run toward him to show him I understood. But I needed to try on this Tim. When the boy said it, I wasn't sure it was me.

The girl filled a metal tub with water that she carried from the house in a bucket. She mixed the water with other water from a hose, stirring it like food. When I went over to sniff it, she swept me up and put me into it. I was surprised by the warmth and wetness on my legs. So surprised, I didn't wriggle until she poured water all over me and started to scrub me with a brush.

"It's a bath," she explained as I tried to squirm out of her hands which were so little and gentle as to be useless in holding down a determined dog. Her mother knelt down beside the tub and held me so the little girl could scrub.

"I don't think he likes it," the girl said.

"You didn't like baths either when you were a baby," the mother said. "When he's older, we'll see if he likes to swim."

"I bet he will if we throw a stick," the girl prophesied.

Of course, she was absolutely right. Throw anything, and I'll fetch it, especially if I have to swim.

"He looks like a baby seal, all wet," the little girl laughed as I managed to leap free of the mother, my favorite the little girl, and the tub. I shook water all over them so that they shrieked, "Tim, Tim, oh Tim, Tim, Tim," and I knew I'd better like it because it was my name.

They introduced me to the neighbors, a huge Rottweiler named Gretchen who let me crawl all over her hulking frame as well as bite her feet, her ears, and any loose flesh I could get my teeth into. She yelped and moved away, but allowed me to start it all over again. Kilo, an aging, blue-eyed husky mix down the road was not so welcoming, and we had little to do with each other from the beginning. I kind of liked a handsome, lean Doberman named Max in a house nearby, but the owners didn't last, and Max moved away.

I even met some of the neighbors on my own, including a family of skunks who lived under our deck. Since they lived so close, it seemed we would get to know each other well, but every time I ran into one of them, something went wrong. The big people in the house had a fit after these encounters. The man put me in the tub with tomato juice that turned my black coat auburn until the rain washed it clean again. The woman cried, "P-U, Tim!" and put perfume under her nose. I agreed with her. The tomato juice smelled pretty bad.

We lived in the mountains with majestic views in all directions. There were several places I could sit and command the valley or the peaks like a king. The little girl was my queen, even though many days she had to go to school. I didn't like the big bus that came to pick her up at the bottom of the hill below our house. I followed her down to the bus day after day with great suspicion and loathing. The bus smelled, it roared, it took her away during all of the hours of sunshine when she missed most of the interesting events that ever happened in the neighborhood.

"Go home, Tim," she urged as the awful bus squeaked to a stop on the road. "I'll be home soon."

Which was a lie. Hours would pass – the sun would curve through the sky; squirrels would leap between trees; birds would feed and disappear, calling information to each other; hundreds of insects would hum and die; I would chew and sleep and yawn and sleep again – before she would come home.

Even in a dream, I could hear her footsteps as she climbed the hill after school with her brother and the children of the neighborhood. They

147

took their time on the steep hill. They talked and laughed at a handful of silly stories while I woke from the dream and waited.

All day I had guarded the house and the yard – the castle, the mountain, and the kingdom of the little girl. It was a long time to spend with no one but squirrels, birds, and a bunch of bugs. I stopped waiting and ran to greet her, barking great, deep throatfuls of love.

"Tim, Tim," she laughed when she saw me.

The children gathered around, touching me on all sides, rubbing my head, grabbing my tail. I twisted and turned under their hands. I licked their fingers and their faces which were sticky and smelled of the strange place called School, where there must be bitter soap, rough paper towels, masses of sweet paste, dusty chalk, tomato soup and cheese sandwiches for lunch, women with perfume, old linoleum with layers of wax, crayons also made of wax, sometimes paints, slightly sour milk, other children's bodies moist with sweat, games with rubber balls, books and paper made of wood (smelling of sap, of lumber, of branches, of bird nests). The children smelled of all these when they came home laughing and hungry.

They stormed the kitchen to devour dill pickles and huge, crunchy bags of chips. They drank juice and cocoa and cider. They nibbled cookies and popped corn. The little girl filled my dish with hard, loud nuggets and ran the faucet to give me cold, fresh water. Her fingers played silent music on my head as she murmured, "Good boy, Good Tim, I'm home, we're home, how-was-your-day-I-missed-you."

And then she let me outside again where I stretched in the yard, my head held high in the breeze so I could catch the scent of dinners being cooked across the mountain. With views in all directions, a sliver of moon beginning to show in the dusk, I no longer had visions of running away as I had in the beginning. Perhaps I was complacent, lulled by a full dish and a warm place to sleep. Or maybe it was the little girl, who loved me as much as I loved her. Every night she kissed me goodnight on my nose, and I didn't expect to find that kind of love very often or every place I might look. I might dream about freedom, about running free and wild (barking, leaping fences, snarling at evil forces, ferocious and brave in the face of larger dogs). But really, when it came down to it, as I settled my head on the ground between my paws, I was content to leave sleeping dogs lie, especially me.

Wild Bill and the Dolton Pet Parade
by Kimberly O'Lone

P ut down that book," said Pearl. "Look, I've got a great project for us." A half-page ad, complete with illustrations of dogs and cats in Monday's *Dolton Pointer* read:

Kids 12 and Under - Howdy!
Dress Western Style and Join the
Pet Parade for
Dolton Roundup Days!

In smaller print it said, *"Parade: 1:00 Saturday, July 23, 1967. Real and Pretend Pets Acceptable."*

"With some red gingham I could turn you into Dale Evans," said Pearl, setting down the paper and looking at her manicure. "With your height, you'll look like a real little lady. And you could bring that broomstick horse as your pet."

Gale's brown eyes grew large. "Mom!" said Gale, "I have a real pet."

"That rodent!"

"Pepper's a guinea pig," Gale emphasized. "And Dale Evans is just an actress. I want to do something from the real West, like on vacation. Remember, Wild Bill Hickock's grave in South Dakota?"

"Hickock! Wild Bill Hickock?" Pearl lowered herself carefully into the damask upholstered wing chair.

Gale continued, "My wagon could be Boot Hill. I could make Wild Bill's gravestone, and Calamity Jane's, and all the rest. Pepper could be the undertaker."

Pearl smoothed her flowered dress carefully before answering. "The undertaker. *You'll* be?"

Gale paused. "Colorado Charlie, Wild Bill's best friend. I would be Chief Mourner."

Pearl forced a smile. "Honey, why not be something … nice?"

"The West wasn't nice." Gale called as she ran up the stairs. She returned triumphantly with picture postcards of a hilltop cemetery. The hand lettered wooden tombstone read:

> WILD BILL
> J.B. HICKOCK
> Killed by the Assassin
> Jack McCall
> In Deadwood, Black Hills
> August 2, 1876
> Pard we will
> meet again in the happy
> Hunting ground
> to part no more.
> Good bye
> COLORADO CHARLIE

"This will be so cool. Gotta tell Veronica." Gale was out the door, leaving Pearl slouched back in the chair, worry lines deepening between her eyes.

❖ ❖ ❖

Veronica was putting bows in her long red hair. "Just like the dance hall girls in the Old West," she said. "I'll make my wagon into the Long Branch Salon."

"Saloon," insisted Gale.

"No. Salon. Saloons are smelly, dirty places. *Mine* is a salon."

Her white rabbit Flopsy would be Miss Kitty, complete with candy pink polished nails and a slender ribbon around her neck.

Gale secretly thought the Gunsmoke TV theme silly, whereas she would depict a real life gunfighter.

As the two girls worked on their wagons, Sally, who was only seven, showed up. She wanted to turn her red Radio Flyer into a covered wagon, but didn't know where to start. Gale drew a Conestoga wagon. "You could make a frame of wire hoops and spread a sheet over it," she said, and drew a rabbit looking out of the wagon, Sally's Mopsy.

❖ ❖ ❖

That night at dinner no one could get a word in edgewise as Gale spilled out facts about Wild Bill. "He was playing poker when he was shot in the back. Holding a pair of aces and eights." She paused for effect as Pearl frowned. "Gamblers still call it The Dead Man's Hand." Pearl sighed. "When they dug up his body, they found it wasn't rotten at all. It had petrified and turned to stone. Sounded just like a log when they hit it with a stick." Pearl almost choked on her meatloaf.

Tuesday morning Gale glued aces and eights on the back of the wagon. She and Sally built a paper maché hill and painted it green. They stuck tombstones made from Popsicle sticks into the hill. Gale made a little sidewalk out of white pebbles running up to Bill's grave. At the foot of the hill she placed a wire arch with a small sign saying "Boot Hill." Across from the arch was a shoebox painted to look like Saloon Number 10, where Wild Bill met his fate. Gale used an ashtray she made in ceramics class as a horse trough in front of the saloon's door.

When Pearl checked on Gale, she found her filling the trough with water. "You made this all yourself?"

"Sally helped. She had to. Her dad's making her a covered wagon, and won't let her touch it." Gale surveyed her work. "How am I going to make Pepper's clothes?" she muttered.

Pearl was bent over a teddy bear's tuxedo when Gale came down to breakfast Wednesday. She looked up. "I'll rip out the seams and use it as a pattern for Pepper's coat."

"You'll help?" Gale beamed.

"Yes, but I'm not going to touch that rodent." Pearl scowled. "How many inches from the nape . . . uh, bottom of his neck to his waist?"

"He really doesn't have a waist."

Pearl shook her head.

Gale put newspaper on the red Formica kitchen table, and got Pepper. The guinea pig calmly wrinkled his nose, smelling Gale's hand as she laid a ruler lengthwise next to him. "Four inches," Gale reported.

Next, Gale held Pepper with her left hand and tried to wrap a tape measure around his waist with her right. He wiggled free and ran toward the table edge. Gale froze. Pearl grabbed Pepper just before he fell. Clutching him to her chest with both hands, her face crinkled in

151

disgust. She held him away from her, revealing the small wet spot he'd left on her dress. He squealed in panic, struggling. Slowly, Pearl brought him to her again and began stroking his head. "Shhh. You're OK," she repeated as Pepper whimpered, then fell silent. "He's quieting down. Measure him now."

"Exactly a foot."

She frowned. "Hmm. I always thought he was a little on the chubby side. Take him, but be gentle."

Pearl sewed throughout the day and distractedly put a Swanson Salisbury Steak TV dinner in front of Gale's dad for dinner. As he stared at the small, wrinkled peas and carrots in his tin foil tray, he was about to complain, when he looked at his wife and daughter. They were intently gluing a rubber band to a small top hat. He ate his peas silently.

Pepper's first fitting was Thursday. This time, Gale fed him a carrot while holding him. Pearl gingerly lifted his front legs, one at a time, and guided them into his sleeves. She basted the seams with white thread. Pepper shifted as Pearl pinned his hem, causing her to jab him. The little animal screeched, then dashed again for the table edge. Pearl caught him, exclaiming, "It was my fault, I should have just marked it, but I was hurrying." She examined him as he squealed. "Just a pinprick." Pearl cradled him and began to rock. "You're fine." she said, and sang, "Hush little baby, don't say a word..." Pepper quieted down.

"Mama's gonna buy you a mocking bird..."

Gale stared, amazed.

"You liked this song, too." Pearl smiled. "A long time ago." She handled him over. "He's had enough for today."

❖ ❖ ❖

Friday afternoon Pearl said, "He really isn't bad looking, almost handsome." Pepper stood quietly in his coat and hat, accustomed now to being fussed over. Pearl stood back appraisingly. "A bath," she pronounced.

"Mom, he's not going to like it."

"Let's try. I think a nice cream rinse will help make his coat easier to brush, too."

"Brush?"

"Of course," Pearl said, petting Pepper. "But not until after he's blow dried. We don't want split ends."

Pepper struggled as Gale lowered him into the lukewarm water that Pearl had tested with her elbow. Gale's dad stuck his head in the room. "Is this the Baptism?" he asked.

"Shut up, John," snapped Pearl, "We're busy."

Pepper endured the bath, but enjoyed being dried off. Pearl set the dryer on low and carefully kept it at a distance. Then she gently brushed him with Gale's baby brush, finishing by parting the hair on his head neatly down the center. "There, you look like a little gentleman."

Saturday, parade day, was 78 degrees and sunny. Gale, Veronica and Sally lined up to walk together.

Veronica wore a cowgirl outfit her mother had bought at the corner Woolworth's. The skirt and vest's brown and white fake fur looked like cowhide. Her red hair flowed from under her white cowboy hat. Flopsy was chewing the end of her pink ribbon, peering warily from inside the Long Branch Salon.

Sally pulled a wooden covered wagon, with Mopsy inside the wagon in a wire cage. Dressed in her Indian Halloween costume, Sally had red streaks painted on her cheeks and a single blue feather stuck on a leatherette headband.

Pepper scurried about Gale's wagon in his black coat and hat. A woman screeched, "Is that a rat?" and hastily retreated. Gale, as Colorado Charlie, dressed in cowboy boots, old jeans, shirt and battered brown felt hat. She sported a handle bar mustache. Just before the parade started, Pearl, who'd dressed for the occasion in a turquoise silk dress and matching hat, brushed the few gray hairs that stuck out of Pepper's coat. He put up no resistance.

Fifty kids walked through downtown Dolton. When they reached the parade's end in Dolton Park, the Chamber of Commerce Women's Auxiliary gave them vanilla ice cream in cups. As they ate with flat wooden spoons shaped like figure eights, the girls talked excitedly about Mopsy's escape attempt.

"I thought she was going to knock the wagon over," said Gale.

"So did I," agreed Sally. "Thanks for quieting her down. I never saw anybody sing to a rabbit in the middle of the street."

The Chamber of Commerce president said into the microphone. "Our pet parade winners, and recipients of the AM/FM transistor radios are..." A hush fell over the crowd. "In third place, Veronica Ryan and Flopsy. In second place, John Black and Butch. Our first place winner is Sally Boulder and Mopsy."

153

Gale felt her stomach tighten as the other girls rushed to claim their prizes. She met her mother's disappointed gaze, and could no longer contain her childish tears by the time they reached their Dodge.

"Store bought clothes and they won!" her mother mumbled. "Pepper looked so nice compared to those ratty looking rabbits with their runny, pink eyes. Pepper's eyes are a beautiful deep brown." Pearl snorted.

"I should have been Dale Evans and left Pepper behind, like you wanted," Gale said, sniffling.

"No. Wild Bill was right for you. You're just tall, so you look older. Judges always go for little kids."

"Look at them, with their radios." Gale said sadly. "It was our idea."

Pearl stroked Gale's hair, "Honey, you've earned a radio. Let's get Pepper home and go to Woolworth's. A radio is a good idea for you, anyway. I'll teach you to dance. You're getting to the age where that will matter."

Gale stopped sniffling and rolled her eyes. "Let's think about this," she said, and got into the Dodge.

Diva on Deck
by Carolyn Paprocki

She looked like some
Funereal bird:
Bleak plumage,
(Black talons curling from her hat)
Pearls like teeth
Of ancient archaeopteryx
At her throat,
Fumes of dead fur
Under a sharp mouth.

Her cellophane skin
Testified to the fossil beneath;
She was a skeleton
Decked with treasures,
A specter risen from the deep.

She could sing; oh yes, she could sing,
Better than any bird;
But could she live?
No warmth, no spark flowed
From that vapid vulture body,
Fabulous cadaver.

She wanted to be worshipped,
To have candles lit before her
And she in a gilded cage
of *de rigueur* elegance
Would take pity
On poor mortals.

But instead she was alone
On a wide gray sea,
Cape crossed
Like folded wings
About her;
Too cold to move,
Too stiff to join the flight of the gulls.

155

Mark

by Arthur Melville Pearson

In the stillness, Mark can actually hear the water turn to ice. The sound seems to him a chorus of tinkling death rattles, each tiny molecule exhaling a faint, final *chink* as it passes from liquid to solid. With no force of nature but the cold to disturb its surface, the small lake freezes clear and fragile as the night.

Mark lightly taps his foot on the new shoreline ice. It has the feel of a storm window, sturdy but not unbreakable. He applies steady pressure. The surface holds. He leans more heavily and finally comes the crack. Mark snatches back his foot and studies the hairline fissure that runs to where the lake is not yet frozen – a pool of blackness that more resembles oil than open water. The high moon's reflection does not appear on the water. Mark wonders if some law of physics determines that just before freezing, water molecules become too cold, too dense to reflect light, creating a watery black hole.

He hasn't been back to this lake in years. As a kid it cost him just five bucks for a junior Izaak Walton membership. This entitled him to seasons of leaving his fishing line in the water while he went in search of tadpoles, turtles and bird nests. Every spring, he could hardly wait for the return of Canada geese and mallards that soon were followed by the appearance of small clumps of down called goslings and ducklings. All summer long, the fish picked clean his hook while the boy marveled at a belted kingfisher's ability to dive beneath the water and re-emerge with a wriggling perch fry in its beak. Fall weekends would find him at the lake in the hopes of glimpsing migrant waterfowl stopping over before continuing south for the winter. As much as he loved the colors, shapes and habits of these visitors, he loved saying their funny names perhaps even more: canvas backs, buffle heads, widgeons, ruddies, shovelers, coots and grebes.

One winter, the lake had frozen not only smooth, but exceptionally clear. Skating atop the perfect surface, Mark could see the sandy bottom in the shallows and in the deeper waters, the tops of seaweeds whose root ends disappeared into nothingness. Far out in the middle of the lake, he came upon a small school of fish. As surprised as Mark, the fish banked but stayed close along the underside of the ice. The little devils that stole his bait all summer were now his to ride roughshod over. He stayed right on top of the rattled school, cutting, stopping and starting like the world-champion fish wrangler he was proving himself to be. For hours he pursued his charges until the light began to fail and the world upon which he played faded and grew unfriendly. The fish disappeared into darkness. The young boy came to an unsteady stop in the middle of the void. The black water welled up and melted the ice entirely from view. Mark's brain insisted that the ice remained firm beneath him but his fears informed him otherwise and froze him – he was about to drown.

❖ ❖ ❖

Orion and his entourage have marched halfway across the heavens. The black hole in the middle of the lake is frozen closed, completing a perfect picture window. Mark rises up on the twin glass-cutter edges of his skates. His knees bend and he pushes off.

The ice holds. At least around the perimeter. Mark's stomach serves as an internal safety barometer, rising against his Adam's apple if he ventures too far from shore. The first time around the lake, he never looks down. His breaths remain high in his chest and shallow, his stride short and stiff. Three slow, rim-hugging laps later and all's well. Mark glides to a stop. His breathing is a little deeper for the gentle exertion. His stomach sits near to where it should. He looks to the middle of the lake. His exhalations idle on the air about his face like he's just warming up. But it's very late. It was foolish to skate even the edge of the too newly-frozen lake, foolish to come here at all. Time to go home. Mark drifts toward his boots. He reaches down and grabs a lace. Straightening up, he lets his left skate drift forward. He leans hard on the outer edge of the lead blade. His body follows the ensuing tight circle and gathers momentum. Like an Olympic hammer thrower, Mark spins three-sixty once, twice and releases his boot in a towering arc toward the middle of the lake.

With bursting strides, Mark accelerates hard after the boot. His legs churn, his arms in opposition pump. The ice receives each elongated stride as crystal takes cuts from a master craftsman. He zeroes in on the boot as if it were prey. He's seen a peregrine falcon ball its talons and literally punch a pigeon from the sky. Mark curls a fist and, streaking by his boot, cold cocks it into the dead center of the lake. He lets out a whoop and takes a long, sweeping arc in preparation for the kill. Crouched and crossing right foot over left, he picks up speed as the boot comes back into view. Lame, lying on its side, the boot's fate is now inevitable. It hovers just ahead, suspended between the dark of the water and the dark of the air. Mark's nostrils flare as they pick up the scent of imminent death. His face prickles with the racing cold. Tears freeze on his cheeks and his blood shrieks with the impending blow. Half a stride from his victim, his weight shifts back, both skates go parallel to the target and the boot is showered with the shavings of a power stop.

Mark's heart cannot stop so quickly. It races on in an internal victory lap – triumphant, vibrant and alive. Mark shoots his fists toward the heavens and throws back his head to see Orion echo the gesture. Gulping deep, starry space, a quiet laugh stirs in his lungs. Each hard breath tickles the impulse until a giggle crystallizes and mingles with the midwinter air. Giggles quickly give way to chuckles to open-throated laughter. He cannot help himself. His eyes shed a second course of tears that freeze his laughter into heaving sobs. Alone in the middle of the lake, Mark weeps uncontrollably. His heart floods with adrenaline. Then comes the crack and the plunge into darkness.

He has no sensation of cold, wet or even panic. The darkness is not so dark. Mark can see the fish he angled for as a boy. A pang of guilt shoots through him as there idles by a few bluegills with ripped lips, victims of his childhood sport. But none of the fish appears bent on revenge. They do not nip at him as he feared they might. The perch, sunfish and carp take no notice of him at all until they assume human features. No longer does Mark look into any cold fish eye, but the benevolent face of his father. He's been gone too long. As has his mother, swimming in perfect sync with her husband as she did during their fifty-two year marriage.

There follows a school of fish bearing the faces of other relatives long dead. Grandparents, aunts and uncles. Some friends, too, who have passed. Drowning up to this point is effortless, almost pleasant. But with the sight of a living face comes the first cold trickle of water into Mark's lungs. There swims the face of his best friend, dearer to him than his own. His best friend's wife and their children. Mark feels his body's air sacs fill with water. The face of the woman he loves is followed by the face of the woman he divorced. The trickle increases and at last triggers panic. There is one face he must see before his eyes fail.

Mark flails his swelling arms and legs. The school disappears in a cloud of silt. Mark hovers in the roiled void, his lungs steadily flooding, his sight growing dim, when out of the murk emerges the shape of a nine-year old boy. Mark recognizes him instantly. Not living, not dead, this is the boy who thirty years ago stood frozen with fear on the dark ice above the dark water. What happened inside the boy that day is hard to say. But the quality of fear that froze him would re-surface at the wedding of his best friend. As the woman he loved walked away for the final time. As he heard himself say, "I do" to another. When his mother could no longer recall the name of her husband. When his father slipped into a coma and Mark could not reach across the void to save him as his father had rescued him from the invisible ice of Izaak Walton Lake.

The particulate-laden waters settle. The shape of the nine-year old boy draws closer. His features come more sharply into view. Mark looks into the face, not of his younger self, but of his own son he has not seen since the divorce. Tears come to Mark's eyes a third time but underwater they do not matter. He tries to raise his arms but they no longer obey him. Only now is drowning a torture. His boy is so beautiful. Why have all those fish returned to pick at him? Fish, not with human faces, but with the heads of birds – picking, pecking and raising an ear-splitting squawk.

❖　❖　❖

Mark's eyelids flutter in response to the sound of pre-dawn birds – a cacophony that ought to raise the dead but through which most of the world sleeps.

"You all right?"

His eyes open and struggle to bring the question into focus.

"Sit up slow."

Lying on his back, Mark raises onto his elbows.

"Cold one, last night, huh?"

Mark's eyes finally work in concert. He sees a thermal coverall-clad man seated on a low campstool.

"Here."

A Thermos-lid cup is held to Mark's lips. He tips his head forward and drinks. Hot coffee laced with whiskey instantly de-ices everything but the couple of toes he will lose. Coverall-man downs the rest of the coffee himself, then returns his attention to setting the flag on a trip device set above a six-inch hole in the ice. From this device dangles a short line and baited hook. Mark looks out over the ice and sees half a dozen more flags poised to indicate a catch. A shiver runs through him as a far flag pops up. A whiff of sulfur stings his nose. Coverall-man adjusts the burner on his propane stove. Two more flags. Pop. Pop. Olive oil splashes into a frying pan. The flag at coverall-man's feet releases. A massive hand yanks a six-inch tiger perch onto the ice. Half-expecting to see the face of a loved one rather than the unblinking eye that greets him, Mark is further unnerved as a thin blade dislodges the flank of the still twitching fish. Fat fingers flip over the perch and perform an identical cut. The fillets are rived of ribs and skin, rinsed in the ice hole then slapped into the sizzling oil. From his coat pocket, the man takes a pinch of something and sprinkles it on the frying fish. With bare fingers, he flips over the solidifying flesh. Mark closes his eyes and concentrates on the whiskeyed coffee racing through his veins.

"Here."

Fat fingers hold a flaky morsel to Mark's mouth, which opens. And receives.

The Kindness of Strangers
A Novel Excerpt by Doris Popovich

Cool morning dew soaks through the seat of Allie's faded thin jeans, as she stretches across the grass, only half-ready to begin another day. Joey is curled up next to her, his front paw extended and touching her leg. Quietly, Allie breathes a soulful sigh, almost a whimper. Her eyelids are red, heavy from another restless night. The handlebar of her rusty silver bike is balanced against the park bench directly in front of her, casting its dawn shadow on the grass. Her few possessions are draped majestically on this bike. Joey's cage is wired in place, lodged between the handlebar and the front fender. A stack of blue-green paper towels from a gas station lines the cage, with dead leaves and grass softly packed on top.

A musty green water-fountain stands five yards south. All night the sound of the water trickled in the fountain. The winds are beginning to pick up now and the sound of waves slapping against the boats docked in Belmont Harbor intensifies. After seeing the morning's first jogger, Allie feels relieved. The sun gently washes her face with color. When she closes her eyes, transparencies of yellow, red, and orange spin uncontrollably before her. Soon it will be time for her to rest. Another night, another quiet night. Quickened by her good fortune, she makes a mental note to return later to this same spot.

Joey stretches and gently pumps his white front paws. Allie delights in this ritual. She loves Joey. She adopted him eleven summers ago, in what seems like another life. Gracey, the grey tabby who belonged to Hanna, her next-door neighbor at the time, gave birth to three grey tabby kittens and Joey, who much to everyone's surprise, was stark white. A flush of nostalgia warms her cheeks as she remembers Joey as a kitten. He used to sit perched on the outside sill of her kitchen window staring into the house for hours. Allie never cared much for cats, but she found his incessant interest in the goings on of her life quite flattering. Before she knew it, Joey had found his way to the inside sill of her kitchen window. There he would sit for hours, looking out with an equal mix of interest and disinterest, like only a pampered cat can do.

❖ ❖ ❖

Early morning is their preferred time of day, quiet and usually safe. The lakefront is deserted except for the familiar parade of early morning bikers and joggers. Traffic on Lake Shore Drive hasn't picked up yet.

"OK, big boy. Back in a second." Standing slowly, she feels dizzy from the rush of blood to her head. She staggers and waits for it to pass. When she catches her balance, she makes her way to the water fountain. Using her hand as a cup, she rinses her left arm to the elbow, then her right. She unties the red handkerchief from her neck, soaks it, and uses it to wet her face. The water feels cool against her forehead and eyelids. She leans down to drink but loses her balance and falls, landing on her left knee. Gently she removes a small brown shard of broken glass from the skin of her knee, and she starts to bleed. Looks worse than it is, she thinks. There's no one around to complain to, anyway. The hazy orange sun peaks half out of the water, far across the lake. Another day beginning.

Each day proceeds much the same as the next. No hurry. Find a good spot and stay there. Running water is nice. At first she required a toilet, now a secluded bush at night does just fine. Less competition that way. Safety is another consideration, though more difficult to predict. This morning's spot has lots of shade, private toilets, and the promise of picnic leftovers; a spot of relative good fortune.

Allie wakes up hours later. The bench is hot and the sun is burning her face. When she fell asleep the park bench was shaded. She is startled by a stray toddler standing directly over her, staring intermittently at her and then Joey. The park is crowded with picnickers. She looks over to Joey's cage. He is wide awake, peering suspiciously back at this little girl. Both Joey and the child have grouchy looks on their faces. She wonders whose youngster she is. Before long, a young Hispanic girl, maybe seven, comes and retrieves the toddler. The girl looks tired. She grabs the hand of the baby and drags her away without making eye contact with Allie or Joey.

"Time for breakfast." Allie reaches for a plastic bag inside another plastic bag, inside a paper bag. Joey stands up and paces the circumference of his cage when he hears the rattle of plastic. He may be old, but there's nothing wrong with his appetite. He lives to eat, and much to her pride, she makes sure he eats every day.

Coyote's Chocolate
by Rochelle Rhodes

The coyote licked its nearly frozen paws and stared into the lit window of the house. It had been a long trek, but the coyote loved the snow and delighted in the journey. It was the curiosity of what lay ahead in that small town, Caribou, which kept the coyote yearning. It was the need to see the woman that had compelled her to push faster and farther than she'd ever gone. This was the coyote's first time in New England and the landscape she witnessed as she traveled was more enchanting than she'd imagined.

The trip had taken longer than she had estimated and the ground was much colder here. Canada, after all, wasn't that far away. The December wind tore at her fur and howled in her ears. Wisps of moisture left the coyote's mouth as her ragged panting gradually began to subside. She reached into the pouch that was draped around her neck, and with her mouth, carefully pulled out the crumpled envelope that had made the trip with her from the Midwest.

I must be crazy, the coyote thought to herself as she crept up the front steps. The last thing she needed was for the woman to look out her window and find a tattered and weary coyote on her stoop. The coyote had no idea what the woman might do if she were to find herself confronted with a creature of solitude and obscurity. Perhaps she should have morphed into a crow – a creature that would have adapted to the temperature – and flown the distance rather than trot hundreds of miles on foot into the New England winter. The air had been balmy and unusually kind for this time of year when she had left the fields of Indiana at the end of November. Now, she shivered.

She didn't know the woman very well. Come to think of it, she didn't know her at all. Their connection was the result of a mutual friend playing matchmaker. The coyote had made a concerted effort to woo the woman into a correspondence, using all of her best words and clever lines. Well, she mused, shaking her paws in turn, it's as Forrest Gump says: pick your chocolate and hope for the best. The coyote could only hope that tonight wasn't going to be a cherry or vanilla filling. She preferred chocolate over chocolate.

She had played this scenario over and over in her mind. She had received only one response from the woman – encouraging though noncommittal – weeks ago, but it was enough to cause the coyote to venture north, to wrap her heart in Christmas paper and take a chance. The coyote dropped the envelope and scratched twice on the door before darting back into the night. She waited at the edge of the yard to see if the woman had heard her sound. The porch light went on and the door opened. She stood there, as breathtaking as her friend had described. Penetrating eyes that had the capacity to bore deep into the coyote's chest, peer into her mind and read her every thought. Short dark hair that framed an exquisite face.

The woman moved to the edge of the porch and squinted at the coyote with its tongue still hanging from its mouth, uncertain as to whether it signified anticipation or exhaustion. The woman raked a handful of snow from the porch railing and packed it into a solid snowball. "Scram!" she shouted. "Before I wing this Maine fast ball between your eyes."

The coyote held her ground, and her breath, unprepared for this hostility. Without moving, she braced herself for a line drive. The throw was high and to the left. The coyote leapt into the air and caught the snowball in her mouth, then gently dropped it to the ground. The woman shrugged and turned to leave the animal to the elements. Before returning to the warmth of her fire, she glanced at the envelope lying on the porch. Confused, she opened the letter and began to read as the coyote looked on. "Another letter," she muttered to no one in particular, shaking her head. "Why couldn't she just send this through the mail like everyone else?"

"Because the last thing in the world I want to be is like everyone else."

The woman spun in the direction of the sound. She gasped as she turned, her body immediately surging backward. The coyote had vanished. Instead, a woman with serious green eyes and a mischievous smile stood not more than six inches away. The green eyed woman instinctively grabbed the shoulders of the startled one and pulled her safely upright and closer to her still.

"Who are you?" the woman demanded.

"Well, you can call me friend, or even beguiled, but please don't call me chicken thief."

The woman sighed and allowed her visitor to pull her near in an embrace that suggested all manner of good things. She felt the chill in the stranger's cheek from the bitter wind as she lingered in her arms, and realized that the lunatic on her porch was the one responsible for the multitude of mail she had recently received. "What on earth are you doing here?" she asked.

"It's just as I thought," the visitor replied, brushing her cheek against the woman's forehead. "You're perfect in my arms. Perfect for a hug. That's what I'm doing here."

"You are weird, weird, weird."

"I suppose so." The visitor smiled to herself, undaunted. "But I think you like it."

The woman snorted. "You are mistaken, my coyote friend. I don't know how you can make such bold assumptions, because I never indicated anything of the kind." She stepped out of and away from the embrace. "Wasn't my silence a clear enough message?"

The visitor leaned back against the porch, grimaced, then moaned aloud. "Oh, Jesus, I'm wounded." Tears welled in her eyes.

"Sorry, but that's how it is."

"What?" The visitor looked bewildered for a moment, then a flicker of understanding registered. "Oh, it's not that." She reached her left hand behind her back and made a wrenching movement before bringing her hand back around. "It's this." She clutched an ominously shaped eight-inch icicle with a broken tip. "This stalagmite wants to joust with my left cheek."

"How could you possibly have leaned into an icicle?"

"I didn't. I'm positive the hand of fate pulled it from your awning and poked it into my butt. I have the feeling it's trying to tell me something."

"Are you ever serious?" The woman bit her bottom lip to suppress a smile.

"Rarely." The visitor tossed the chunk of ice into the yard. "It gets me nowhere." She wiped the tears that had begun to slide down her cheeks. She squeezed the tears in her fist, and when she opened her hand, several glittering diamonds lay in her palm. "This is what I would give you." She smiled at the woman. "But it is not what you need. And obviously not what you seek."

The visitor leaned over the porch railing and flung the diamonds into the nighttime, scattering them into the frozen darkness. They shimmered with the brilliance of stars strewn across a moonless midnight, then slowly began to fade until they vanished, like sparklers being twirled by a child on the Fourth of July.

"You're right." The woman spoke with contrition. "Please forgive my lack of manners, but I am not in need of diamonds or coyotes or the endless lines of verse and prose that you send." She stood behind the visitor with her arms folded. "And I don't need anyone else in my life."

"I understand," The visitor replied, gazing up at the sliver of a crescent moon. "People are motivated only by that which they do not already possess. But I wasn't asking you to marry me." She inhaled deeply, the frigid air causing her throat to feel as brittle as a twig on the tree.

The woman rubbed her hands together and disregarded the visitor's observation. "It's cold. Would you like something to drink before you leave...a bowl of warm milk, perhaps?"

The visitor looked over her shoulder and laughed. "No, thanks. Warm milk is for pussies. I'm going home – a different way, though, a faster way." She grinned as she turned and pulled the letter she had delivered only moments before from the woman's hand. "Someone tried to hitch me to a dogsled just outside of Bangor." With resignation, she looked once more into the woman's eyes and traced her jaw line with the tips of her fingers. "Vanilla," she whispered.

"What did you say?" The woman frowned in confusion.

"Nothing."

"You're a strange woman."

"No, not strange," she replied. "Vulnerable, maybe, but that's because I refuse to be ordinary." The visitor sprang from the porch, vaulting over the steps to the sidewalk, slick with ice and snow. In midair she metamorphosed back into her coyote form and landed in a snowdrift along the edge of the walk. She began to prance in a circular motion, as though chasing her tail, her speed increasing with each rotation, until she was a blur of fur and wind. In seconds the image resembled a miniature funnel cloud swirling back and forth along the porch as if waving good-bye.

"Ever been kissed by the wind?" The voice came from inside the spinning mass.

The woman stood holding on to a post and closed her eyes as the wind enveloped her body. It was not a violent wind, nor was it cold or brutal. Rather, standing in its center, she experienced a sensation of alternating warmth and coolness, a clarifying mist that caressed her body with tranquillity and light. The source of this light was undeniably born of love; a love which was of a purity, kinship and innocence not yet understood or even known to the world, to those who claimed consciousness while spending their waking hours in a kind of sluggish sleepwalk.

It did not frighten her; it took nothing from her.

It simply existed – briefly.

As gently and as deftly as it had surrounded her, the wind departed, leaving her in a hush of serenity. The woman smoothed her short hair into place and touched her fingers to her lips. She knew with certainty that she would never hear from the coyote or the human visitor again, but she had been kissed by the wind, and nothing would ever be the same.

The Last Chicago Bear
by Jill Riddell

After exiting the subway at Clark and Lake, I purchase nineteen dollars and twenty cents worth of stamps at the postal branch inside the State of Illinois building, and step outside onto the pink granite sidewalk lining LaSalle Street. I've come here on a nature pilgrimage. One hundred sixty-four years ago, on October 6, 1834, the last bear in Chicago was killed in this vicinity, and I've come to trace the path of its last few moments of life.

I discovered the description of the bear's last stand in a book called Chicago Antiquities, self-published by Henry H. Hurlbut in 1881. The text on the flyleaf describes its contents as "original items and relations, letters, extracts and notes pertaining to Early Chicago." According to Hurlbut's interview with John Sweeney, the carpenter who shot the animal, the bear first appeared in the area of Randolph and LaSalle, a corner currently anchored by the two State of Illinois buildings, City Hall and the Bismarck Hotel. Though they appear on plats from the time, the streets in this area didn't yet exist on the ground. According to Hurlbut's reconstructed account, the bear "happened to be rambling through the thicket, or woods, in the neighborhood of Randolph Street, somewhere between LaSalle St. and the River" when it was encountered by Samuel George, a man who made his living baking bread in a shop on Lake Street.

There's no sign of anything resembling a "thicket" at Randolph and LaSalle, and precious little nature at all as I contemplate my surroundings on a chilly November afternoon.  The stone walls of the buildings rise up at right angles from the rigid plain of sidewalks. Across the way from me, on the west side of the street, a line of frail locust trees shiver in the wind. To my left, seven ginkgos grow out of metal grates in front of City Hall. All have lost their leaves, and appear forlorn in their naked state.

Feathers, Fins & Fur

Upon spotting the bear, Samuel George bolted back to the settlement to alert the residents. According to Hurlbut, "the wild deer, and the wolf, and the Indian, still lingered about, and many a settler who had journeyed to what they termed this faraway frontier, had brought from Ohio or New York, Pennsylvania or Vermont, his trusted rifle or shotgun. In short, many had the shooting-irons ready loaded; and, of a crowd of villagers, whom the hullabaloo had aroused, among the first who answered the summons were Ashbel Steele, who kept the...tavern on Lake Street, and John Sweeney, a carpenter, who had arrived here in the spring of that year. Bailey Courtney, a tailor was also electrified with the news, and Courtney had a dog, and the dog too was excited, and they all hastily pushed forward to the onslaught. Coming in sight of the bear, we may say that Steele got the first shot at the varmint, which had started off on a trot, but the charge failed to hit him, and, as the dog was yelping at him furiously, he was induced to climb a tree."

The crew headed south after the bear, so I walk in that direction, too. Across the street, on the west side of LaSalle near Washington, six hawthorns stand like bare-limbed sculptures in black granite planters. On the east side, where I'm walking, tropical crotons and fig trees are clustered together behind the windows of American National Bank. A thin sheen of steam clouds the glass that separates them from the cold. For the next two blocks, there are no trees at all, no signs of any representative of the natural world, until I reach the Harris Bank on the south side of Monroe where a few tall locusts stand. City trees have a rough life; it's a rare one that lives to be more than forty. These are the most mature specimens I've encountered thus far, but I suspect even these guys weren't around when Kennedy was shot, much less the bear.

"Sweeney's turn now came and as the bear was quietly resting at the base of the limb [of a tree at the intersection of LaSalle and Adams]...he says he deliberately took aim at the bear's head just back of his ears.' Mr. S. assures us, that before he had time to blow smoke from the rifle, bruin came tumbling down very carelessly."

The bear would have a rough time finding a tree to climb at Adams and LaSalle today. There are none in front of the Rookery, 208 S. LaSalle, 190 S. LaSalle, or the LaSalle National Bank buildings, and their stone facades reveal nothing of the bit of natural history that unfolded on this spot.

"Briefly we may say, the bear was dead; he was drawn by an ox team on a sled to the meat-market of Edward Simmons on Lake Street, where his weight was found to be 400 pounds, and where he was skinned and dressed....the prevailing and notable food of the village then for some days was bear meat; all the taverns and most of the private houses had each a piece; every frying pan and gridiron in the settlement...was for a season redolent and reeking with bear's fat," concludes Hurlbut.

As I explore this stretch of roadway and history, I'm puzzled by the idea of the "thicket" and "brush" that recur in the description, and by the presence of a tree large enough for a bear to climb in the midst of what was known to be prairie. Upon my return from the pilgrimage, I call Jerry Wilhelm at the Morton Arboretum. A coauthor of Chicago's botany bible, *Plants of the Chicago Region*, he's more likely than most to understand what transpired in the downtown landscape.

Jerry reminds me that Jean-Baptiste DuSable and various white settlers started moving into Chicago in the late 1700s. By 1834, downtown Chicago had already experienced thirty years of their influence – part of which was suppression of wildfires. "This was more than enough time for parts of the land to grow up in brush," he said. Though the areas surrounding the settlement weren't "improved" in the sense of being built or cleared, they were already being affected by the European presence.

"It wouldn't have been a land anyone would describe as forest," Jerry says. "But there could have been scattered trees." The best guess was that the bear in its desperate attempt to escape its enemies climbed a black oak, a tree that thrives on sandy prairie soils.

Odd to think of the landscape of 1834 already being under the influence of the culture that would transform the prairie into the cement jungle where I ride subways and run errands today. Strange, even, to think of a book being written in 1881 about the "antiquities" of a city only 50 years old. Hurlbut acknowledges this irony in his introduction, justifying the title by the colossal nature of the change that occurred during the period. "A few decades have affected what in most cases the efforts of centuries have been required to accomplish," he writes.

Since then, we've piled on another hundred years, a blink in time by Eastern hemisphere standards. But it's been more than enough time to have shaped the land into a state that would be unrecognizable to Sweeney – and even less so for a 400-pound black bear.

Full Moon

by Jude Rittenhouse

Right there by the fence
hidden in bushes at the top
of the hill, at the edge
of my childhood yard,
Snake drapes great white folds
over branches. Enormous,
radiant, she shines light against bark
of a single-century tree. Despite
my distance, I notice
a faint black-lace pattern of scales.
She sees me,
begins moving. I stand still,
my bare feet deep in green
on this full moonlit night.
My right hand rubs two
black disks together. They
feel warm, alive. I throw them
to Snake: make an offering of these
magnets like fire, like a child. I know
they hold power. I know
their control would consume me.
They belong to Snake.
Only she can absorb
their blackness. I turn,
enchanted by glowing green grass,
and do not see Snake again
in this dream. But I know
where to find her: by that
long ago boundary, in the elm
where my brothers
shot at just-hatched starlings
at the top of the hill, at the edge
of my childhood world.

Snake

by Jude Rittenhouse

Snake magic
knows how to make a man
freeze and how, without hands
or claws, to climb
impossible trees.

Yet she must rest
two full days,
undisturbed and alone,
after devouring prey.

At any moment,
she can appear
out of nowhere,
her muscles rippling
like waves in ocean.

Yet when she sheds
outgrown skin,
exposes body transformed,
she must hide herself
tender and blind for a time.

The Goddess knew
how to choose a symbol:
mighty and fragile,
omniscient and blind.

The Goddess knew
how to choose a symbol
who would make men
remember.

Picasso & Me 4-Ever
by Christine Rusch

icasso was a great painter. Every night precisely at twelve I kiss his picture, the one thumbtacked to the wall next to my studio sink, which is also my kitchen sink and my bathtub. I love water, and I use the sink a lot. I use it to clean my brushes and to wash my dish – it is blue as the sea – and my spoon – it is real silver, from a flea market on the Slope. I use it to cleanse myself as I paint, and to wash away the shapes and colors that might have been but never will be, and to watch them as they ripple down the drain. Great painters always keep their brushes clean, and so do I. In this way I, too, will someday become a great painter.

Tonight I am tired and hungry, but I must try to work, because great painters work even if they are tired and hungry. They also paint what is in their hearts, but tonight I am having some difficulty identifying what is in my heart. I am having difficulty because I feel that all the pictures that have been painted since time began have not begun to tell the Truth, and that it is up to me to do it now. This is a large responsibility, and I do not know whether to start with the green or the white, or the brown, so I am just standing here, trying to decide, staring at the empty canvas. Beyond it, my dusty little TV set, which smoked and sparkled and made a poofing noise when it was hit by lightning last March, stares back at me.

A noise: it must be my stomach growling. I decide that I am hungry, but I notice that there are only two things in my refrigerator, a head of pale green lettuce, and a white plastic container of chocolate lowfat milk. I reach for the lettuce, but it is frozen, fused to the wall of my little refrigerator. I pull out the container of milk. The date stamped on the label tells me that the milk has not been safe to drink for two months. I would have trouble drinking it anyway, because the liquid has crystallized into little brown snowflakes that make me think of the slush on the side of the road on the way to school back in Kalamazoo. I realize that it is late – too late for supper, too late for Kalamazoo, and too late for great painters and their paint. I yawn. I hear the noise again. It is louder this time.

I catch my breath: right in front of me, on the screen of my broken TV set, is the man of my dreams. I don't believe it. I can't. This big lightning storm broke my TV last spring, and it does not work now. It definitely does not work. I have a receipt somewhere from Arnold's TV and Appliance on Seventh Street, that has two words scrawled on it in black magic marker: *Can't Repair*, but they still charged me $35.00. I have a certifiably broken television set, but there he is, on some kind of live talk show. This is really strange. How can anyone appear on a live TV show if he isn't alive? As I sink to the floor and watch him, he grins and casually mentions my idea for everyone to hear.

Mine! He's got everything – money, fame, and even death, but all I've got is my idea, and who does he think he is, telling it like it's his? I use my sleeve to brush away the dust on the TV screen. I start to bite my nails for the first time in seven months, two weeks, and five days. I look closer. It's not a talk show. It's water. A lake, maybe. Or the ocean.

His bulging eyes are watery. His skin is translucent, with layers of where he's been and what he's done lined up in rows which look a lot like scales. I adjust the set. They *are* scales. I check the contrast knob to make sure.

He founders, and through the static I can see that he is drowning. But he has always been an excellent swimmer, and, in fact, used to help me with my butterfly at the Y. I catch my breath again, for the look in his eyes tells me that he doesn't need my idea, and when I move a little closer to the TV set and squint, I see what I have always known: he has plenty of them; he is drowning in them. They break over him, pounding him into the surf, and when I see him disappear I feel an urge to help him, but I restrain myself, because after all, he is long gone, and my TV is broken, and in real life nobody can drown from ideas. I have a sudden craving for popcorn, but I would settle for frozen lettuce. Still, I don't move: I can't take my eyes off the TV.

Then he surfaces again, and I realize that my craving is not for popcorn at all. I try to get his attention, but he avoids my burning eyes.

A splendid wave approaches. I see it coming before he does. I cry out to warn him. He tries to outswim it, but then, to my horror, he disappears without a sound under the very salt ripples he used to call earthblood, under turbulent water which looks a lot like the sparkling waves we would lie in, on the nights he used to whisper against my temple as we worked, *earthblood. Earthblood.* I cannot help myself.

I plunge into the swirling broth and paddle kick to his ripples. If he weren't drowning, I know he would ask me where I've learned to paddle kick like a well oiled steamboat, because he's asked me many midnights, and I have always been able to sketch the answers.

"Can you call to mind Malaga?" I would reply with a sly smile. But when I reach his ripples, he is gone.

Then I see him farther out, bobbing up and down, and sputtering. He waves to me and then, again, he goes under. This time I power kick to him so quickly that if he weren't out of breath, I know he would ask me where I've learned how to power kick like a sleek amphibian, and I know what I would say.

"Do you recall a clandestine estuary near San Sebastian?" I would respond with a wink.

Unable to find him in the remnants of his sputters and bobs, I am about to give up though, when I catch sight of his head, just ahead. My heart leaps, and I lunge for him as I have never had the courage to lunge for him before.

However, it is not to be. Inexplicably, as I inch closer, he yardsticks along a riptide. I chase him, but he manages to stay just beyond my grasp. When he turns to look back at me, I think I see a smirk on his face, on the face I have kissed every midnight for more years than I want to count. No. Impossible.

Then, suddenly, in the brilliant   promise of the rising sun, I watch in terror as he surfaces only inches from the jaws of a painter-eating shark. There is only one thing left for me to do.

I shift into rocket kick, and in fractional seconds I catch him, snatch him from the incisors of the cartilaginous beast. But it does take time. And in that time, if conscious, he would surely ask me where I've perfected my rocket kick, and I would only have to say, "Remember that little cove near Tarragona?" And oh, he would remember.

Now, however, he remembers nothing. I carry my Pablo to the safety of the shore. But it is too late.

I bury him in the seaside forest near his favorite cinnamon ferns and, laying my head on a bed of bloodroot to rest, I dream of currents running alone and then together, of separate trickles down a mossy glen, merging in a secret waterfall where all wet wishes meet.

The wish I make is that my idea was his, too. But no sooner do I blow out the candles than something brushes my leg.

I awake with a warm shiver to find him there, rooted to the ground above the trembling cinnamon ferns. He smiles down on me as his arms bend gently in the ocean breeze.

"It was an idea we had alone and together," he declares.

But all I want is to know is how he did it.

"Resurrection baloney," he grins. "That soil is full of minerals."

Idyll 1968, Age 18

by Anne Scheetz

Cheek caressing
smooth curve of wood
on sun-soaked hay I
sit, bales above
the ground, fingers
picking over
drowsing strings. Cattle
gather, dark and solid
shapes, moving
only tongues to chew
the cud, and ears
erect. When
silence comes, they will
drift away,
but will have
been there.

Informal Concerts
by Whitney Scott

"Where were you so long?" No answer, just a shrug of his big shoulders as he hangs his jacket on the coat tree, then a glimpse of his back in a blue oxford shirt as he disappears into the bathroom, closing the door behind him. Does he think I'm some kind of animal, less important than a dog or cat or canary, so not worthy of acknowledgment? Does he think I'm half asleep? Dead? Not yet. Not this morning. He can't hear me, so I'm not asking again. I just lie back quietly and plan.

First he runs the water, now he's flushing, now he runs the water again. But there's something to be said for waiting him out. Sooner or later he'll have to face me. That's one thing I've learned well, confined as I've been the last two months: to wait.

The act of waiting, if consciously sought out, if practiced rigorously and with devotion, becomes an almost religious dedication. Over time you learn little calibrations: the slow pulsing in the arteries beating with the expansions and contractions of the natural wood beams overhead, the tick of the mantle clock, the counting off of these small divisions of life.

He's flushing again! *What* is he doing now? Everything in me wants to yell, "Come over here now, you self-centered bastard! How much time do you think is left, anyway?"

But I don't. I won't. I'll wait until he comes to me. I can still do that.

In fact, even though I sometimes feel caged up here, there are quite a few things I can still do. Like beating Susan at gin rummy while he's at work. Or managing the walk to the bathroom on my own.

Or calling in to those radio talk shows, masquerading as a Bible-thumping fag hater who loves our wonderful President Reagan and wants to say once and for all, that this here country – no, make that this here *great* country – ain't no place for bums and sicko homos, welfare queens having all those babies without any fathers – that we, the hard-working, honest, taxpayers support.

Announcers love me.

Yes, one finds ways to pass the time. Usually I save my talk-show calls for the weekday afternoons, after Susan's left to get her boy from school, and the shadows extend. When they disappear in the dusk, I know it won't be long until he's home again.

Now it's the shower! My God, is this washing and flushing and showering some kind of Lady Macbeth syndrome? What does he think water's going to do, cleanse and absolve him, lead him on the path of righteousness to a new and better life? Is this some sort of baptism of the shower head? I'll give him a shower head where he'll appreciate it most.

Thinking of happier times gone by, I wonder what ever happened to Stephen. Now *there* was a marvelous looking sailor, all tattoos and muscles, a joy of a sight for an old British seaman like me! He was in some clinic for awhile, then died back in his parents' two-room flat in Iowa City. Best not to dwell on that. Happy times, that's what they said to think about at the support group – builds endorphin output or positive hormones or good vibrations or some damn thing, an old hippie idea. That must make it, oh…20 years past its time, I'd say. "Nature's natural high," that new doctor says. I'd give a lot for an unnatural high right now. Or at least to get in the john and pee.

Well, memories of things past are past, after all, and one must have grace under pressure, no matter what, must keep our powder dry. Have to do it for those around us, you know, that's what Mum used to say. To the very end, she insisted on dressing and being helped down the stairs if necessary. She'd sit downstairs in her music room each afternoon, wearing those fabulous raw silk tunics and ballet slippers, and with her wonderful red curls swept up in a ribbon and off her face, showing her long, pale neck. She'd look out at the pigeons and mourning doves, doubtless refugees from bombed-out London, just like us. She'd sip her sherry and leaf through sheet music she'd played not that long before.

I remember those informal twilight concerts of Debussy and Mendelssohn, the Chopin nocturnes and Beethoven sonatas she gave us every evening as we were growing up. During The Blitz she played in darkness, though we were thought to be safe enough, far from London as we were in the country house. Sometimes she'd play for hours in the long summer evenings, until she'd suddenly remember us, my little sister Hermoine and me, seated just outside in the garden, never wanting it to end, that sweet flow of sound, liquid in the warm, summer air. "To bed now, not another song, not a note, no," she'd say, but sometimes we could wheedle a short, sweet encore from her before going up to bed.

Those Mendelssohn *Songs Without Words!* I never tired of hearing her play them, would nag and whine for them in fact, and she would look at me from the piano, saying, "Ned, Neddy, there's more to music than the *Songs*. Bach, for instance."

But stringent and thrilling as he was, Bach couldn't titillate and entice like the Romantics. The delicate nuances of emotion, the soaring choruses, the romance and grandeur of the pale, tubercular heroines dying gloriously, gracefully, in the heroes' muscular arms as the spotlights dimmed into twilight – *there* was an era for me.

Born out of my time, my mum used to say, especially at the end. "So sweet, my little Romantic," she'd say when I brought her bouquets from the garden, and she'd touch my face with her long, slender fingers, rearranging my hair, a darker version of her own. "So Byronesque, my young hero. Let me rest now. Come up again after supper."

On those times when she managed to remain awake in the evenings and we talked, she was often foggy from her pain medicine. But even if she wasn't up to saying much, I could still talk, and that I certainly did – about the ocean voyage I would take her on that would change our lives, restoring radiant health to her and transforming me from a pasty, frail boy to one of those robust, strapping youths ready for 'round the world adventures befitting a hero. Except I often saw myself more as the heroine in full, ruffled skirts and flowing curls, swooning with rapture into supportive, masculine arms.

"You'll be who you are, Neddy, and I will always be with you, no matter what," my mum would say, and I knew it was true.

On the weekends when Father was home from his government work in London, I wasn't allowed to go up to Mum's room and chat after supper, so I'd sulk instead in the kitchen. Nearly drove cook 'round the bend, I should think, but she was a patient old soul.

She'd see me with my face screwed up tight from wanting to be with my mum and worrying so about her, and she'd sit me down by the old stove and tell me about her growing up days in Dorsetshire, all plough horses and cows, farms and haystacks dotting the green rolling hills, lush and lovely; a place where old horses were turned out to pasture in retirement for whatever time they had left, free at last to roam and relax.

Bess had been cooking for Mum for as long as I could remember, so her lined face and pale eyes were as much home to me as our big house in the city had once been. The move from upper class London to an old fashioned country house must have been hard on her, but she never complained, just told me how nice it was to have a bit of the old ways back in her life again. She'd tell me stories about harvesting crews, show me the finer points of feeding a wood stove and demonstrate the art of carrying two full buckets of water without spilling a drop. Then she'd send me off to my sister with a ginger cookie – miraculous with wartime rationing – and a reminder to make sure I shared. Sometimes I did. Eventually, the bloody weekend would end and I'd have Mum back again. Until I lost her for good one cold, short day as she sat downstairs contemplating the doves and I had to take "The Moonlight Sonata" from her cooling fingers.

At last! The shower's off. Shouldn't be long now, and I'll get in there and take a good, long pee. I can just see him grabbing a towel to wipe his eyes, then stepping out onto the rug with rivulets streaming down his body. Ah-ha! Just on cue as the houselights dim. Do I know him or not, eh? First, that tentative clearing of the throat and a few warm-up notes before the melody actually takes shape, and he finally bursts into song. What will it be today? Rogers and Hart? Sir Noel? Cole?

Talk about tacky – "Swing Low, Sweet Chariot." What next? "Just a Closer Walk with Thee"?

Actually, I've been seriously considering that one for when – the inevitable. I want it all very stately. I want to be well-remembered, for people to think back on an occasion that was properly done, with dignity and refinement, nothing ostentatious, but absolutely memorable for its taste. Elegance and grace will be the keynote, which reminds me, "Amazing Grace" is another I'm fond of. Yes, definitely that one, and I'll wear my good blue suit and the Italian silk tie, since the colors compliment my hair ...well, there is no hair any more, not since the clumps started coming out in the comb...

Mustn't think on the small things, after all. There's a kind of purity in having one's head shaved, so austere and priestly. Besides, Susan says this look has a certain nobility, and *he* says I look cute. God knows, it's no bother to keep up.

He shows no sign of stopping, but at least he's switched from hymns to Gilbert and Sullivan. Certainly, he's the perfect model of a modern something – but damned if I can remember what, and now the blasted water is running again and I feel caught in some kind of Niagara Falls. If I don't get to the bathroom soon, I'm going to pee in his precious Swedish Ivy.

At last! The door is opening, and if I run for it, I just might make it in time. Wouldn't you know it! Trapped in a twisted bed sheet and two blankets, a prisoner of flannel with only one foot out, but maybe – damn! Now I've gone and wet myself, all over my pajamas, the sheets, everything, and there's nothing I can do and I can't cry, no, I can't show tears, not around him. My mum was brave, refusing to weep when a bomb killed her closest friends. I saw her pain, but she would not cry, not that night nor during the funerals, but maintaining dignity for all around her. I still don't know why his errands took so long, but there's nothing anyone can do, anyway, and what does it matter, after all? I'm such a mess. I can't look at him. Oh God, please let him go back in the bathroom or back out or something, but don't let him see me like this, it's more than I can bear, it's more than he can bear, poor thing, having to watch me go like this, little by little, first the spots, then the hair gone, now I've wet myself like someone's old granny in a home, for God's sake, and the next thing you know it will be …

"It will be all right," he says quietly, holding me now and stroking my bare head.

He draws away slightly, regarding me, and I return his gaze, taking in his dark, red-rimmed eyes, those fine high cheekbones. Together we can see the rolling green hills of the future and he pulls me to him again, close.

Love Story
by Alice Sellars

He was blond, big chested and proud. She was dark with long, shapely legs, and a little sassy.

They met one hot 4th of July night when the air was heavy and sweet with summer. She was young and inexperienced, and he was a man of the world, seasoned and tough. Her name was Sheba and his, Sundance.

As the years passed, their mutual devotion to one another grew. Sundance was fine as long as he knew exactly where Sheba was. But if she was separated from him, a loud bellow would explode from his chest, and heaven help the one standing in the way of a berserk palomino.

Sometimes we left the gate open to let Sundance and another gelding roam the land around our property. Sheba spent long hours watching the road, waiting for Sundance to come home.

He always came home to his lady.

They spent hot summer days standing together, brushing each other's faces with their tails. Summer or winter, they stood exchanging love nibbles. They had their picture taken together and it was published in the newspaper.

Life was good except for an annoying fly or two.

After 13 years together, it all came to an end one cold February day. An obstruction in Sundance's intestines slowly poisoned his body with toxins. There was nothing we or the veterinarian could do, but give him a lethal injection to end his suffering. He had stood stoic through it all, but he stumbled as we led him to a patch of pine trees.

Swallowed by my own grief, I forgot Sheba. As my big golden horse fell to the ground, she screamed and tore up and down the fence line in panic.

It was fitting that the last thing Sundance heard was not my good-bye, but Sheba's.

Who really knows the mind of a horse? Even after a year had passed, she still stood looking at his grave, then down the road where he used to come home. Eventually it seemed she looked down the road more. Perhaps she had more hope in that route.

I don't want to think Sheba and Sundance's love affair is over. After all, who's to say they won't be together again someday? And life will be better than good then.

There won't be any flies.

Of Wolves, Ashes and Prairie Gold
by Alice Sellars

More than anything else, Anna Richardson wanted peace. The burden of guilt and remorse had been with her for too long. She found it when the reporter came. She looked him in the eye and let her old wounds bleed.

He stood on her front porch, impatient energy bound up in him like a mountain lion ready to spring. Intense brown eyes behind gold-rimmed glasses were focused on deadlines. Behind him, dust hung over the gravel road like a bloated snake.

He had flown to Billings from Boston the day before, spent the night, rented a Nissan Pathfinder, and had driven most of the day through endless miles of country to reach a cattle ranch near Cameron, Montana. He wanted an opinion about the re-introduction of wolves into Yellowstone Park from a rancher that lived nearby, he'd said.

She had agreed, though she imagined him figuring he could get a few lines of meaty words from the old lady, head back down the road, and get back in Billings that night. He could catch an early flight out the next day. Be back in time for the weekend.

He licked his lips nervously. Perhaps he was unused to such open spaces, she thought. Or was it too quiet for him?

Anna ushered the young man into the library, gestured to a large leather armchair, and settled into her wooden rocker. She studied him across the room, an energetic youngster dressed in a casual, but expensive shirt, pressed slacks and wing-tip shoes.

His feet shuffled on the wooden floor in a lop-sided two-step. He scribbled something on a yellow pad.

She had something to say that she had kept to herself all these years. It was time to say it – she didn't have much longer. He was from another world, but he would have to do.

"I met my first and last wolf when I was 17," Anna stated matter-of-factly.

Aware of the reporter's look of surprise, she continued, knowing she was going to say what he didn't want to hear.

"I named him Spear," she said softly, with a hint of a smile like a lover remembering.

"The first time I saw him was when I was out riding, checking the fence lines. I looked up and there he was, high on a ridge. He stood there in his thick furry coat, white and gray dusted with black, like ashes from a prehistoric campfire, rimmed in gold from the late afternoon sun.

"I was terrified," Anna said, her hand clutching the buttons at her throat. Wrinkles deepened with her wry smile, flowing into the silver hair that was swept up into a bun behind her head.

"But I looked into his eyes and something happened between us, even then, something that surpassed all the horror stories about wolves I'd heard growing up," she said, nodding at the man across the room, who had stopped writing and was looking at her incredulously.

"Then he leaped off the ridge like a spear, and before I knew him, his name was planted in my heart."

She told of seeing the wolf again, and how she followed him one day to a den hidden away in sandstone boulders and junipers. She returned many times and watched the family at a respectful distance during the summer. They were keenly aware of her and indulged her presence with aloof goodwill.

Spear's mate was a slender, almost white wolf with tawny undertones. She was a devoted mother to four pudgy puppies, but when greeting her mate she acted like a coy teenager. Crouching before him, she bit him gently on the lower jaw and licked his cheek. He in turn nosed her lovingly, puffed out his chest, and waved his tail like a plume.

On one occasion Anna witnessed the whole family joining together in song. After a standard greeting of sniffing, nipping and wagging tails, Spear barked, hit a high note and crooned. As his voice rose and fell, his mate sang out her own sweet melody and the pups yipped, leaping and tumbling over themselves in their excitement.

Anna felt something rise from deep inside her, wanting to join in a fierce yowl of her own as she felt primitive drums beat in her ears. She was running barefoot over tundra, skins flapped against her thighs, lichens spread in green and gold, moss caressed her cheek. She hunted with the pack and sang in their choir.

The rocking chair creaked, disturbing the beat of the drums. Anna blinked. She was once again in her old body in a chair and a young man with glasses stared at her from across the room, pen suspended.

"Then wolves began killing a calf or two during one long winter," Anna said as she smoothed her dress.

Her face changed and her eyes grew cold as she recalled riding to the den one cold day in February. Steam poured from her horse's nostrils as he plunged through the sun-struck crust of knee-deep snow. Crystals sparkled with abandon in contrast to the bloody, torn meat the pups were snarling over in front of their den.

She saw the hide, her father's brand, and Spear standing, watching proudly from a distance.

"Oh, God, why, Spear?" she had screamed.

Startled, the big wolf had flattened his ears and showed his teeth, while wagging his tail. But she had stumbled away, not wanting to hear his side of the story. The awful pain of the decision she had to make was all she could bear.

After another calf was killed, Anna did what she felt she had to do. It was the way she was raised. In the battle of hearts and heads, the head always won.

Her knuckles turned white against the blue of her veins as she told of being in town a few days later when a group of men rode in, yelling and shooting in the air. As they drew near, she saw the limp body of a wolf being dragged through the mud behind a horse. Her eyes glazed at the sight of Spear's once-glossy fur coated with blood, snow and mud. To her horror, the rancher jumped off his horse, took out his hunting knife and began sawing off the wolf's head. Someone brought a pole, and as she turned away, the scene panned before her eyes, another furry body, once white, a pole being erected with the head of a wolf...

As she stumbled away, the shouts told the rest of the story.

"Those blasted pups won't grow up...."

"$100 bounty for these sonsabitches..."

Anna's blue eyes burned brightly against her pale skin. "I changed after that. Up 'till then I had been a tomboy, working alongside my father on the ranch. But after they killed Spear, I became more like my mother, got married, and had a family."

The rocking chair creaked again. "My father never understood why – it was too painful to think about fathers and their role in life after Spear's death. I told myself it was time to grow up, be responsible and do what I had to do."

Anna looked out the window, pale eyes gazing past the scene behind the glass. The reporter took off his glasses and wiped his eyes. He studied the objects around him, old things, older than anything he'd probably ever known. The musty smell of old leather filled the corners, blending with the rich tones of polished wood. Long shadows stretched across the room and the antique clock ticked loudly.

Anna sighed. "We killed 700,000 wolves in Montana between 1870 and 1877. We wiped out the buffalo, the Indian, the wolf and the wild horses – all for our cattle, which we also kill in the end."

She was tired. It had been festering in her for 60 years and now it was out. But she wasn't through. The sun touched the top of her white head and lit it up like a halo as she leaned forward. Now she had a question for the young man from the far away city.

"Who really has the right to decide who lives and who dies?"

The reporter from Boston bowed his head. The library in the ranch house was a church as quiet settled around them. He drove over the plains in the Montana dusk a few minutes later.

Anna Richardson gazed out the window as the sun sank beneath the ridges of sandstone boulders and junipers. She was alone again. But that didn't hurt so much anymore. Her children had grown up and left years ago. She had married her father's hired hand, and he had been a loving husband. They had a good life. She was the only one left. The one to live with all the memories.

She heard the howl out of the long ago then, and she remembered reading somewhere how the Indians asked forgiveness of the animals they killed for food.

She shut her eyes and called him back. He stood proud and noble and whole once again, looking at her with those golden eyes filled with intelligence and age-old wisdom. The multicolored hairs of gray, white and black framed his face and bristled with life and vitality.

"Forgive me, Spear," she whispered into the coming darkness.

Peace came then. Like a floating wisp of gray ash on Montana's golden prairie.

The Goat Goes Sight-seeing
A Novel Excerpt by Dominique B. Slavin

1. In which the goat takes on Edinburgh traffic

The goat paused, staring at the front that massed before her – the last, protective vanguard to the garden. They were poised on the verge of outright attack, rumbling imprecations, spitting black smoke into the sky. She was nervous. How not? Even the Greeks, seeing the size of the Persian army at Thermopylae – even they, brave as they were, felt some slight twitchings of fear. How many, after this fight, would still be standing? To whom would be devoted the funeral pyres, the funeral games? Would their names, one day, be inscribed upon the stele before the temple – of those who died for freedom, who gave up their lives so that their people would not be forced into slavery?

The goat cocked her head slightly to the side. She had every right to be afraid – before her, in all its splendor, lay the entirety of mankind, bent against stopping her from reaching her goal. And yet, she took on this quest not for some puny, punitive reason, nor even as a lark. The motivations that impelled her were the noblest ones. No longer could she be caught between four walls. She was neither a sheep nor a chicken, at home in monotony. She was a goat, and goats *must* be free.

There was a sudden, high-pitched wailing. The armored mass began to move toward her, gathering speed. She waited for the last possible moment, then dashed across the bed of the valley, toward the hill. The army, ponderous in its greatness, screeched too late to a stop and began to collide with itself, buckling, screaming. The goat didn't look back to see the damage her nimble feet had done. She had somewhere to be. Goats are nothing if not punctual.

195

2. In which the goat counts serious coup on Marks and Spencers.

The cabby hit the brakes without warning, sending them all flying forward. "Bloody Hell!" Frank shouted. "Would you watch where you're going?"

"Ah am," the man replied. "Look."

In the middle of the intersection, right before High Street, four cars lay spewed across the road. Out of their steaming, hissing wrecks staggered blood-covered, gesticulating individuals. They shouted; they threatened; they pounded on the tops of cars and waved their hands at the passers by. One of the car horns wailed incessantly. Behind them, a hundred thousand other irate travelers – unable to get around – expressed their irritation and their intent to do nothing helpful or even useful about the predicament by honking on their horns and screaming imprecations.

The cabby, intelligent as he was, studied the environs, tallied up the time necessary for different routes, backed up two feet and, hauling vigorously on his steering wheel to the outraged chorus of the horns behind him, spun into the other lane, narrowly missing a parked car and the old lady who had wandered out from behind it to get a better glimpse of the gore.

"Nicely done," Frank said. The man smiled bashfully. "By the way," Frank added, inching up behind the cabby so that he spoke into his ear. "How *are* things these days?"

"No' too good," the cabby replied, swerving sharply to the right and down the hill.

"Yes," Frank said calmly, "Don't seem to be feeling much of the effects of this famous economic 'recovery,' eh?"

"Tha's tha' truth," the cabby answered with some enthusiasm.

"Does he always try to convert everyone?" Socorro asked Joe.

"Of course," Joe replied. "If you believed in something, wouldn't you?"

"I'd rather like to believe in something," Joy said pensively.

"Oh, for God's sake," Faith snarled, pulling her seeking eyes from the window, "haven't we gotten past belief yet?"

"Technically," Peter said, "that should be impossible."

"Right," Socorro concurred. "If you believe in nothing, it remains a belief."

"No," Guerric said, "it remains a word or concept."

"No," Peter retorted. "You're involved in the same activity. You're still believing."

"Not necessarily," Guerric replied. "You're just using the same word for it. That's all."

Hope sighed. "Could we move beyond philosophizing and try to see how we're going to get ourselves out of this situation?" she asked. Everyone – knowing quite well that predictions (and therefore planning) were of utterly no use with this goat – ignored her completely.

"I don't see," Peter said, "how you can argue that unless you want to say we have no conception of reality whatsoever."

"No," Guerric replied as the cab pulled into Prince's Street, "just that language has no conception of reality whatsoever. Denotation is not signification."

Peter sat in his seat, his expression befuddled.

"What the hell does that mean," Joy asked.

"I have absolutely no idea," Guerric answered, grinning at the frowning Peter. "But it certainly stopped him, didn't it?"

"Here y'ar," the cabby said, pulling up before the milling Marks.

"Superb!" Hope cried, plucking the twenty-pound note from her sister's fingers, handing it to the cabby, and leaping out of the cab. The others followed.

"Girls," Grace said calmly, unflappable as always as she walked through the swinging doors of Marks and Spencers, every spare body angle laden with purchases. "What the hell are you doing here?"

"The goat's escaped," Hope told her.

"Bloody hell," Grace moaned despairingly. Then an overweight woman leapt three feet into the air and screamed at the absolute top of her lungs, and mayhem descended on the crowd. The goat, walking around the recently accidentally-but-quite-enjoyably butted backside, saw the girls just as they saw it. Glancing around for an avenue of escape, it decided to do the dashing thing. Filled with *elan* and bolstered by the alacrity of four feet, it shot between two young women walking out the door. Hope – having, by dint of long acquaintance with the goat, premeditated the action – threw herself in that direction. Flying through the air, she catapulted straight into the screaming girls, taking them both with her through the doors of the shop and onto the ground, pushing through the passers by like a full-scale avalanche down the slopes of Mont Blanc.

"Help!" screamed one of the girls, justifiably alarmed.

"Rape!" cried the other, just before she hit the ground and had all the wind knocked out of her.

The sisters, thanks to the gap made by Hope's daring plunge, followed the goat through the shop and down the stairs, into the grocery store.

"Get off me, ahh, help!" screamed one of the girls, regaining her breath. Hope peeled herself off the floor and after her family.

"Left!" Guerric shouted. "Head it off in the vegetable sections!"

"Where the bloody hell is it?" Faith cried irritably.

"Try milk and cheese!" Hope cried, running through the onlookers.

"The sandwiches!" screamed Prudence, to all extents and purposes on the verge of a nervous collapse. Darting as a pack around the corner, they came upon the vegetable row and stopped, staring.

"Wow," Socorro said.

Before them, straddling a mountain of fresh vegetables with all the pomp, circumstance and self-congratulation of Sir Edmund Hilary atop Mount Everest, was the goat, chewing a stalk of celery. At her feet, Patrocles to her Hector, lay a young, uniformed lad, stunned by a combination of goat horns and a passing orange. At a safe distance stood a small crowd of plump Scottish folk, mumbling like a Greek Chorus. The Aspenalls heard the foreboding pounding of furious feet. The Chorus fell to an anticipatory silence. A suited, overweight man came running around the corner, the wisps of his fading hair waving madly in the air. Three, uniformed, well paunched security guards followed.

"Cor!" said a businessman. He reached into his cart, pulled out a package, unwrapped it, and began to eat what smelled like a ham and cheese sandwich.

"Ah theenk it's an advertisement for tha' telly," a woman whispered to her mother.

"I dunna ken eef Ah'd buy those vegetables, afta tha'," her mother replied doubtfully.

The general manager of the grocery department – James T. Falkirk the Third of Ballynahinch, Northern Ireland (a village in the vicinity of Slieve Croob, glorious mount of five hundred and thirty-five towering meters) – was not the most mellow of men. To call him high-strung would be to put it mildly. Excitable was more along the correct lines. Permanently wavering on the verge of a cataclysmic psychotic episode would begin to capture his personality. This character flaw (if we may call it that) was accentuated by his recent demotion from the sandwich department of the Glasgow branch of Marks and Spencers for reasons unknown but indubitably serious. He was, to put it simply, already leaning well over the chasm of total despair. "What is te meaning of tis?" he screamed with the usual Irish disregard for the fricative, dental consonants of the English language.

"I have absolutely no idea," Guerric said calmly. "I'm not even sure what it denotes."

"And as for signification..." Peter added, shaking his head.

"Exactly," Guerric said, grinning.

"To whom does tis animal belong?" Mr. Falkirk cried, his voice high with the indignity of it all. Everyone looked at Prudence. Prudence smiled hopefully. "Get tat ting off my fresh foods stand!" he shouted.

"Well," Prudence said somewhat sadly, "I'm afraid it's not quite that..."

Mr. Falkirk turned to his aides, trembling with overwhelming irritation. "Get it!" he screamed. His aides saw in that rousing call the possibility of swift promotion and jumped into the fray.

"Wait!" Prudence cried. Sadly, it was too late. The goat, perceiving her assailants, waited with all the cunning of a guerrilla force until the last possible moment and leapt off the produce bar. The guards, flying through the intervening space to intercept her, missed and landed instead on, respectively, cucumbers, green peppers and Israeli oranges, knocking the vast majority of them to the ground.

The Greek Chorus, given their opportunity, did what a Greek Chorus should do. They sighed. They gasped. At the appropriate moment they hissed, moaned, and covered their eyes. And when, finally, the goat descended from the mound and landed before them, they collectively threw their hands into air, dropped their belongings, screamed loudly, and fled.

At that moment the door to the lift opened. The goat, perceiving through the assembled and swiftly exiting bodies the image of another garden on the far side (and in it the figure of another goat), dashed through. The sisters watched in amazement as the goat bounced off the mirror on the elevator wall and back against the closing doors.

The manager screamed incoherently.

"Upstairs!" Faith shouted.

"Stop the bloody lift!" Hope cried.

"I don't know how," Guerric said disconsolately. A loud scream rang out from one of the upper levels of the department store.

"Too late," Joy said dejectedly. "Come on. We have to catch it before it gets to designer clothes." The rest exchanged horrified glances and ran for the stairs.

Bug Tales
(or why I'll never even try shoo-fly pie)

by Carol E. Smith

When we were young, our mother made a wonderful dessert called banana pudding. It was a beautiful concoction to see and an even more delightful treasure to eat.

The first step was the layering of rows of vanilla wafers and sliced bananas in a clear glass bowl.

Next, she prepared vanilla pudding. Not the instant cold milk kind but rather the variety that required her to stir a pot on the stove top. I loved to watch it magically thicken to the rhythm of her spoon. Then she would pour the warm, thick pudding into the bowl. The smooth yellow liquid would flow into all the crevices and spaces between the bananas and the cookies.

The bowl would be placed in the refrigerator so the pudding could gel completely.

This was my favorite sweet food. When we scooped out the first serving, the different parts were discrete – cookies that had some crispness, firm banana slices and yummy pudding. It would not stay in the refrigerator long once we started eating it and once we started scooping out of the bowl, the contents became mixed and mushy.

The cookies would get mashed into the pudding. The brown spots on the banana slices would mix into the pudding. The dessert changed from an ordered, tiered thing of beauty to an indistinguishable mess. But it was a mess that tasted wonderful. I loved it.

I loved it, that is, until my dad tried to tell me what was really in the pudding.

One afternoon I stood at the kitchen counter scooping pudding into a bowl. Dad was beside me, watching my work.

"Having some fly pudding, I see."

"No," I grunted, "it's banana pudding."

"Well, can't you see the flies in it? Your mother puts flies in it."

"Dad, no, she doesn't."

He pointed his finger to a congealed glob of banana-spot-speckled pudding.

"See, flies right there."

I rolled my eyes at him and sighed. However, when I sat at the table to start eating, I did select my spoonfuls carefully. Unless I could clearly see just cookies and/or pudding, the spoon would not touch my lips. I ate slowly, considering the texture and flavor of each bite.

My mind rambled.

"She wouldn't put flies in this stuff! But she is swatting flies in the house all the time. Where does she put the dead flies?"

Suddenly I felt something that was harder than pudding that did not feel like a cookie crumble against my tongue.

My mind raced.

"Fly guts!"

I spit the food back in the bowl. I rubbed – no, I scrubbed my tongue with the hem of my t-shirt.

Fly pudding. I wasn't going to take any chances.

Whose World is it, Anyway?

by Grazina Smith

My mama always said, "Even a blind chicken pecks a corn occasionally," and that's just how my life has been. Good luck never embraces me; my search for a country home was no exception. Real estate agents showed me only wrecked farmhouses; then one day, when I was aimlessly driving the back roads of Indiana, a "For Sale" sign blinded me. Its new paint gleamed in the sunlight. A quick snoop around the building convinced me the place was ideal. A Perfect Victorian House! I met with the Realtor and acted cagey, not letting her know how much I wanted the house. There were four acres of land and two gnarled apple trees, laden with fruit, stood just outside the kitchen door waiting for me to bake pies. Best of all, there was a heated, floored attic that could easily be converted into a library.

I moved in late summer. Two teenage boys from Medairyville, the nearest town, helped me settle in the house. I made only one change that day. A large, curved antique mirror sprawled above the fireplace. Because the glass needed resilvering, everything reflected in it darkly like a nineteenth-century sepia reproduction of life. I planned to have the mirror repaired; but for now, it was condemned to stand in a corner of the attic. The boys struggled with the mirror and with sixty boxes of books, clothes, and odds and ends to store up there. They grumbled when I paid them five dollars each for the afternoon's work; but they hadn't negotiated a salary in advance. I taught them a valuable lesson about the mores of today's business world.

I don't remember falling asleep that night; but I woke to a discordant symphony of tree frogs serenading each other. The rich scent of apples filled the room. A night breeze billowed the sheer bedroom curtains, as if allowing restless spirits to float in and out on currents of air. Confused, I lay in the dark and wondered where I was until I realized this was my country home. Before I could close my eyes again, a soft shuffle came from the attic.

Sitting up, I heard the sound again. Something was slowly dragging along the floor upstairs! The shuffle would start and stop, like a person with an injured leg. Here I was, a woman alone, miles away from my nearest neighbor, with a maimed prowler in the attic. As I dialed the sheriff's office, it dawned on me who was making the noise. It had to be Frank and Billy, the two boys who'd helped me move. They must have decided to frighten the "old lady" for getting the best of them. Before I went down to meet the law, I locked the oak door to the attic. Let them explain themselves to the sheriff, I thought.

When I told Sheriff Chapman about the noises, I was careful to avoid any hint of the culprits' identity. The attic was deathly silent; and when the sheriff beamed his flashlight into the darkness, the room appeared empty. However, turning on the dim overhead bulb revealed that some of my storage boxes were ripped open. Winter sweaters lay scattered everywhere, some were partially unraveled and their yarn stretched from box to box like a booby-trap maze.

"Where are those two boys?" I whispered.

"Who are you talking about?" The sheriff asked, eyeing me suspiciously.

"The prowlers, of course."

The sheriff said, "I think they're here, under the floorboards."

He couldn't be serious. "Those boys wouldn't fit under the floorboards."

"I don't know who you think is up here, but I know it's raccoons," the sheriff said.

"Raccoons!"

"Yeh. See the little paw prints all over your boxes?" He examined everything like a TV detective. "Their hairs are caught in the masking tape that sealed the flaps. If you check the soffits around the roof, you'll find boards they pulled away. Before you do repairs, you'll have to get rid of the nest."

Sheriff Chapman explained that raccoons, as fur bearing animals, are protected by law and must be trapped and released alive.

"Call County Animal Control," he said. "They'll bring you live-animal cages." He gave me a stern look. "Don't try to poison them, it's against the law." In case that wouldn't deter me, he added, "They'll die under your floorboards and really stink up the place."

The next day, I learned animal control covered two counties and only had four cages. My cage would come in three weeks. Every night, I woke to thumping and shuffling. The raccoons seemed particularly fond of my favorite books, nibbling pages that had traces of chocolate on them. I weighed boxes down with bricks, but that provided them a challenge, and the crescendo of toppling bricks became my nightly serenade. I knew the boys would want a large bribe to move the boxes again, so I kept a long pole near my bed and pounded the ceiling when I heard the Raccoon Shuffle. After all, whose house was it, anyway?

I complained in town and Mr. Sweeney at Medairyville Hardware guaranteed the smell of mothballs would drive the raccoons away. He suggested I scatter them all over the attic, even drilling holes in the wood floor and rolling mothballs under the boards. Armed with my new electric drill and fifty pounds of mothballs, I went to work.

The following morning, a reek of naphthalene assaulted my nostrils. A milky, chemical haze hovered over the lawn. Intermittently, the mist parted and revealed small mothball eggs peppering the grass like buckshot. From the corner of the roof, the raccoons had hung a triumphant banner. My sheer black nightgown was snagged on the gutter, gaily flapping in the breeze, informing everyone on County Road 238 of my foolish brush with Frederick's of Hollywood. A good deal of negotiation got Frank and Billy back to the house. They had learned their lesson well and charged me fifty dollars each before they agreed to play amateur acrobats and climb forty feet to retrieve my flimsy nightgown.

The animal control officer appeared later that week. I greeted him with a zeal disproportionate to the one, long wire cage he carried. He gave a short lecture on how to use the trap. It was simple. The metal cage had a kick plate at the bottom. All I had to do was bait it, adjust the door and wait for the raccoons to shuffle in for treats. One step on the kick plate and the trap slammed shut!

I arranged a feast of grapes and honeydew melon balls, set the trap and left, whistling Beethoven's Fifth Symphony. The next morning, the fruit was gone, the cage was on its side, and the kick plate dangled harmlessly in the air. Again I baited the trap, wedged the cage between two heavy boxes, and left, quietly humming "I'll Be Seeing You." This time the trap was exactly as I left it, but the fruit was gone. A souvenir backscratcher lay next the cage. It had been used to push the fruit into the eager paws of the parasites that inhabited my home.

A gleam in the corner of the attic caught my eye; and I thought the raccoons were staring at me. Instead, I discovered the shambles those animals had made of Aunt Judith's Victorian Christmas ornaments. For as long as she lived, Aunt Judith had designed and sewed two confections to hang on my tree each Christmas. The wooden storage crate housing these treasures was pried open; an obscene tangled rainbow of sequins, colored beads, rickrack and gold braid spilled out and disappeared into the darkness. Like the bloodless massacre of exotic birds, colorful silk and brocade ornaments lay ripped open and white feather stuffing leaked from the gashes. I picked up a tattered blue orb and touched the delicate stitches along the side. Aunt Judith's lilac talcum powder wafted up from the ball and I remembered the needle flashing as her long fingers carefully wove the thread. The same fingers had often pushed a stray lock of hair from my face or lovingly traced the curve of my cheek. I squeezed the delicate cloth and vowed vengeance. When I realized my nails had cut the palm of my hand, I threw the tattered ornament back in the chest. It landed in a cloud of feathers.

I approached my raccoon problem in the same manner I had used for science fair projects in grammar school. First, I spent the afternoon at the library. After studying books on electrical conductivity, I gutted an old radio for its high voltage transformer. I wired the transformer to a metal grid and firmly attached an aluminum pie plate in the center. Melons and grapes floated in a saline solution in the pie pan. After carefully arranging everything on the attic floor, I plugged in the electric cord and activated the transformer. The prototype electric chair for raccoons that I designed and built would have made Dr. Frankenstein proud. The raccoons would fry for their sins, dimming the lights of houses in all directions!

That evening, I imagined the pleasures of my peaceful home once the intruders were eliminated. Anticipating victory, I woke at dawn and made my way carefully upstairs. When I pulled the light chain, the overhead bulb swung in an arc casting grotesque shadows on the wall. Even in the flickering light, I could count my successes. Three furry bodies sprawled on the floor, their jaws stiff in the rictus of death, their small sharp teeth flashing with each sway of the light. A war whoop escaped my lips and I began to dance around in a circle. In my peripheral vision I caught a hint of movement in the corner of the attic. Shocked, I turned to confront the intruder and beheld a madwoman in a white nightgown shaking her gnarled fists at me. Although the figure was murky, its black malevolent eyes flashed in triumph. It took ten seconds to realize the apparition was my own reflection in the antique mirror. I stared at my phantom self, observed the hard, crafty lines of my face and the echo of a sneer that still twisted my mouth. I could not force myself to gaze again into my eyes. The evil that shone there suffocated all human compassion and made me afraid of who I had become.

Geese

by Gregory Stall

It has never been said
that bounty overstayed its welcome.
But just when the wildlife
get fat and lackadaisical,
an alert sugar maple
waves a leafy red warning flag.
Thus a hard frost
bullies the countryside in darkness
and caught at first light
breaks into a cold sweat,
then cowers in the shadows
until all is exposed.
It's too late though
for all the brave asters are lost.
And small flying things
oblivious to time
and obsessed with abundance perish.
Now the tree's prophecy has come to pass.
To flourish has been slain.
The geese know and mobilize.

Between These Worlds

by Margo Tamez

Our mountain moves itself toward the herd.
Nudges them inward to her crease
and they feed.

I have seen them run through fences at night,
in front of cars doing fifty
on a single-lane road.

Gallop across and leap through headlight funnels,
into a thin fog between this world
and a sloping berm of dark.

In day I look to both sides,
see where they went, how could they run through?
What about the barbed wire?

But nothing like that matters
above the mountain's jaw,
where their heads are bowed tight to her lip.

A Habitat and Strings

by Margo Tamez

She can't have this room,
Or take the corners, crevices and walls,
Be fixed to the underside of the table
With her ear to the fold behind my knees,
When I laugh at his jokes and squeeze
Thoughts through my calves during meals.

She can't have the arm resting on my thigh,
Have her infants use it like a plank or map,
Hold the wind in a tunnel, then throw its weight
Against the windows during monsoons,
Repel down her string flaunting sex
Like a slut upon my nose,
Or aim towards my toothbrush

While I'm in the middle of the upward stroke.
I pick up scattered shards,
See the mutual fragments – week lips and curves.
O her peripheral waiting, months below the shelf
Trussing the prey when I wash his chipped cups. . .
They fly by, fly by me, yet I say and do

Nothing. It is her skill, patience, that mesmerize me,
so I pretend death is not the thing.
I sweep and wipe
Brush away what she leaves – faithful.
I am out to see desire, what is embedded
Near her eyes,
My eyes,

When she impales one through the wings.

Of Little Girls and Ponies

by Sandra Tatara

I had a pony named Lady when I was little. Actually, I had two ponies: Samson, the larger of the two, was a rusty brown color, shaggy and not too bright. He had foundered and resembled an old man shuffling around in sloppy bedroom slippers on the wrong feet. The only way to get a good ride on Samson was to catch him out in the pasture when he was headed toward the barn. Lady, on the other hand, was a beautiful pony: black and white with a long, thick mane and flowing tail that swept the ground. She had a generally sweet disposition but could be ornery as ponies tend to be. One day we were galloping flat out toward the barn; she ducked in a low barn door and knocked me on my butt. I was a smart little kid and I learned to ride low whenever we were close to the barn. I rode Lady bareback, often without a bridle. We explored the pastures near our home enjoying the idyllic, carefree, hot summer days of my childhood. I brushed and cared for Lady and fed her sugar cubes. Lady was beautiful; I loved her and she was my best friend.

Some years ago after my mother died, I was sorting through her old papers and boxes of photographs. I came across photos of me with my beautiful pony. I looked the way I remembered I did at that age – a skinny, freckle-faced kid of about ten or eleven with a crooked-tooth grin, glasses sliding down on my nose, long auburn hair in disarray. Lady...well, she didn't look as I remembered her. She *wasn't* a beautiful pony! I must admit she wasn't even a pretty pony.

I couldn't blame it on bad photography of someone who didn't know how to shoot equines to their best advantage because there were several photos from various angles.

Her little legs seemed too short for her fat body. Her head was too large, out of proportion to the rest of her. Her face didn't look sweet but crabby and...*old*; and she was just a wee bit – okay, more than a wee bit – sway backed.

A tear slid down my cheek and I was sorry I had found the photos; I would rather have held onto a little girl's memory of her beautiful pony. I quickly stashed the box of photos away, fearing I would find pictures of my beautiful dogs and cats!

Clupea Palassi
A Novel Excerpt by David A. Tomasko

T his particular fish, a member of the species *Clupea palassi*, otherwise known as Pacific Herring, was on her last spawning run. At nine years of age, she was one of the oldest fish around. Unknown to her, she was also one of the most prolific herring in the northern Gulf of Alaska. After six successful spawns, this female, now well over a foot long, had already produced millions of eggs, which in turn gave rise, after tremendous mortality early in their lives, to thousands of mature fish. She had good genes.

She was swimming twenty feet below the storm-wracked surface of the Gulf, feasting and trying not to be feasted upon. She ate krill, tiny shrimp-like animals that also make up the majority of the diet of Humpback whales. In the summer months, whales take up residence in the bays and inlets along the southern coast of Alaska. The school she swam in was nervous. Hake, a fish not too different from their better-known cousins the cod, and spiny dogfish, miniature versions of sharks, would strike into the enormous shoal of fish, causing the mass of herring to scatter and reform later on, like potbellied ex-athletes leaving and then regathering at high school reunions.

Most of the fish in her school were as old as she was, and about the same size, so would swim at the same speed; a useful feature for a collection of migrating animals. And migrating they were.

Fall was a time of overcast skies, frequent rain, and herring migrations. The vast schools of herring that had roamed the deeper waters of the Gulf of Alaska all summer were moving back toward the more protected areas where the Humpback whales had spent their long summer days. Herring replaced the now absent Humpbacks, which had headed south to Hawaii for the winter, an act repeated by many of the more affluent humans who also called Alaska home.

213

During the course of the long winter the old female herring became lethargic, the cold water and feeble sunlight perhaps triggering her reaction. As winter continued, the huge school once again became restless. She was carried forth, without knowing how or why, to the same spawning ground she'd visited in years past. The water this close to shore was not as salty as the open ocean where she spent her summers, and the bottom was much shallower, only a hundred feet at its deepest.

The pre-spawning tension built day by day, but she knew that the time was not yet right. She had no calendar, of course, and had no idea what day it was. But she wouldn't, she couldn't, move to the shallow waters until seven days after the last full moon. Six times before she had taken part in the mass sexual explosion of a herring spawn, and six times before she had waited until the weak high tides, neap tides, of seven days past the full moon.

When the tides were finally right, she joined the school as it splashed and wallowed in the shallows along the beach. She released her eggs close to shore in three feet of water. The sea around her was cloudy with sperm, giving her every chance that her eggs would be fertilized and could start on their long, hazardous road to maturity. Her eggs sank slowly to the bottom, penetrated by the surrounding sperm.

The shallow waters where the herring came to spawn were rich with kelp plants carpeting the rocky bottom. These sea weeds determined whether her fertilized eggs would become more than just food for the crabs and shrimp and other small animals living on the bottom of the bay. Her eggs sank, as did all good herring eggs, and they were sticky. The luckiest of her eggs stuck to the undulating blades of the kelp plants, and began the slow process of developing into their next life stage.

An underwater nursery. Lose the kelp, and you lose the herring.

This particular bay, the one where the nine-year-old herring was undergoing her latest spawn, was like most others bays in south central Alaska. With one exception. This bay, Prince William Sound, was made intimately aware of the devastating price to be paid when a country's insatiable appetite for oil teams up with a man's insatiable appetite for vodka straight up.

❖ ❖ ❖

More oil has leaked out into the world's oceans through natural processes than has been spilled by humans. Many scientists know this. Every oil company public relations hack knows this as well, and will recite it without even being asked. In many places along the seafloor, seeps of oil form the basis for unusual food webs, with the oil replacing sunlight as the primary energy source upon which all other life forms depend.

The problem with oil spills, like the one in Prince William Sound, isn't that a foreign substance is introduced into a previously pristine natural world. The problem is one of scale. Too much oil. Way too much. Delivered in too little time. Way too little time. Into too small a place. Way too small a place. Even if the place is something as grand and seemingly boundless as Prince William Sound.

Oil is liquefied life. In most power plants, coal or oil is used to heat immense volumes of water into steam. The harnessed steam turns giant magnetos. These magnetos strip off a constant current of electrons and send them coursing down power lines. These electrons can stream across the interior of a light bulb and cause its metallic filament to glow in rhapsodic excitement. The act of reading can be a bridge across millennia. Sunlight from millions of years ago could be the original source of energy for the light now illuminating this page.

Indeed, oil can do great things. But too much oil, in too little time, in too small a place, can do horrible things.

❖ ❖ ❖

In Prince William Sound, horrible things were beginning to happen. Luckily for the old female herring, she wouldn't know the fate of her last spawning effort. The oil spill wouldn't kill her offspring, not outright. Not directly. Instead, the oil spill killed off her genetic line, her lineage.

While her progeny would live, those that made it past the normal terrors of growing up in the wild would be severely and permanently crippled. The males would produce damaged sperm and the females, damaged eggs. Joined together, their offspring would be even worse off. In combination with the high mortality expected from even normal spawns, the old female herring's transmitted heritage would disappear in eight short years.

A genetic library that took tens of thousands of years to create would be eradicated from the global web of life by the reckless behavior of a single man on a single day.

Accompanying the demise of the vast schools of herring was the collapse of the herring fishery. As the fishery collapsed, so did the local economy of towns like Port Ashland, a place where options in life were few. Work on a commercial boat. Or leave.

In the scattered small towns that ringed Prince William Sound, the lively streets and bars and stores slowly crashed in on themselves. A ghost town from a hundred years ago might have somewhat of a romantic quality, but a town in the process of becoming one of these places is about as appealing as a spreading infection.

Prince William Sound, known for its magnificent vistas, its diverse and prolific sealife, was becoming a faded memory of its former self. Outward appearances proved deceiving. Except for a few areas where oily deposits had not yet been scooped out and shipped off to hazardous waste dumps, the bay looked remarkably unchanged.

But changed it was. The unseen damage, the molecular rearrangements, the genetic disruption, continued to devastate the fish and crabs and shrimp and seals and whales and humans who were left to deal with the spill's aftermath.

Long after the last oil-covered sea otter had been bathed and scrubbed and blow-dried, the last cormorant buried after its toxin-loaded liver gave out, long after this, the bay continued to suffer.

Sea World

by Claudia Van Gerven

I. The Sadness of Eels

They hang from crevices
of pot rock, vanquished
and superfluous
as flaccid penae.
Small pinched faces
random set of wrinkles
in crimped, torpid
ribbons of flesh,
suggesting a nest
of aquatic vampires, debauched
and remorseless, turning
weary appalled gazes
on our voracious
curiosity.

II. Underground Sharks

Lean shadows dart
across vast tank, like
over blue hills.
Hunters without ruse
        or scruple, they soar
sleek and effortless
through aeons of water,
elegant angels
of hunger.

Strange Elements

by Claudia Van Gerven

The geese lift
themselves lingeringly
from dark water. Each
sensitive, splayed foot
questioning perilous
solidity of earth.

Mourning Cloak
by Claudia Van Gerven

He hovers almost aggressively
in dank air as I approach.
Somewhere in the lake below
a carp rubs his brown back
against brown belly of water.
Crayfish plait green silt
with hinged legs. Scent
rises from my sweat-slicked
skin, like heat from the far meadow,
where pairs of coupling cabbage moths
tumble above the dusty heads
of drooping loveroot. I feel
the weight of his furred legs
against my knee. He opens
and shuts crisp, sooty wings
slow and melodic as a heart
or a star cluster. I look into the secret
indigo of his multiple eye
spots. They skim my aging face
dustily. An unaccountable longing
stirs the fine invisible hairs
of my arms, my breasts.
Then he floats off lazily
into the slumping willow,
where he slowly circles
another pair of dark wings.

Across the Street

by Elizabeth Wheeler

Martha sighed and thought, this could be a long week. She'd looked forward to Michael's visit from Nebraska, only the second time Martha had been brave enough to invite her nephew by himself. Motherless herself, she'd felt adrift, panicky almost, at the thought of mothering a boy she barely knew – for a whole week. That had been five years ago when he was only nine years old, so she'd settled on being a Big Sister instead. They'd had a great time; a full and tiring week of dinosaurs in museums, monster movies, hot dogs, pizza, chips, nachos with cheese, and amusement parks. Martha had hoped he could come every summer after that, but with soccer and a new baby sister the years had passed without plans.

"Houses are too close together in Chicago," had been the first thing out of his young mouth on that trip. The thought had never crossed her mind. What did a nine-year-old kid know, anyhow? It had reminded her of the reasons she had left Nebraska all those years ago – too much space, all emptiness. Chicago had been her answer – tall buildings, traffic, people all over, people who looked different, and talked of different things, not crops and weather. Chicago was the haven she had been looking for since she was five years old and rode the bus to school each day. She would run down the lane and cross the road to wait by the mailbox. Riding with her nose plastered to the window, it was a time to be safe and alone, and to dream. She watched the cornfields go by, looking off at the horizon, longing for a world she was yet to explore.

She had shed no tears at her high school graduation; there was just relief. Relief knowing she was on her way, out of Nebraska where one brother's dirty face blurred into another's and yet another's as they'd bullied her, touched her, even when she'd been so little, forcing themselves on her. How hard to find differences in them, in anyone, let alone find any differences in the days. No one to listen or really talk to, no dream except escape, nothing to relate to. Stationary, isolated, boxed in, She'd carefully held herself silent in her still world where even greater stillness blocked the pain. Even now after so many years in Chicago, her chest still caved in every time her mind wandered back.

Lately, though, the city was starting to feel closed in to her, too. And now her nephew wasn't coming. Her brother had called few minutes ago; Michael had the chicken pox, and would stay inside for a week, doctor's orders. Martha couldn't change her vacation; she didn't want to, anyway. She ached for a vacation, time away.

She sat on the front porch thinking about the week. The concrete was cold. Martha loved being outside but always forgot that until she was there. The porch was a quiet place to enjoy her neighborhood. She let herself relax and look around. The once tiny evergreen was taking over her front yard. Should she cut off the bottom limbs where the dogs peed? This side looked pretty good but the branches on the other side were dead. The people across the way were working on their house. The clean, sparkling windows, the caulking and painting, the pruned evergreens all combined to remind her of her own building's shabby, unswept porch with paint curls peeling away from weathered, gray wood.

Across the street seemed so far away. A car rumbled by, blaring out loud music whose vibrations shook the porch. Why hadn't she gotten rid of those old flowerpots? They had never been used, and just sat there. She might spend the week cleaning her apartment, maybe even painting it. On the other hand, she could go to the beach and take Spike and Buttons. She loved the lake in the early morning with the dogs. Cool, fresh wind against her face. The roar of the lake and its huge openness let Martha forget she lived crammed in the first floor of a two flat, neighbors so close she knew more about them and their living habits than she did of her own family back in Nebraska. Yet, what did she really know of them besides the fact that Mrs. Winslow got up at night to use the bathroom and he coughed a lot in the mornings, and together, the Winslows fought frequently, especially on weekends? She'd never made any attempt to cultivate them as acquaintances, let alone friends, had not shared any more than the usual surface courtesies if she ran into them on the back stairs. Still, she'd made that choice many years ago.

The dogs were already at the water's edge as she headed on the long walk across the cool, sandy beach, heavy with moisture. They didn't get much chance to feel this free. The city was a hard place for them, with their abundant energies compressed within their small bodies and within the cramped lifestyle of the city.

Here on the beach they could run fast without constraint and make as much noise as they wanted, yapping at each other as if what their barks said made a difference. They dashed around, leaping, landing on top of each other, then parting, then coming back together. Without neighbors to yell at them or at her, they could embrace their real selves, perhaps some primal memory of running in packs under the freezing moonlight, returning to her only occasionally as if to touch base, then racing off down the beach again, continuing the adventure.

Martha was jealous of their wild and natural passion for life, and watched them in the distance, trying to understand what it was she had lost or never had. Was there something to learn from them? Let it go, she told herself as they ran off again. She was thinking too hard.

From the edge of the water she could see the bathhouse, cars on Lake Shore Drive, and the apartment buildings just visible beyond the other side of the beach, buildings adjacent to the one she'd lived in when Michael had visited five years ago. She thought again about what he had said: "Houses too close together." Now it made her stop and think as she gazed at the dogs playing on the long expanse of sand drying in the sunshine. Buttons, the little black and tan one, had a behavior problem, mostly what seemed to be a super-energized anxiety. Buttons was a mix, supposedly calm and well adjusted, but instead of all the hyper genes being diluted, they concentrated in her. For four days straight last summer, she had escaped through the back kitchen window. Every day Martha had

tried something new. The first day she closed the window; the next day she locked it; after that, she wrapped the safety bar with wire mesh and nailed wooden slats on the outside. The fifth day she moved the refrigerator in front of the window and it stayed there until she got a metal enclosure for Buttons. She didn't like the word "cage," but was still struggling to think of it as the "crate" people often called such pens for their dogs. When she moved the refrigerator back she'd found dog prints in the dust on top of the refrigerator. So the beach was what Buttons needed for all that energy yearning to burst the confines of apartment life; a place to run fast, free and powerful, swallowed up by nature.

And what did Martha need? A place to feel full – completely alive, but not cluttered with baggage left over from childhood. She lost the thought as the dogs ran back. With the sun warming the day, the lake's smell became noticeable, fishy with overtones of chill in the breeze. Spike, the Australian Cattle dog, ran up, sand and seaweed hanging from his body. He looked up at her and laughed. Spike was the only dog she knew with a sense of humor. Both his face and body seemed to laugh as he wriggled with joy, and then he fell over in excitement, his fat body rolling on the half-wet sand, his legs pawing at the humid air, motioning for her attention. Maybe it was because he was the younger, like the youngest child – silly to be noticed. Like all her dogs he'd come to her secondhand. Someone moving away had left him; now Spike was part of the family. He had taught her to pay attention and enjoy the moment. Who knew when another good one would come?

The sun moved higher into the sky. Waves slapping the sand and dogs yipping into wind filled up her senses. Today that was what she'd needed. Too easily the city and work and bills could fill up all the spaces, leaving no room for thoughts and feelings, for simple contemplation of the rain falling in sheets against her window, blurring the pale glow of the streetlight outside.

She needed to connect to something bigger than herself, something so big she could let herself become lost in it. This day, this morning, she needed to feel the hugeness of nature. She pulled off her sneakers and ran toward the dogs, feeling the wet sand pack beneath her feet until it gave way to the shallows, and then she was standing in the chill of the water up to her knees. When the cold penetrated her back and neck, and made the hairs on her arms stand up, she called the dogs and walked back to the car feeling full, rested and complete.

When they returned home, Martha sat again on the concrete front porch, feeling its cold grit beneath her thin cotton jeans. One of the guys was working in his yard. Something made her get up and walk toward him. The sun was still shining and the brown leaves rustled as she walked.

"Hi. " His hair was damp, curling down halfway over his eyes.

"Hello. I live across the street. I just wanted to welcome you to the neighborhood. Well, actually I've never met anyone from this side of the street. I've lived here a long time and I've never even thought about coming over. Something always stopped me. I sit over there and watch." Why was she going on so? "I was looking at you and your house with the paint and the trimmed trees and bushes and all, and I don't know, I just now got up and came over. I didn't even decide to do it, actually. " She shrugged, self-conscious. "My name is Martha. "

"Mine's Skip. " He smiled. "Saw you with your dogs this morning." He paused to extend his hand.

She took it and looked at him. What was he thinking? What did she think? Usually she could tell right away how she felt about someone, and it generally made her stand away, distant. But this was the first time she had so boldly marched into someone else's life. Maybe her own was changing.

The Crests of My Colts

by Karin Wisiol

Springtown Leon, d.1992
Quietude Sterling, d.1994

Now my colts curve
out of the flesh.
Molten in God's late
loss of talent for life, they
harden.

Pursuing and not, I call
"Good-bye, good heart, good speed"
"Good-bye, good heart, good speed."

So scored, bone holds
ever and ever
the first, last,
first death.

I will not walk
this lakebed, its people
salt in my silence.
Conjuring, fist caging
a charred paper charm,
I invoke instead
those beasts who will answer, echo
my skin, give back
my sound.

Ah, surely I can ride
cadence,
air thick as rhyme below,
certain of welcome as
a goose-borne child.

Drawn by my right hand
and left, see curving
the crests of my colts as we
flash down.

Family Day at the Izaak Walton League
by Dan Witte

It's Saturday, Family Day at the Izaak Walton League, which resides in an antique Georgian style house along the overgrown banks of an inky, run down river. Parents disembark from station wagons with swarming children in their wake, drifting through buggy sunlight into the club where hunters and anglers discuss conservation. Today the centerpiece of an expensive remodeling project will be unveiled: a two-story, house-wide plate glass window that will allow club members to gaze at the woods and river outside while they go about their activities inside.

My father believes that the League is important to environmental preservation efforts. Technically, my mother agrees, but only insofar as it preserves the environment for hunters. She doesn't understand why men continue to hunt, and would prefer that my father didn't. She hopes that I won't develop an interest in hunting, and today wants to insure that my attention is directed away from the sport and toward conservation. I have yet to form any real opinion on these matters.

As more families arrive the scene begins to assume the proportions of an adolescent riot. My mother walks me through rooms with exhibits and diagrams that explain the role of wetlands, prairie and biological diversity, concepts that have no meaning to me. I am instead interested in a group of kids who appear to be playing a full-contact version of croquet, and I finally, bravely introduce myself to their game by jumping onto and smothering one of the wooden balls.

We have been here for about an hour when a large khaki-clad man approaches a microphone and asks for our attention. He welcomes us to the Izaak Walton League on this sparkling spring day, hopes that we've all had a chance to get a sandwich and some salad, that the children have all had some soda pop and cookies, and now it's the time we've all been had some soda pop and cookies, and now it's the time we've all been waiting for. Behind him is a floor-to-ceiling canvas drape, and as he gestures toward it, my mother finds me in the crowd and walks me over to a table where my father is seated with some other men. The ceremony has broken up what had turned into a satisfying game of something or other, and frankly I don't appreciate the interruption.

The room is mostly hushed when, with a faltering bow to drama, the khaki man tries to tease us with a peek under a corner flap of the canvas. It is not possible for me to care less. Voices increase in volume, there is some polite laughter, and with a clumsy flourish the master of ceremonies finally strips the drape away from the window, revealing a bright landscape of woods, water and sky, which rises blue and cloudless well above the purview of the two-story window frame.

So clean and smooth is the glass that one is barely aware it is there, and the effect is indeed impressive. One believes there is no window at all, but rather an open and natural entryway to the forest and all of its inhabitants, and I find that even though I lament the interruption, I am mesmerized by the view. There is some initial cooing and clucking, and then there is a noise like a " thunk" that comes from the direction of the window, and outside something flashes and flutters to the ground, like a white leaf. This is followed by another " thunk," and another white leaf flutters to the ground.

The room becomes noisier as conversations pick up, and as the emcee warbles something about nature's splendor and migratory duck watching in the fall. There are several more thunks heard from behind the man, who now turns to see the source of the sounds, and – forgetting to lower his microphone – mutters, " Oh my God" so that we all can hear, and can share in his sentiment. Many of us in the room have made the discovery at the same instant, and we move forward, closer to the window, where we can see a little more clearly the missile-like trajectory of small birds who don't know about things like glass and windows, who only recognize the reflection of trees and sky as a continuum of their habitat, and who are now bashing themselves into it.

It is a fascinating sight for me, though a horrifying sight for most others, notably the adults, and particularly my mother, who doesn't want me to see this. But I *have* seen it, and in fact I've got my face pressed against the glass down near the ground, where I can see a small brown bird with a white belly and wings struggling to stand up and move, one wing hanging derelict and bloody. The bird's mouth opens, but I cannot hear it. It may be that the glass is too thick, or that there is too much commotion around me. It may be that the bird makes no sound.

By now I have forgotten about the makeshift croquet game and the group of kids I was playing with. I've also forgotten about the soda pop and cookies, and even the undeniable beauty of the forest as it was first glimpsed through the window. What transfixes me is the crippled bird on the ground in front of me – and now here comes another one, which lands a foot or two to the left, and then another, a few feet out, and it's like a small storm of falling birds, and it is this spectacle that has me captivated when my mother picks me up by the shirt and drags me outside, where we wait for a few moments before my father follows, fishing in his pocket for the car keys, hunting the lot for our car.

The Freshening

by Nancy Means Wright

(for Tom Buttolphe: Shoreham, Vermont)

Here in the midnight barn
kerosene lamps kindle the labors
of forty cows; the boards groan
but no wind squeezes through.
The cows chew like films in slow re-
wind while in the birthing pen
Charlotte cramps into a swollen
sigh: the birth sack heaves with each
soft bellow. Her waters break
in a rush that brightens the air –
an ivory hoof kicks toward breath!
I tug and the head comes like a bulb
suddenly shooting out of a freshly
planted garden but its stem
is still in the ground. Brown

shoulders ease out, then the ribs
like furrows of hard earth.
The calf is only halfway here
but it opens an eye and the storm
enters my heart. I've strength
now to pull the whole way!
Charlotte stumbles to her feet
and we balance against each other's
spent breath. She licks the soaked
heifer and trumpets her prize.
The snow beats against the door
like stones from an ancient
enemy's sling but inside the barn
old Lute Buttolphe built
this calf will stand a chance.

Two-Way Glass

by Nancy Means Wright

If I were an artist I would paint
four women at lunch in an old farm-
house where the knives click
on the chipped plates and the talk
flutters in and out on forks:
a grandson's prank, a child back
home, nesting, the way time over-
laps like quilts tossed on
a pumpkin pine bed. Outside,
a feeder swings from a golden oak
and just after the carrot-yogurt

salad a lady cardinal jabs
at the windowpane with her bold
red beak; black eyes fix the eight
inside as if this is a two-way
glass: a woman out in the cold
fall afternoon and staring in
at those four old birds at lunch:
all of them laughing now
at the greedy rebel looking
to trade her sunflower seeds
for hot lemon pound cake.

Canada Geese

by Robin Wright

So there I was, nearly divorced and wretched,
to fly or not, the question, new life and all a
cliche in the making, but clinging still to what
had or might have been, when, on a sudden,

as I rounded the turn of a track I knew they
were about to leave. I had watched them
for days as I ran, the geese, a grey and noble
covering on Paradise Pond, a feathery cloud,

had felt their strength in its strange merging
of light and heavy, sinking into the water
yet floating, the air a second nature they
no longer question or second guess,

when, silent, they shaped themselves, a v,
and in a second they were aloft and gone.

Music for a Dead Cat

by Paula Yup

for Eric Turkington

Woke up this morning to a phone ringing,
then sounds of a sonata,
my friend's boyfriend at the piano,
crying over a dead Persian cat,
the day after the big LA earthquake,
after buildings collapsed,
after cars slid on the freeways,
after a man in a shower jumped out a window
to his death, and my friend cries.
They dig a hole in the ground,
put the white cat in black dirt.

We are survivors, like the mechanics
in a Pasadena body shop, who hearing
'earthquake', ran out quick,
three seconds before the building went.
We inherit tears,
this disturbing
of the earth.
The limp Persian
is quickly covered.
May this earth be calm.

I Feed the Pigeons

by Paula Yup

I'm in Haarlem after a morning spent strolling Amsterdam streets
and part of the afternoon drinking coffee in a Den Helder restaurant.
After getting off the train,
relieved that our gear is in an Amsterdam locker,
unburdened we stroll Haarlem streets.
It's quieter than Amsterdam and lovelier than Den Helder.
He snaps a picture of me in front of the Ten Boom Museum.
I sit by a statue to rest and he wanders off. His feet never hurt.
I see pigeons and pull out bread I found in the campground trash.
I feed one pigeon, then two, then three, then ten
and soon there are forty pigeons. One keeps landing on my hand.
Shoo. Shoo. I say. A man strolls by and takes a picture.
As the bread disappears I feel a frenzy.
It's the feeling I get in life drawing class. A happiness.
My husband returns. He takes a picture of me.
Any bread for me, he asks? I'm hungry. All gone, I say. He's mad.
Let's look for food, he says. I know of a restaurant here.
We sit on a sidewalk facing a church. The bells ring.
A ginger cat entertains us. Same color as the wicker chairs.
It's our last day in Europe, he says. Let's feast.
We order two salads with our last thirty-two guilders.
I had fun feeding the pigeons, I say. It's OK, he says.

237

About the Authors

❖ **Lucy Aron** of Santa Barbara, California, has had her essays and short stories published in magazines, newspapers and anthologies including *The Phoenix, The Cleveland Plain Dealer, Where the Heart Is,* and *An Ear to the Ground.* She received the 1995 Santa Barbara Arts Fund Individual Artist First Prize in Literature. Her essay, "Bat Showers," in *Feathers, Fins & Fur* won SECOND PLACE in the Prose Division.

❖ **Denise Bachman** is a native of northern Illinois, currently residing in Lindenhurst with her husband of 18 years and their two cats, Tigger and Miss Muffett. Denise just began the creative writing process a few short months ago and has found the experience to be challenging, frustrating, fulfilling, enlightening and rewarding.

❖ **Janet Baker** of Encinitus, California, is a university professor, writer and outdoorswoman who grew up in an Iowa farm village. Her work has appeared in *Prairie Hearts.*

❖ **Gail Bauman** was born and raised in Chicago, earned a BA degree from the University of Chicago and a Master's Degree from Governors State University. She has worked for years as a sculptor, exhibiting and selling at the Art Rental and Sales Gallery of the Art Institute. As her emphasis shifted to painting, she exhibited at Chicago's Matrix Gallery.

❖ **Cynthia Belmont** is Assistant Professor of English at Wisconsin's Northland College, where she teaches creative writing, composition, literature, and women's studies. She received her Ph.D. from the University of Wisconsin in 1996. Her poems have appeared in literary journals including *The Cream City Review, Iris,* and *Poetry.* She has received two Academy of American Poets Prizes. "Dinosaur Dreams" won SECOND PLACE in the Poetry Division of *Feathers, Fins & Fur.*

239

❖ **Steven Bigden**, a native of Chicago, now resides in Beach Park, Illinois with his partner of eight years, Robert. He has been writing since childhood, but has only recently started submitting work for publication; his short fiction has appeared in *Tails from the Pet Shop*. He writes short stories and poetry, has studied creative writing with poet Diane Williams and is currently working on a novel. Steven, a TallGrass Writers Guild member, enjoys visual art, music, and spending quality time with friends, family, and his dogs, Scooter and Snowflake.

❖ **Donna Black** is an actress in the Chicago area doing films, print work, industrials and theater. A multi-talented artist who has studied creative writing with Whitney Scott, she has been published in *Prairie Hearts*, first in Outrider Press' acclaimed "black and white" series of anthologies. She went on to win First Prize in the *Alternatives* Short Fiction Division.

❖ **Kate Boyes** writes by the light of kerosene lamps and candles since she chooses to live without any utilities. Her work has appeared in journals and anthologies including *American Nature Writing: 1996, Great & Peculiar Beauty, Tumble Words*, and *Of Frogs and Toads*. Forthcoming writings will be published in *Catalyst, Canyon Echo* and *Petroglyph*. Her work has been featured on several public radio programs including *Facing West*. She teaches writing at Southern Utah University.

Kate Boyes' essay, "Confluence," won FIRST PRIZE in the Prose Division of the *Feathers, Fins & Fur* anthology contest.

❖ **Harker Brautighan** is a web developer, writer and video artist. A Midwestern native, she currently lives and works in San Francisco. Her hobbies include spending time in the ocean and spoiling her two cats rotten.

❖ **Lisa Brosnan's** works have appeared in *Freedom's Just Another Word* and other literary journals and reviews including *Literal Latte, Pandaloon, Earth's Daughters* and *Whelks Walk Review*. She says, "All of my animals have been neurotic. I am starting to wonder if maybe it's me."

❖ **Anne Clifford**, who lives in Oakland, California, writes, "I am a free-lance grant writer and have published short fiction in the Portland-based weekly, *Tonic* and a local 'zine, *Get Off My Wagon*; most recently in *A Short, Short Night*, a publication out of the San Francisco State Extension Program. But most important, I love birds."

❖ **Cathryn Cofell** of Appleton, Wisconsin has been published frequently in magazines and anthologies including *Poetry Motel, Rag Mag* and *Freedom's Just Another Word,* third in Outrider Press' "black and white" anthology series. Her awards include first place in the Wisconsin Regional Writers' Association Jade Ring Contest and Outstanding Poem from the Wisconsin Academy of Sciences, Arts, and Letters for both 1996 and 1997. Her first chapbook, *Her Religion*, came out (and sold out) in 1998.

❖ **Nancy Cook** teaches at Cornell University and holds both an MFA in creative writing from American University and a law degree from Georgetown University. Her stories have appeared in *Southern Anthology, The Harvard Women's Law Journal, Circles, The Virginia Journal of Law & Social Policy* and *Seven Hills Fiction Review.* She has taught creative writing courses to women prison inmates and to undergraduate students. She lives in Ithaca, New York.

❖ **Lee Cunningham** was born on a Wisconsin farm, has experienced life in rural, small town, and big city settings, and moved to Chicago in the 1960s. After several years of teaching English, speech and drama, Lee worked in the publishing industry, then entered the business world as an executive secretary. Eventually, she become a publicist for not-for-profit music and drama groups. She lives in the Chicago area with husband Ted and two cats, and is a TallGrass Writers Guild member.

241

❖ **Joanne Dalbo** works for the Mental Health Association in Kingston, New York as a Family Specialist and teaches writing at SUNY New Paltz. Formerly, she directed the YWCA Battered Women's Services in Duchess County. Ms. Dalbo's publication credits include *Freedom's Just Another Word* and *The Chronogram*. She shares her home with her boyfriend and two cats, Marmalade and Spock. Spock is currently very jealous of Marmalade's literary achievement and waits patiently for his mother to create a Spock sonnet.

❖ **Jeanne Desy** received an Ohio Arts Council Individual Artist's Fellowship for her work on a recently completed comic novel. She holds a Ph.D. from Ohio State University, with dual specialities in creative writing and critical theory. Her numerous publications include essays, humor, scholarly work, poetry, and free-lance features. Her feminist fairy tale, "The Princess Who Stood on Her Own Two Feet," has been widely reprinted and studied.

❖ **Jo Lee Dibert-Fitko**'s poems and cartoons have received publication in over 100 presses nationwide including *Prairie Hearts* and *Freedom's Just Another Word*, two of Outrider Press' anthologies. Her editor, Simon, a secure and decidedly spoiled feline, occasionally approves "diversionary doggie material."

❖ **Alexandria Elliot**, M.A., L.C.P.C., A.T.R., is a professional counselor and art therapist practicing in the Chicagoland area who is also known in the visual arts for her black-and-white photography. Her short stories excerpted from her novel-in-progress have been published in *Kaleidoscope Ink* and *Freedom's Just Another Word*. She has performed her work in Chicago's Footsteps Theatre.

❖ **Dianne L. Frerichs** is joyfully counting down to a retirement with her husband, George, and her Schnoodle, Gypsy. She enjoys RV travel and adventures that range from off-road four wheeling and hot air ballooning to scuba diving and sky diving. She hopes to reside in the mountains and at the sea shore. Dianne, a member of the TallGrass Writers Guild, has had stories published in Outrider Press publications *Alternatives* and *Freedom's Just Another Word*.

❖ **Cynthia Gallaher** is the author of a new book of Chicago poems, *Swimmer's Prayer* (Missing Spoke Press, 1999), as well as *Private, On Purpose* (Mulberry Press, 1994) and *Night Ribbons* (Polar Bear Press, 1990) which was honored by the Illinois Library Association and the Chicago Public Library. Her collection of animal/environmental poems, *Earth Elegance*, is being published in the coming year. This recipient of three arts grants from the City of Chicago has recently completed a manuscript for a children's book, *Monkeys Meet Monsters Mostly on Mondays*. She is a member of the Chicago Park District's Green Team who educates the public about tree conservation and recycling.

❖ **Margaret Glass** is a Chicagoan who has been writing and telling stories as a hobby since second grade, when a teacher gave an assignment of keeping a journal. Thirty years later, she still writes each day about the events of her life. She is working toward a Master's degree at Northwestern University.

❖ **Leonard Goodwin**, a retired professor/researcher in areas of social psychology and public policy, now lives in Virginia's beautiful Blue Ridge Mountains. He is presently writing narrative as well as spiritually oriented poetry, and is in the process of setting some of the latter poems to music.

❖ **Jane Haldiman**, whose "Mayan Fragment" tied for (THIRD PLACE) in the Poetry Division, is a writer and illustrator who has lived in Chicago for six years. This TallGrass Writers Guild member has published poems, fiction and essays in previous "black and white" anthologies published by Outrider Press and in *Lip Magazine*, a small press publication.

❖ **Janice J. Heiss** lives in San Francisco with her orange tabby, Tinkerbell. Her prose and poetry have appeared in various publications including *Jewish Currents, The Ecstatic Moment: The Best of Libido, There's No Place Like Home for the Holidays, Frontiers: A Journal of Women's Studies, Women's Words* and *Freedom's Just Another Word.*

❖ **Shari Hemesath** is a part time poet, writer and has the propensity to become a crazy cat lady if left unchecked. Her work has appeared in *Alternatives: Roads Less Traveled* and *Freedom's Just Another Word*. She's performed her poetry at Chicago's Footsteps Theatre and has attended University of Iowa's Summer Writing Festival. Before she let her creative spirit flourish, she worked as a journalist for international and national radio networks.

❖ **Tina Jens** is a founding mother of the Dangerous Dames troupe as well as the executive producer of Chicago's "Twilight Tales" reading series. She also edits a Twilight Tales series of chapbook anthologies including *Dangerous Dames, When the Bough Breaks* and *Tails from the Pet Shop*. This self-described "recovering board chairman" of the Horror Writers Association has authored over 30 published stories of horror, fantasy and erotica. Her most recent work has been anthologized in *More Monsters from Memphis, Horrors: 365 Scary Stories* and *Cemetery Sonata*.

❖ **Fran Kaplan,** a retired jewelry designer, is a free-lance writer. In her career as a welder-designer, she was offered a job on the Alaskan Pipeline years ago, at $40,000 a year; "A lot more than I make as a writer," the author wryly notes. Her awards include National Writers Association, Dancing Worlds Press, Writers of Kern and California Roundtable. She lives in Palms Springs, California, where she edited the *Palm Springs Writers Guild Newsletter.* She was chosen as a finalist in the 1997 *Writer's Digest* Writing Competition's Personal Essay category for work that has recently been published in *Northeast Corridor*. Her essay, "Milestones and Hot Potatoes" was winner in non-fiction, writers' choice, Black Hills branch of the National League of American Pen Women in 1998. She also has work forthcoming in *Alligator Juniper, Belletrist Review, The MacGuffin* and *The South Carolina Review.*

❖ **Tanya Kern** is a registered massage therapist in British Columbia, Canada. Her poetry has appeared in many journals including *Antigonish Review, Event Magazine, Minus Tides* and *Midwest Poetry Review*. A reader at the 1996 Open Space Emerging Writers series, she was a poetry delegate in the 1997 British Columbia Festival of the Arts. Her chapbook, *Glory Days,* was published in 1997.

❖ **Wilfrid Rumble Koponen, Ph.D.,** is the author of *Embracing A Gay Identity: Gay Novels as Guides.* He lives in Albuquerque, and teaches in the Department of English at the University of New Mexico. He has two completed novels submitted for publication. His short fiction, "Quoth the Raven, 'Mortimer,' " won (THIRD PLACE) in the *Feathers, Fins & Fur* prose competition.

❖ **Jill Angel Langlois** was born in 1964 in Aurora, Illinois. She grew up and continues to live in Park Forest, now with her husband, Aaron. A member of the TallGrass Writers Guild, she has been writing poetry since the age of twelve, has studied with Whitney Scott and has read her poetry and short stories throughout the Chicagoland area in venues including Borders Book & Music and Footsteps Theatre. Her work has appeared in *Surprise Me.* She holds a BA from Governors State University and currently works at La Grange Memorial Hospital as a Physician Relations Coordinator.

❖ **Lyn Lifshin,** a literary diva in the world of small press publishing, has been dubbed "A modern Emily Dickinson" by poet Ed Sanders. *Small Press Review* calls her "the most published poet in the world today." Her poetry, praised by Robert Frost, Richard Eberhart and James Dickey, has appeared in virtually every poetry and literary magazine of note in America. She has written more than 100 books including *Blue Tatoo, Marilyn Monroe* and more recently, *Cold Comfort,* a finalist for the Patterson Award. Other finalists were Maxine Kumin, Philip Levine and Marie Howe. This internationally known *grande dame* of the small presses has received a Jack Kerouac Award and been the subject of the award-winning film *Lyn Lifshin: Not Made of Glass.* A resident of Vienna, Virginia, she has edited four anthologies of women's writings including *Tangled Vines: Mother and Daughter Poems* and *Ariadne's Thread: Women's Diaries and Journals.* Her 1999 book is *Bruised Velvet.*

❖ **Ellaraine Lockie** has authored two articles for *Once Upon a Time* and has two children's short stories in forthcoming issues of *Talking Story for Coastal Kids.* This award-winning children's writer is at work on a collection of essays on women's menopausal years. "Cat in an Empty Nest" is excerpted from it.

❖ **Bobbi Mallace** writes, "I cannot imagine living without dogs, since I constantly learn from them." She and her husband currently own two Lowchens and a Louisiana Catahoula Leopard Dog. She has written a regular column for a national breed club newsletter.

❖ **Terry Martin** of Yakima, Washington is an English Professor at Central Washington University, where she teaches Composition, Fiction, Young Adult Literature, and Poetry & Prose about Women & Nature. Her poetry has been published in *English Journal, Evergreen Chronicles, Inland, Voices from the Middle, Poetry Motel,* and two anthologies – *On My Honor* and *Freedom's Just Another Word.*

❖ **Karen Laudenslager McDermott** lives in Geneva, Switzerland, where she is a teacher, a visual artist/ photographer working in clay and wood, and a writer of short stories, poems, and essays for local English-language media. Her writings have appeared in *Offshoots: Writing from Geneva,* Volumes III and IV, and in *Tanzania on Tuesday – Writing by American Women Abroad.*

She is a member of the Geneva Writers Group. She also directs The Ensemble, a theatre troupe for adolescents, working primarily with original material.

❖ **Pamela Miller** is the author of *Fast Little Shoes* and *Mysterious Coleslaw.* Her third collection of poetry, *Recipe for Disaster,* is in progress. Her poem "Resignation Letter to the Boss from Hell" was recently published as a limited-edition broadside by Outrider Press. A frog enthusiast for over 25 years, she shares her Chicago home with a collection of over 700 froggy objects – from figurines, toys and puppets to books, artwork and clothing – and attends the annual Frog Collectors' Convention in Eureka Springs, Arkansas.

Pamela Miller's "Fish Story" is the winner in the 1999 anthology's Poetry Division.

❖ **Eliza Monroe** of Vallejo, California, earned her MA in creative writing from Antioch University, has won numerous awards for her writings, and has had her short fiction published in literary journals and magazines including *Amelia, Sweet Annie's Press, Salt Hill Journal, Onion River Review, Writers of the Desert Sage, Pacific Coast Journal, Sonoma Mandala* and *Widener Review.*

❖ **Rita Naughton** of Chicago has worked as a medical secretary. A lifelong animal lover, she's had parrots, rabbits and all breeds of dogs. This is her first publication.

❖ **Ellen Nordberg** relocated to Chicago from California several years ago, and while still seeking a sufficiently warm coat, moved back. She lives with her boyfriend and their collection of bicycles and kayaking gear. Her short stories have been published in *Kaleidoscope Ink, Alternatives, Freedom's Just Another Word* and *Moon Journal,* and her creative non-fiction has appeared in *Windy City Sports.* She free-lances for the *Chicago Tribune* as a special features writer, and is currently at work on a novel.

❖ **Nancy Nye** of Green Mountain Falls, Colorado, has published fiction in *Bananafish, Negative Capability, Writers Forum, Anemone, Blue Moon,* and an anthology, *Higher Elevations: Stories from The West.*

❖ **Kimberly O'Lone** holds a Master's degree in Public Administration from the University of Illinois at Chicago. She is an award-winning auditor with the U.S. Environmental Protection Agency, and a native of Chicago. Kim and her husband are the proud parents of two little girls, Elizabeth and Rosemary. A member of the TallGrass Writers Guild, her short fiction has been published in *Kaleidoscope Ink, Moon Journal* and *Tails from the Pet Shop.* She has a book of creative non-fiction in progress.

❖ **Carolyn Paprocki** performs her poetry in Chicago venues including Barnes & Noble, Borders Books and Music and Footsteps Theatre. Her work has been published in *Hair Trigger* and *Puerto del Sol.* She hosts the monthly reading series "Poetry by Candle Light" at the Logan Square Branch of the Chicago Public Library, where she works as a librarian. She recently published her first chapbook, *A Routine Omelette Becomes the Big Bang,* whose title poem was first published in Outrider Press' anthology *Alternatives – Roads Less Travelled.*

❖ **Arthur Melville Pearson** is a 1999 Illinois Arts Council Fellow for playwriting/screenwriting. He has received numerous awards for his work including first place in the Midwestern Playwright's Festival for the stage play, *Cairo.* He has published fiction and creative non-fiction based on his extensive travels throughout the Midwestern and Western states. When not on the road or at the keyboard he contributes his time to the restoration of the landmark community of Pullman where he lives, and the recently established Midewin National Tallgrass Prairie.

❖ **Doris J. Popovich** is a native of Chicago. Two of her poems were recently published in *Blister and Burn*, a Scars Publication (1997). Sometimes this TallGrass Writers Guild member prefers animals to humans.

❖ **Rochelle Rhodes** of Indiana has worked as a medical professional, played in a rock band and sold men's underwear, providing the "element of truth" in all she writes. She has had poetry, fiction and creative non-fiction published under various pen names in periodicals including *Common Lives*.

❖ **Jill Riddell** writes about nature for *Chicago* magazine, *Garden Design Magazine,* the *Chicago Tribune,* and other publications. She is a regular commentator on *Eight Forty-Eight,* a radio show on National Public Radio's WBEZ-Chicago. She is the author of *The Big Middle,* a novel that appeared as a daily serial on the Spiegel web site and now awaits conventional print publication. Born in Liberty, Texas, she was raised in Posey County, Indiana, and now resides "amidst the natural wonders of inner city Chicago," she writes.

❖ **Jude Rittenhouse,** a member of TallGrass Writers Guild and Regional Representative for the International Women's Writing Guild, is a Rhode Island based free-lance writer, editor and teacher. She has won short story and poetry awards, including a 1998 Writer's Grant from the Vermont Studio Center, and her work has appeared in publications such as *Sistersong: Women Across Cultures; Wish Women; Pudding Magazine; Freedom's Just Another Word;* and Wild Dove Press' 1999 anthology *Jane's Stories II.* She is at work on a book-length manuscript, *Snake Hands.*

❖ **Christine Rusch** lives in South Carolina. Her fiction appears internationally in *Mississippi Review, Freedom's Just Another Word, Abiko Quarterly* (Japan), *A Room of One's Own* (Canada) and *Breakfast All Day* (France). A member of the Dramatists Guild, her plays have been presented in New York and published in regional magazines such as *Southern Exposure.*

❖ **Anne Scheetz** was born in 1950 and grew up on a small farm near a small town in Western Colorado. She now lives with her husband, and near her dearest friends, in the city of Chicago. She works as a physician, specializing in geriatrics and home care. She writes regularly, she tells us, "and has been published but not paid."

❖ **Alice Sellars**, whose short fiction "Of Wolves, Ashes…" won the (Outrider Press Award) is a free-lance writer and photographer, currently working on an historical novel. She has worked as a news reporter and human interest feature writer for *The Roundup Record Tribune* for several years. She currently lives in Roundup, Montana and works for a conservation district, publishing two award-winning newsletters. Her real passion is animals.

❖ **Dominique B. Slavin** of Dorado, Puerto Rico, was born in Seattle. She writes of herself, "Aiming to get in touch with her roots, she moved to Scotland. Then it started to rain. Now she lives in Puerto Rico. Draw your own conclusions."

❖ **Carol E. Smith** is proud to have a short story in a TallGrass Writers Guild anthology for the third time. She has also been published in The College of Lake county's *Kaleidoscope Ink*. Carol, who has a Master's degree from Northwestern University's Medill School of Journalism, lives and works in Chicago and tells us, "she has chosen to avoid anything too cutesy-cutesy for her bio this year."

❖ **Grazina Smith** has had her work published in previous anthologies published by Outrider Press. Her work has also appeared in *Weekly Magazine, Women's World, Kaleidoscope Ink,* and has been published in the national best-seller, *Chicken Soup for the Woman's Soul.* She reads her work throughout the Chicago region.

❖ **Gregory A. Stall**, whose poem "Geese" tied for (THIRD PLACE) in this year's Poetry Division, is a veteran of the U.S. Navy who served in Vietnam. He lives in a suburb of Chicago, where he works as a free-lance artist and woodworker. "Geese" is his first publication.

❖ **Margo Tamez** lives on a small, organic farm that she, her husband and children own and manage, in southern Arizona. Periodically, she teaches creative writing at Arizona State University and Cook College, both in Tempe. She recently completed a second book-length collection of poems, and both are now in circulation. Her poems recently appeared in *Americas Review, Abya Yala, Cimarron Review* and *American Poetry Review*, and are forthcoming in *Flyway Literary Review, The Peace Review, Two Girls Review* and *Frontera Literary Review.*

❖ **Sandra Tatara**, a member of the TallGrass Writers Guild who serves as secretary on its board of directors, has been published in *Alternatives – Roads Less Travelled* and *Freedom's Just Another Word* and won Second Place in the 1997 Writer's Contest sponsored by National Organization of Women. She raises and shows Registered Quarter Horses, paints in oils and watercolors and lives in the rural arts community of Crete, Illinois with her husband, horses and cats.

❖ **David Tomasko,** whose parents were stationed overseas, was born in Ankara, Turkey on Thanksgiving Day, 1960. After being raised in Turkey, Greece and Iran, he returned to the United States with his parents and settled down in to a normal American childhood. Following high school and college, he went on to earn a Master's degree and then his Ph.D. in marine biology, and works as a research scientist in Southwest Florida. He and his wife enjoy boating, scuba diving and collecting fossils.

❖ **Claudia Van Gerven**, is a resident of Boulder, Colorado, where she teaches writing. Her work has appeared in numerous magazines including *Prairie Schooner, Calyx,* and the *Lullwater Review.* Her writings have been widely anthologized in collections including *I Am Becoming the Woman I've Wanted,* winner of the 1995 American Book Award. Her chapbook, *The Ends of Sunbonnet Sue,* won the 1997 Angel Fish Press contest. *Spirit String* was a finalist in the Backwaters Poetry Prize contest in 1998.

❖ **Candace Walworth** lives in Boulder, Colorado, where she is an associate professor at the Naropa Institute.

❖ **Elizabeth Wheeler** spends her days at Chicago's Lincoln Park Zoo recruiting volunteers who talk to the zoo visitors about wild animals; by night she lives with three dogs and many cats. She is currently training her dog Edward to behave in public. "Across the Street" is her first published work.

❖ **Karin Wisiol** and her husband live in Grayslake, Illinois. After a career as a book editor, she retooled with a Ph.D. in biology to do work in ecology and agriculture. Horses and poetry are longtime passions. The first poem she submitted to a national publication appeared in Outrider Press's 1998 anthology, *Freedom's Just Another Word*.

❖ **Dan Witte** is a vice president of marketing and sales for a Chicago-area utility management company. He co-authored the article about Printing in the 1994 *World Book Encyclopedia*. He spent ten years in trade publishing and free-lance writing before opting for a corporate job with respectable pay and benefits. He was on Bozo's Circus when he was ten years old.

❖ **Nancy Means Wright** has published poems recently in *Carolina Quarterly, Bellingham Review* and others; anthologies include *Claiming the Spirit Within* and *Generation to Generation.* Her seventh book, *Harvest of Bones* a novel, was published by St. Martin's Press in 1998. A former Bread Loaf Scholar, she lives, teaches and writes in Vermont and in New York's Mid-Hudson Valley.

❖ **Robin Wright** is a professor of English and Director of Women's Studies at Harold Washington College in Chicago. She earned a Ph.D. in the Sociology of Language from the University of Chicago. She edited *Wyrd Women, Word Women,* a collection of women's writings from the Writing Workshop for Women she directed for a decade. In 1991 she was the recipient of an Illinois Arts Council Fellowship for non-fiction. Her publications include scholarly work on women's language as well as essays and short stories.

❖ **Paula Anne Yup** was born in Phoenix, Arizona and attended college in Los Angeles, California, and graduate school in Montpelier, Vermont. She currently makes her home in Spokane, Washington. Her work has appeared in *Mid-America Review, Passages North, Black Buzzard Review, Earth's Daughters* and other journals and anthologies.

About the Editor

Whitney Scott, a major force in Chicago's literary scene, plays many roles in the publishing industry. She is an author, editor, book designer, and book reviewer whose poetry, fiction and creative non-fiction have been published internationally, earning her professional listings in *Contemporary Authors* and the *Directory of American Poets and Fiction Writers*. Her work has appeared in many literary journals and magazines including *Howling Dog, Pearl, Potomac Review, Art & Understanding, Amethyst, Dangerous Dames, Tomorrow Magazine* and more.

She edited Calhoun Press' *Words Against the Shifting Seasons - Women Speak of Breast Cancer*, a collection of writings by breast cancer survivors. Scott is also editor of the well known "black and white" series of Outrider Press anthologies, often publishing many previously unpublished talents who have gone on to national recognition. She has performed her work throughout the Chicago area, and has been a featured guest author in the Illinois Authors Series at Chicago's Harold Washington Library. A regular reviewer for the American Library Association's *Booklist* magazine, Scott runs a variety of Chicagoland writers' workshops and has headlined the Taste of Chicago Writers Conference at St. Xavier University. She says, "I'm easy to recognize – I'm the one in a straitjacket, with a rose in my teeth."

Long-stemmed, of course.

About the Judges

Maureen Seaton of Chicago won an Iowa Prize and a Lambda Literary Award for her 1996 poetry collection, *Furious Cooking*. She won the Capricorn Award and the Society of Midland Authors Award for the *Sea Among the Cupboards* (1992), and the Eighth Mountain Poetry Prize for her 1991 collection, *Fear of Subways*. Her awards include an NEA fellowship and Illinois Arts Council grant, 1996 and 1997 Literary Awards for Illinois Arts council, and two Pushcart Prizes. Her poems have appeared in magazines and anthologies such as *The Atlantic*, *The New Republic*, and *The Best American Poetry 1997*. She teaches poetry at the School of the Art Institute's MFA in Writing Program.

Yvonne Zipter, judge of the Prose Division in the *Feathers, Fins & Fur* anthology contest, has authored a number of books, most recently *Ransacking the Closet*, a collection of humorous essays. Her book of poetry, *The Patience of Metal*, was runner-up to John Frederick Nims for the Poetry Society of America's 1992 Melville Crane Award. This Lambda Literary Award finalist holds an MFA in Fiction Writing from Vermont College, teaches creative writing at the University of Chicago and writes the nationally syndicated column "Inside Out." Her essay, "A Season of Unity," was selected by WBEZ radio for a live performance on stage that was later aired as part of its "Chicago Matters" series.

About TallGrass Writers Guild

The TallGrass Writers Guild, a not-for-profit corporation, provides publishing and performance opportunities for beginning and established national and international writers via monthly Open Mikes, twice-yearly formal, themed readings and an annual anthology of worldwide writings on a given theme. The guild publishes a bi-monthly newsletter for its members, is sponsoring a 1999 Creativity Conference in Greece, holds monthly writing development workshops at Chicago's Sulzer Regional Library, and makes possible leadership opportunities via election to its Board of Directors, which meets on a bi-monthly basis.

End Notes

Feathers, Fins & Fur is published by Outrider Press, Inc., in affiliation with the TallGrass Writers Guild, whose national contest and call for manuscripts yielded these submissions among many others. Details on Outrider Press may be had by calling 708-672-6630 or faxing 708-672-5820.

Every effort has been made to locate and credit any prior publications of writings in this book. If any have not been credited, please notify the publisher so that corrections can be made in future printings.

❖ ❖ ❖

"Samson! Where's Delilah?" by Steven Bigden originally appeared in slightly altered form in *Tails from the Pet Shop*, ©1999.

"Tiger" and "Whale Song" by Cynthia Gallaher were published in *Swimmer's Prayer*, © 1999, and will appear in *Earth Elegance*, to be published in 2000.

"Gators in the Sewers" by Tina Jens first appeared in *Horrors: 365 Scary Stories*, Barnes & Noble Books, ©1998.

An earlier version of The Last Chicago Bear" by Jill Riddell originally appeared in *The Reader*, ©1995.

Pamela Miller's "Gigantic Frogs…" originally appeared in *Tails from the Pet Shop*, ©1999 and has been accepted for publication by *Pudding;* Miller "Fish Story" originally appeared in *Zuzu's Petals Quarterly Online* and *Clutch*, ©1998.

"Wild Bill…" by Kimberly O'Lone first appeared in *Tails from the Pet Shop*, © 1999.

"The Crests of My Colts" by Karin Wisiol was first published *Willow Review*, © 1999.

"The Freshening" by Nancy Means Wright first appeared in *Clockwatch Review*, © 1995. Her "Two-Way Glass" was first published in *Rockford Review*, © 1994.

Illustrations by Art Parts

255

Outrider Press Publications

Feathers, Fins & Fur $15.95
Short fiction, creative non-fiction and poetry on animals and animal themes ....

Freedom's Just Another Word $14.95
Poetry, fiction, and essays: international authors on freedom ....

Alternatives: Roads Less Travelled $14.95
Poetry and fiction from across the nation and around the world on counter-culture lifepaths ....

Prairie Hearts — Women View the Midwest $14.95
Writings on the Hearland by authors from all parts of the country ....

Dancing to the End of the Shining Bar $9.95
A novel of love and courage ....

Listen to the Moon $4.00
Poetry of family love and loss ....

Illinois resident add 8% (.08) tax ....
Add shipping charges
$2.25 for one book ....
$3.25 for two books ....
$4.00 for three books ....
$4.50 for four books ....
$5.00 for five books ....

Total ....

Send check or Money Order to:

Outrider Press, Inc.
937 Patricia
Crete, IL 60417